LOVE, FRACTALLY

LOVE, FRACTALLY

KIERSTEN SCHIFFER

Published by Sweet Light Press

ISBN: 979-8-9857701-6-2
e-book ISBN: 979-8-9857701-7-9

Cover Design and Formatting by Damonza

To my Mom (my own Angel Guide),
Thank you for staying so close.
I might not be able to see you anymore,
but I feel you all the time.
And that's enough for me.

PROLOGUE

Somewhere *else*...

HE STANDS IN front of me, light beaming forth from his every ethereal pore, looking around in wonder. I know how he's feeling. It's the same way I feel each time I come back here, too.

"Hello sweet boy, welcome home," I say, reaching out to hug him to my breast. "We're all so happy to see you!"

When I let go, he steps back, gazing out upon the other light-bodies flanking me, his smile growing even wider. Them...his grandparents, great aunts and uncles, he recognizes. Me...not so much.

"What is this place?" he asks, swiveling around, trying in vain to take it all in.

"It's the place from where you came. And to which you will return. And from where you will leave again. Over and over in the great cycle of eternal life."

"Yes!" He pumps a fist in the air. "I knew it! I knew it was like this. All this time I knew I was right!"

"Yes, you were right. Everything good is always right."

Later, he will realize we are not speaking out loud. That our minds are linked, so we communicate without words. But our exchange is so natural he doesn't notice it now.

He squints as if he's trying to make out my features. Which is probably hard since I have myself turned up pretty bright. It's better if he only sees a little of me now. Later, he'll recognize me. When the time comes.

"You didn't know me in the physical world this time around." I answer his unspoken question.

"But in others?"

"Yes. We've always been close."

I let him digest that for a moment, then go on. "We're all so proud of you…you know that, don't you?"

Hearing this, he starts to cry. The blessed relief swelling, then washing away, leaving him clean and glowing with pure bliss. Ahhhh, what a feeling that is. That knowing of pure love. He deserves this joy. He chose a bit of a bumpy road this time around. But then again, he's always been one who craves a challenge.

"You have a choice now," I say.

His eyes go wide. "I do?"

"Yes. You can choose to stay here or go back."

"Go back? Why would I ever do that?" The thought seems to horrify him.

I understand his reluctance. I could remind him he was the one who wrote the story he lived, so the only person he can complain to is himself. But that might sound a bit petty since he's not fully merged back into his knowing yet. But it's better to keep him that way, still a bit in the dark, until he makes his decision.

"It would be different if you went back. We would see to that." I gesture to his loved ones and when he nods, I know he understands.

"Here, let me show you." I wave a hand behind me. We step out into a dark, expansive space where all his trajectories of lives are lit up. There are myriad geometrical facets and lines. Choices upon choice upon choices, splintering off and joining up in a vast, interconnected web of all his possible futures.

"They're all so beautiful," he marvels softly.

"They are, aren't they? You can't see it clearly when you're there. But from our perspective…they're all perfect just the way they are."

He nods, accepting easily like always. Such a porous soul, this one. "But up here is beautiful too," he says, gazing around in awe again. "And wouldn't starting over with something new be easier than going back to what I left behind?"

"Maybe. But there are still many, many lives you could touch if you go back to the life you just left."

He surveys the fractals all around him, taking time to soak them all in. "They all look similar in a way…. except for that one." He points to the particularly bright path that veers off and merges with another next to it. I knew he'd find that one. They always do.

"Why is that one different?" he asks.

"Oh, that's the Intertwined Path," I explain, as if it's nothing. When in fact it's so very, very, much. "One where two souls meet in a lifetime and agree to work together toward a common goal."

Only then does he turn and realize someone is standing next to him. A light that's faint, but still there, brushing up against his own glow with age-old familiarity.

His face brightens in recognition. "It is extra beautiful, don't you think?" he says to the one beside him.

There's agreement. And laughter. So much laughter. That's another part humans get wrong. We're not half as serious up here as everyone thinks we are.

His partner pipes up, still more rooted in her physical limitations than he is. "But it looks like it would be a one in a million…no, more like one in a billion chance of finding that single intertwined path." Practicality is an attribute she chose this time around. Sometimes it serves her. And sometimes it doesn't.

She goes on. "Goodness, how many decisions would we both have to make to get to that point? It's mind boggling. If we even decided to go for it…how would we even find each other to start?"

I smile at the oh-so-logical question. Her role as a skeptic will definitely spice things up for the two of them. That is, if their paths ever do cross. No, he won't be the obstacle for their future. The memory of the love he's felt here will erase most of his doubt. His partner, however, she's going to be a bit harder to convince.

Smiling my most angelic smile—lots of twinkling teeth and rays of light shooting out everywhere —(it's a bit cliche, I know, but it gets their attention) I point to one particularly bright fractal close to us. It plays a single moment in time, over and over again, like a snippet of a movie running on endless repeat. A moment that, could…if all their other choices line up just right…change everything for them.

"Oh, don't worry about finding each other," I tell them with a wink. "I can help you with that."

CHAPTER ONE

Indiana, 1989
ANNIE

I STAND OUTSIDE the dining hall doors at Camp Boundless, wondering for the millionth time why I agreed to take this job.

"You took it because you said this job would help round out your resume," my sister Caroline reminded me this morning, after I'd voice my fears out loud. "Then you could get a job at that fancy camp on the east coast after graduation and leave us all behind."

I hadn't missed the exasperation in her voice as she talked about my intended career path. My sister still thinks my decision to get a college degree in Outdoor Recreation is some kind of a joke. Just last week, she accused me of settling for what she calls "the world's easiest college major" because I don't have the confidence to try anything harder. At least that was a little nicer than when she'd flat out called me lazy.

Caroline has obviously never been a camp counselor before. Because if she had, she'd know this job is exactly the opposite of being lazy. I've spent the past six years—starting the summer after my freshman year in high school—working at Camp Cheyenne, the Girl Scout camp I'd attended since I was a little girl. And working with kids in nature is paradoxically both the hardest and the most fulfilling job

I've ever had. Which is why I've chosen to make a career out of it. (And also because a Recreation degree doesn't require any math classes.)

But this job I'm about to start—which, for some strange reason, I'd accepted with barely a second thought—is a far cry from working at good 'ole Camp Cheyenne. My old job there was easy. I already had a set of ready-made friends, a predictable routine, and (most importantly) I knew what to expect. In fact, I was so established at Camp Cheyenne if I'd gone back this summer, I would've been Assistant Director. But instead, I'd taken my college professors' advice and pushed myself to try something new here at Camp Boundless, a fully inclusive outdoor facility for kids with disabilities.

Yeah. I forgot how much *new* sucks.

Two girls walk up to the building as I lurk outside like some kind of loser. They pause, holding the door open for me. "You going in?" one of them asks kindly.

"In a second." I gesture to my foot. "I just have to take care of this first." I crouch and pretend to tie my tennis shoe, hoping they won't notice it's already tied. God, why am I always such an awkward mess? Why can't I just relax and take things in stride, like apparently everyone else at this staff orientation can?

The girls cheerfully say they'll see me inside, but I only nod, keeping my eyes trained on my laces, as if forming this fake knot requires my utmost attention.

Once they're safely gone, I get to my feet and resume my stall tactics, hovering in the entrance's overhang, peeking through the windows, trying to steel myself for what's about to come.

Inside, the large room is made up of log walls and two-story windows that look out on a dense forest beyond. Someone has pushed all the tables to the edges, probably to prepare for some kind of cringe-worthy ice-breaking exercise the staff has planned for us. Believe me, I know them all. I'm the one who used to lead them at Camp Cheyenne.

I dread having to walk in there and make all new friends and learn all new rules and figure out a whole new lay of the land, both literally and figuratively. I pull a crumpled paper from the pocket of my shorts. Like, how am I supposed to find this Franklin Cabin where I've been assigned?

Kids cluster around the room talking animatedly, waiting for the training session to begin. The closed doors muffle their voices, which makes the scene inside play out like a silent movie; all the characters smiling big and laughing hard; everyone working furiously to put on their best show. One girl is even doing some kind of dance routine with jazz hands and high kicks. Typical new camp counselor energy. I can feel their overloaded circuits even with a solid pane of glass in between us.

Why do they all seem to know each other, anyway? Oh man. That just makes it so much worse.

It's times like these I really miss my mom.

If she were still alive, she would've sat on my bed this morning as I packed and given me one of her totally biased mom pep talks, going on and on about what a natural gift I have with kids. Telling me how brilliant I am, how much I have to share with the world. And how I'm the kind of person everyone can't help but love. Once they get to know me.

My sister had tried to give me her version of a mom pep talk this morning. But right in the middle of saying how proud she was of me, her four-year-old had pulled her out of the room to build a ramp for his cars using wooden blocks. Then baby Emma needed to nurse, so like always, Caroline couldn't finish her thought.

At least I'm getting out of their hair for a while. Her husband Jonathan is a saint, but when he married Caroline I doubt he expected he'd have to take in his wife's high school sister when our mom died of cancer. Luckily, I'd only had to live with them for half a year before I turned eighteen and left for college. Ever since then I've been trying to make myself scarce, flip flopping from the dorms to summer camp, then back again, only making brief pit stops at their house in between. I'm pretty much a vagabond now. Always moving. Always making sure

I have a summer job with housing so I don't become too much of a nuisance to them. And now Camp Boundless will be the next pit stop on my road to who the hell knows where.

Another group of kids approach the entrance. Seeing me hiding in the shadows, one girl smiles my way and holds the door open, gesturing for me to go in front of her.

I guess there's no putting this off any longer. Like it or not, it's time for me to make my fresh start.

∞

Just inside the entrance, two women sit at a table stacked high with papers and nametags. Behind them, Miles, the Australian camp director who hired me, greets each new recruit with a blinding white smile and hearty, "G'day mate!"

Miles is handsome and blonde and looks like he stepped out of Surfer Dad magazine, if such a magazine existed. When I gave him a good looking over during my interview (and I mean a good one…the guy is super hot), I put him at about mid to late thirties. I'm excellent at telling ages because I pretty much only date older men. I like them better than guys my age because they're usually really appreciative and don't want any commitments, which fits my needs perfectly. In fact, it was probably my unconscious attraction to Miles that led me here today. At least that's what I've been telling myself in order to explain my strange behavior at the end of my interview.

Camp Boundless had been the first of three job interviews I had lined up this spring, each with positions that would pad my resume in various ways. I'd planned to go to all the interviews, make a list of the pros and cons, then submit my acceptance to the proper position once I'd made the best logical choice for my career path. But when Miles offered me the job at the end of our conversation, I'd blurted out "Yes!" as if someone else had taken possession of my vocal cords. I'd accepted without thinking about one pro or con. Without comparing one salary, one housing offer, one days-off package. At the time it felt like there was no way I could go anywhere else. But that feeling didn't make any sense. Especially for a girl like me, who thrives on making plans and sticking to them.

Afterwards, I'd stumbled to my car, dazed by how I'd forgotten all reason, reeling at how strong the urge to accept his offer had been. In fact, it had been such a gut instinct I might even think it was fate that brought me here to Camp Boundless. That is, if I believed in something as illogical as that.

In the dining hall, Miles gives me a wave and I try to angle my way over to flirt with him a little (it doesn't hurt to be on the good side of the smoking hot boss, or any smoking hot guy for that matter...) But before I can get to him, a sturdy grey-haired woman at the end of the table stops me.

"Hello. I'm Dottie. Camp Head Nurse," she says with a frown. "Here's your training packet." She hands me a spiral-bound book as thick as my grandmother's family bible.

"Oh uh, thanks." I heave the weighty stack into my arms. Good God. I've printed off a lot of counselor training packets in the past, but none have ever compared to this tome. Is one week going to be enough to learn all of this?

"Make sure you do your reading ahead of each session so you're prepared for the hands-on training," she barks like a drill sergeant. "If you get behind even one day it will be really hard to catch up."

She narrows her eyes at me then sighs heavily, as if she's just sized me up and come to the conclusion that I'm woefully incompetent.... which is woefully true. Dottie might have a silly first name, but the fun definitely stops there. She's all business. She probably has to be with the magnitude of responsibility she bears, keeping all these sick kids alive.

I'm only a few seconds in and already I sense how different this summer is going to be. At Girl Scout camp we were conscious of keeping the kids safe, but it wasn't that hard. We just had to glance over every once in a while and make sure no one was drowning or getting kicked in the head by a horse and our job was done.

But I can already tell (by this encyclopedia in my hand) my role as a counselor at Camp Boundless is going to be *way* more complicated than that. I swallow hard, wondering if I'm really up to the task ahead of me. Or if I'd fooled myself into believing that, just because I have a few muscles and above average stamina, it will be enough to get me through the demands of this summer.

After giving me my name tag, Dottie releases me into the fray of bodies with a clipped "Happy to have you" that doesn't sound all that convincing. I shuffle into the swarm of kids, hating that I have absolutely no idea where to go next.

Inside the two-story room, the drone of voices has grown so loud it's like a physical entity; a cloud of a million buzzing gnats shoving its way into my ear canals, burrowing deep inside my lurching stomach. I have to fight the urge to bolt. To race back to my silver Mustang in the parking lot and squeal off to Camp Cheyenne, leaving only a cloud of dust and a fluttering training bible in my wake.

The further I get into the room, the more I notice how different this group of counselors looks compared to the ones at Camp Cheyenne. For one, there are boys. That will surely make this summer way more interesting than at the girls-only camp I'm used to. There are also kids in wheelchairs, a few with Down's syndrome, an older man in frayed jean shorts and a Metallica tank top who has only two nubs coming off his shoulders instead of full arms.

I'd never thought about how the inclusivity of Camp Boundless would apply to its counselors, too. With how inaccessible most camps are, I bet a lot of these kids have probably never had the chance to work as counselors before. I shudder at the horrible thought. I can't imagine not having access to the woods; not being able to lose myself among the trees and soak my feet in the streams and stare at colonies of ants marching through the leaves for hours on end. Nature is the most healing place I've ever found. It was the only place I could even draw a full breath after my mom died. I've never told anyone, but one of my secret dreams is to open my own camp to help grieving kids like me. Although with the measly amount this career pays, I doubt I'll ever be able to afford to buy my own camp. At least not in this lifetime.

Scanning the room, I notice signs posted along the walls with cabin names written on them. I search for the Franklin Cabin I'm assigned to, relieved I finally have a place to go. Once I find it, I pause for a moment and size up the girls gathered nearby. I hope they're cool because I'm about to be stuck with them for the next three months.

One girl has dirty blonde hair, cut in pageboy style. She looks like she's a few years older than me, so she's probably our Cabin Leader.

Next to her is a taller, extremely pretty girl with really short brown hair who, according to the way the other two are laughing, appears to be telling some kind of hysterical story. My God, if my hair were that short I'd look like a fourteen-year-old boy, but with her big dark eyes and high cheekbones the style looks super chic on her.

Next to Pretty Girl, laughing so hard it looks like she might piss her shorts, is a round girl with dark skin and cherubic cheeks who towers over the other two. My nerves settle a little watching them. At least these girls like to laugh. I can work with that.

As I approach the group, I catch the end of Pretty Girl's story. "…and that's how I learned just how fast an enema takes effect!"

The round-cheeked girl hees and haws and slaps her leg loudly, while our Cabin Leader just smiles politely, looking a bit worried.

I step into their circle. "Hi everyone. I'm, uh… Annie." I feel like I should say more, maybe add to the conversation to keep the hilarity going. But since I have no experience with the timing of enemas, I just smile wanly at them.

"Oh yes!" The older girl says, looking relieved that I've interrupted them. "The last member of our team. Welcome, welcome! I'm Susan, the Cabin Leader." She extends a hand for me to shake. I have to awkwardly juggle my training encyclopedia before I can grab it.

"And I'm Margaret," the hee-hawing girl says, extending a hand.

"But everyone calls me Honey Bear." She points to her name tag where she's X-ed out her given name and scrawled her nickname underneath in Sharpie.

"Great to meet you, Honey Bear." I laugh as I say it because she's still chuckling and it's impossible not to be swept up in her good cheer. Call it counselor Spidey-Sense, but I can already tell I'm lucky to have her as a cabin mate.

Honey Bear goes on. "I used to work at Girl Scout camps, so that's where the nickname came from."

"Me too!" I gush.

"No way! Which camp did you work at?"

"Camp Cheyenne…in Marionville."

"I was at Camp Wai-We-Moe in Ashford. Although…" Honey Bear lowers her voice conspiratorially. "We liked to call *Why We Hoes?* when no one else was listening." We all burst out laughing. Except for Susan, who smiles but scans the room as if she's secretly wishing someone would come rescue her from us.

"What was your camp nick name?" Honey Bear asks me. It's a thing we do at Girl Scout camps: use a made-up name all week, something that alludes to our personality or hobbies, then at the end of the week we reveal our real names to the campers at closing ceremony.

"Freckles," I say, gesturing to my face.

She squints at me, looking skeptical.

"Oh, you can't see them too well now," I explain. "But the more I'm out in the sun, the darker they get. Made even more prominent by my perpetual sunburn."

"You are awfully lily white, aren't you?" Honey Bear scans me up and down, taking in my blonde hair and pale arms.

"Yeah. White like a lily. But not delicate like one, if you know what I mean." I wag my eyebrows while simultaneously cursing myself for making such a stupid comment. I don't even know what the hell it meant, and I'm the one who said it.

Luckily, the girls burst out laughing again, although Susan's grin looks a bit plastered on. Poor thing. I can almost read the thought bubble hanging above her head saying, "How the hell did I get stuck with this bunch?"

Pretty Girl flashes me a warm smile. "I'm Greta. Nice to meet you, Annie." She extends her hand but when I grab it I flinch. It's made of rubber, not skin. When I look closer, I see that almost her entire arm is rubber, attached to a small section of real arm extending from her shoulder.

She and Honey Bear laugh uproariously at my shocked expression as Susan shoots me a sympathetic look. This obviously isn't the first time Greta has played this trick on someone today.

"Oh, sorry to startle you there," Greta says, roughly poking me in the side with the frozen pointed finger of her prosthetic arm. "It's a little party trick I do. Scare the pants off of the newbie. Gets a laugh every time!"

Looking at Greta's lit up face I can't believe how blasé she is about her disability. She doesn't seem ashamed or embarrassed about her half an arm at all. My God, I get a zit on my chin and I'm too mortified to leave the house. Yet here she is waving her plastic arm around for the whole world to see. I think this girl might be my new hero.

"You'll get used to it," Greta says, tapping my cheek with the cold rubber fingers. She proceeds to stroke my hair, pat my shoulder, poke me in the ribs with her fake arm. I'm giggling like crazy by the end of her assault. She's so relaxed, so forward about the way she looks. It instantly puts me at ease.

"Yeah, God kind of dozed off when he was finishing this side of me," she explains, nonchalantly gesturing to her left side. That's when I realize she only has a half a leg too, with a prosthetic attached just below her knee.

"Men," she huffs, shaking her head with disdain. "You can never trust them to finish a job, can you?"

I only manage half a nod before she barrels on. "My mom had

German Measles when she was pregnant. That's why I turned out like this."

"Oh really," I deadpan, already feeling overly familiar with her. "I thought someone told you 'it costs an arm and a leg' and you took them literally."

For a split second, nobody breathes, just waiting for Greta's reaction. Then all of a sudden, she erupts in laugher, and we all join in. My knees wobble a little in relief. Thank God I didn't offend her. It wouldn't bode well for the rest of my summer if I put my foot in my mouth on my very first day.

The clear glee on Greta's face makes me feel like I've passed some kind of test by making a joke about her prosthetics. She squeezes in next to me and throws her fake arm over my shoulder. My God, it's so heavy. How does she haul that thing around every day?

"Welcome to Franklin Cabin, Annie Freckles," she says, squeezing me tight. "I can already tell you and I are going to be best friends."

CHAPTER TWO

I HUDDLE TOGETHER with the girls in my cabin, all of us chatting more quietly now as the last of the new counselors arrive. Then I remember the gifts I brought.

"Here, I made you all something." I pull a handful of friendship bracelets from the pocket of my shorts. I'd been making them ever since my interview with Miles, silently praying with every knot I'd tied that I hadn't made a terrible mistake in accepting this job.

"We did this at my old camp," I rush on, hoping they don't think I'm childish, giving them an arts and crafts project like this. "You make a wish as you tie it on and when it falls off, your wish is supposed to come true."

The girls all murmur with appreciation, thanking me as I tie each green and white band (the official colors of Camp Boundless) around their wrists. I'm not sure why I was so worried they wouldn't like them. From my experience, people willing to commit themselves to the intense work of spending the three scorching hot months of summer in the woods with kids are the friendliest, most accepting group you'll ever meet.

After Greta asks me to tie her bracelet on, we all put our wrists together in the middle of our circle like we're about to break a huddle before a basketball game.

"To an amazing summer!" Susan cries. "May we all work hard and fulfill the goals we've made for ourselves and for our campers."

"Uh yeah," I say, exchanging a subtle glance with Greta and Honey Bear. I can tell they're holding back snickers. Hard work? Goals? There's definitely something very mature about Susan. She's super nice, but she seems like a fifty-year-old woman trapped inside a twenty-four-year-old's body.

"To uh, hard work," Honey Bear says, fighting back a smile.

"And fulfilling goals," Greta says, trying not to crack up.

"Camp Boundless on three!" I wrap it up.

We give a shout and break apart. I hold up the handful of bracelets I still have left. "Guess I went a little crazy, huh? I wasn't sure how many people would be in my cabin."

"Here, let's give some to the guys in the cabin next door," Greta says, tipping her head at a group of boys standing next to us.

She hooks her arm in mine (the real one, not the fake one this time) and drags me over to them. "Hey everyone, meet my new best friend!" She acts so familiar with the boys, I can't tell if she's just naturally outgoing or if she somehow already knows them.

A tall boy with long shaggy hair whirls around, taking a step back to let us into their circle. When his eyes meet mine, his mouth drops open.

"Oh my God…it's *you*," he stammers, looking like he's just seen a ghost.

His strange reaction throws me off. I mean, I'm kind of pale, but I'm not as pale as a ghost.

"Yeah, it's me," I say. "I'm sorry. Do I know you?"

His eyes search my face, his smile becoming wider and wider with each passing second. I've never had anyone look so happy to see me in my life. Including my own mother. Which only confuses me more. Who is this guy, anyway?

When he doesn't explain his odd behavior, just grins and grins like some kind of Cheshire cat in human form, I finally repeat, "Do I know you somehow?"

He startles, like he's coming out of a dream. "Oh, no…no…I guess you don't." He furrows his brows, like he's only just now remembering something. "I'm sorry. I uh….I guess I thought you were someone else."

I look down at myself a bit self-consciously, wondering what it is about me that's made him so flustered.

Greta turns to me. "Sorry, my buddy here can be kind of strange sometimes. Just ignore him." She elbows him with the rough familiarity that tells me they've met before today.

"Sorry, sorry," the boy says, seeming embarrassed. His wavy brown hair reaches all the way down his shoulders and he's wearing a red T-shirt with the arms cut off and bright plaid shorts with striped tube socks pulled up to his knees. He definitely has some unique fashion sense, I'll give him that.

He goes on, looking sheepish. "She's right. I'm weird. It's the most outstanding quality about me."

His voice is warm and melodic, and for a moment I wonder if he might be stoned. With a hairstyle like that, it seems likely. But he's also wearing these nerdy wire-rimmed glasses—the kind that automatically get darker in the sun and never become totally clear—so I can't really see his eyes to tell for sure.

"I'm Annie," I say, craning my head back to return his stare. Goodness, he's tall.

"Hi! I'm Theo, nice to meet you, Annie." He extends his hand but instead of taking it, I hold up a bracelet. "Want one of these?"

Once again his eyes go wide and he stares at the bracelet like it's made of spun gold, not cheap craft store floss.

"It's green…*that's* what was green…" he whispers to himself, smiling big like he's just solved some great mystery.

I'm not sure why the color of my bracelet is so fascinating to him, so I wave it again, hoping to break him out of his trance. "Yeah, it's green." I say, a bit too harshly. "You want it or not?"

He nods furiously. "Oh yeah, yeah…that would be great." He still seems very flustered, which makes me soften to him a little as he holds out his arm. It's kind of nice to meet someone even more awkward than me.

When I reach out to wrap the bracelet around his wrist, our skin accidentally brushes together. The contact sends a shock running through me. Like when you get zapped by static electricity in the wintertime after shuffling around the carpet in your socks. Which is weird because that's never happened to me in the summertime before.

He jolts the same way I do, and we burst out laughing in surprise.

"Geez, sorry about that," I mumble, dazed by the flood of goosebumps cascading all the way down my body and back up again. The visceral sensation sends me flashing back to the night my mom died. When I collapsed on the bathroom floor instead of going to the hospital to be with her. The night I had such a vivid dream…of her visiting me…and telling me to expect someone…someone that I needed to…

I shake my head hard, trying to clear my thoughts. What the hell? Why would that memory come back to me at a moment like this? My goodness, my nerves really must be getting the best of me today.

When I glance up, I realize Theo is doing the same, shaking his head as if in disbelief. And when I look at the bare arm he's holding out to me, it's covered in goosebumps too. I meet his eyes and my heart starts pounding really fast, my skin flushing hot like we've just shared some really intimate moment right in the middle of this crowded room. Which makes no sense since I'm only tying a stupid friendship bracelet on his wrist.

I hurriedly knot the threads, then make a point of stepping away from him. I squint at his face, trying to get a closer look to see if I'd been wrong before. If maybe I do really know him after all.

He gives me a knowing smile, as if we're in on some kind of private joke together. Am I supposed to know the joke too? For some strange reason I think I am. But that doesn't make any sense. He's so distinctive, with all that hair, and height, and a prominent nose that makes him look kind of exotic. He doesn't seem like the kind of person you could easily forget.

I take another step away, trying to get my wits about me. No. I definitely haven't met him before. He's definitely a stranger to me. So why do I want to jump into his arms and tell him how much I've missed him?

CHAPTER THREE

MILES HAS US form an enormous circle around the edges of the room. Once we're all quiet, he launches into a rousing welcome speech, dazzling us all with his brilliant white smile and charming accent. Then, to my horror, he calls out the three most dreaded words in the English language: "Everyone pair up!"

I hold back a groan, but when he adds, "And don't pick a person in your cabin either. You have to buddy up with someone you don't know yet!" the grumble slips out before I can stop it.

As Miles explains the exercise—interview your partner, then introduce them when we rejoin the circle fifteen minutes later—my anxiety soars. I imagine how this is about to unfold: Me, all alone in the middle of the room, facing the humiliation of being the only person not picked as a partner. Once again, the girl abandoned and all alone. Wouldn't that be poetic justice?

I turn to start my search and nearly jump out of my skin. Theo is standing right in front of me, grinning like a damn stoned fairytale cat again.

"Shit! Don't do that…You scared me!" I yell. I don't know why, but I already feel really familiar with him. Like he's my little brother, and I have every right to reprimand him like that.

"Sorry, sorry," he says, holding up his palms. "I just wanted to ask if you'll be my partner."

He looks so innocent I instantly feel bad for yelling at him. Especially since he's just saved me from the clutches of sure humiliation. But instead of thanking him, I say a cool, "Alright, whatever," and charge off to the chairs by the wall, leaving him to chase after me.

I brusquely position two chairs facing each other and motion for him to sit down, as if I'm the one in charge of this situation, which I definitely am not.

He does what he's told and sits down. But I've misjudged how long his legs are and when I get in my chair our knees knock together and we have to scissor our legs in a way that is way too intimate for a first time-meeting. We both chuckle a little at the awkwardness as I frantically scoot my chair further away, trying to ignore the jolt of electricity that shot through me when we touched again. What is with this guy? Is he somehow hooked up to a hidden battery pack? Maybe that would explain his crazy hair.

When I finally get myself properly positioned, I let out a huge sigh.

He sizes me up. "Nervous, huh?"

Something flares in me. It annoys me how he's picked up on my fear so easily. I start to deny it, but when I look at his face it's so open, so accepting, that against my better judgement I tell him the truth.

"Yeah. Just a bit terrified." I honk a nervous laugh. "I haven't had to start somewhere new, where I didn't know anyone in a long time. Making friends isn't really my strong suit."

"But you've already done it!" he says brightly. "See? I'm your friend."

I shrug, grumbling a half-hearted, "Yeah. I guess."

He ignores my subtle snub. "And you got lucky being in a cabin with Greta. She makes friends with everyone. She'll drag you along and before you know it, poof! You'll be friends with the entire camp."

"So you guys know each other?"

"Yeah, she's one of my best friends. We're in nursing school together."

I take that in, trying not to look surprised. It's a little strange for a man to be a nurse. But maybe he's just doing it before he becomes a doctor or something.

Theo begins talking about himself, giving me little tidbits to use in my introduction. I can tell he's purposely taking the lead in order to soothe me, to give me time to relax, and his kindness touches me.

The little brother vibe I got from him turns out to be right. He's two years younger than me, only nineteen, yet he's somehow a junior in college already. Something about skipping a few years in high school, his mom teaching him instead…I don't quite get it all. He goes to nursing school in Indianapolis with Greta and some other friends that he points out around the room. I'm a little jealous he already knows so many people. It probably explains his ease, the puppyish enthusiasm that radiates from his every pore. And how he seems to have so much confidence even though he admits to never having been a camp counselor before.

"I just can't wait until the kids come!" he gushes, rubbing his hands together like he truly wishes they'd all pile through the door any minute. I fight back the urge to bring him down a notch. To inform him it's not going to be as fun as he thinks. I could easily rattle off a long list of all the ways camp sucks: the heat, the bugs, the endless whining from the campers. The monotony and how hard it is to keep your enthusiasm up for such a long time. Oh, all the things this novice doesn't know yet.

I'm not sure why I'm being so negative, since I'm a certified camp enthusiast myself. Maybe I'm just cranky because Theo's unabashed optimism is starting to grate on me. He has no idea what's in store for him, so he really shouldn't be getting his hopes up so high. Believe me, crushed hopes are something I'm all too familiar with.

As he speaks, Theo gestures wildly, long arms flailing and legs bouncing in rhythm like he can barely keep his energy contained to the chair. I try to ignore his uh, *expressive* mannerisms, but when he accidentally whacks me on the shoulder in the middle of explaining where he lives, the strangeness has to be addressed.

"Whoops," he says sheepishly, while I glare at him. "Like I said,

I'm a bit worked up. I've been waiting for this day for a long time." His smile hasn't faded once since we started.

My earlier thought was that he might be stoned. Now I wonder if he's on amphetamines. How can a person be this happy? He's a nice enough kid, but he's a bit too positive, too *smiley* for me. I probably shouldn't be so critical. Caroline is always saying I need to be more open-minded toward people who are different from me. And Theo, with his clashing clothes and wild hair and obvious love of life, is very, *very* different from me, that's for sure.

"I bet you're a runner," I say, pointing to his running sneakers and the black watch with a million buttons on his wrist. Even without those clues I might have guessed it. He has the kind of lithe, lanky body of a runner. Lightly muscled, without an ounce of fat on it.

"You got me!" he says. "State Champion in the 1,500 meters senior year."

"I'm impressed," I say, truthfully. I don't mention I'm also impressed by my uncanny ability to accurately judge people from nearly 1,500 meters away.

The conversation unfolds easily, even though we have to practically shout over the din of all the other get-to-know-you sessions going on in the room. Theo tells me a story of how he once tried juggling tomatoes and ended up accidentally smashing one into the face of his priest and I laugh so hard I forget I was ever worried about this icebreaker. *Ah, that's such a Theo thing to do*, I muse, imagining the embarrassing scene. Then I catch myself. My God, I just met this guy. Why do I feel like I've known him forever?

I scribble notes about him on a paper I've stolen from my training packet. "Are you Italian, maybe?" I ask, after examining him some more. His skin is just a shade tanner than normal, and he has a slight Roman nose that hints at some ethnicity I can't quite pinpoint.

"I'm Polish, actually."

I scoff loudly. "Okay. Well, I wasn't expecting *that*." After all the jokes that went around in high school, I didn't know anyone dumb enough to actually admit to being Polish.

He laughs good-naturedly. "Go ahead, hit me with your best Polack jokes…believe me, with a last name like Teodorczyk, I've heard them all!"

I fan myself dramatically, croon in a southern accent. "Oh dear, I would never do such a thing as to tell an off-color joke in polite company!"

He lifts one eyebrow skeptically and I crack up. "Okay, so maybe I've been known to tell a derogatory joke or two. In fact, my brother-in-law says my humor can be a bit 'caustic' at times, just like my sister's." I air quote Jonathan's description of us. "But I'll reserve the really crass jabs until we get to know each other better, alright?"

"Great! Something to look forward to!"

I give him a strange look. Is he actually excited about me making fun of him?

He goes on, "But I assure you, I can take it. There's not much in this world that bothers me."

It should be a flippant remark, but something about the way he says it so sincerely makes me stop and run the words through my mind again. *There's not much in this world that bothers me.* I could never be that carefree. He's obviously either really dense, or else not looking very hard if he can't find at least a little something to be bothered about in this God forsaken world.

"So," he says, propping his elbows on his knees, leaning closer. I catch a whiff of the flowery scent of his shampoo. Kind of impossible not to, with all that hair waving around as he talks. "Tell me more about yourself, Annie." I swallow hard, trying not to notice how much I like the sound of my name on his tongue.

Usually, I make a point of picking my words carefully when I first introduce myself to someone. I have a strict rule about not giving too much away. You can always give people more later (which seldom happens with me), but you can never, ever, take information back.

But with Theo, once I open my mouth, talking about myself feels easy. Maybe it's the fact that he's younger and kind of nerdy and I'm not attracted to him at all that makes me blabber on so freely. It's actually kind of liberating to be with a boy and not feel the need to win him over in any way. Even if he were older (my requirements are at least 7 to 10 years my senior) I would never consider dating a boy with hair like his. Who does he think he is? Bon Jovi?

Thinking of that, I crow, "Let me guess what music you like! You love Motely Cru, Poison, Bon Jovi, right?!" I gesture to his long, wavy locks. "I mean come on! You've got to, right?"

He chuckles. "Yeah, a lot of people think that. But my hair has nothing to do with the music I like." He hesitates and I think he's going to elaborate more. But he thinks better of it. "I actually listen to a lot of John Denver. Dan Fogelberg. Bob Dylan. More the mellow guys like that."

"Wow," I marvel, surprised. "Mellow guys? I would've never guessed that by looking at you."

For once, he sits very still. Measures his words carefully. "Yeah, I'm used to people jumping to conclusions about me."

Our gazes lock, and even though his eyes are still hidden by his shadowed glasses, something twangs in my chest. His words feel loaded, like he's acutely aware of all the neat little conclusions I've jumped to about him in the past ten minutes. I suddenly realize that out of the three judgements I've made about him so far, only one of them, that he was a runner, has been right. Man, I'm really off my game today. But then again, maybe it's just hard to peg Theo because he's so strange. One second he seems so young and goofy, and the next he seems like a wise old man.

We stare at each other for a few beats until the silence becomes awkward.

"You're really pretty," he blurts out.

I look skyward. Oh boy, here we go. And *this* is why I don't believe in co-ed camps.

"Um, thanks," I say, trying to find a way to gently nip this in the bud. I like the kid. But not in *that* way. "I'm flattered and all, but you probably shouldn't just come right out and say that to a girl," I instruct him, using the big-sister voice Caroline always uses on me. He looks stricken, so I rush on. "I mean, I know you were home-schooled and everything, so you probably just don't understand how things work…"

"I was only home-schooled for a couple of years."

"I know, but…"

He scrunches his face in confusion. "But I meant it as a compliment."

"Yeah, but still. There are certain unspoken rules people go by. You don't just come out and say everything you think. Especially not to a girl."

He looks even more confused. "Why not? I think you're pretty and I felt like telling you that. Why is that bad?"

I struggle for a way to explain it to the poor guy, but I have a hard time coming up with anything.

"It's just…just…" I'm little pissed by how much sense he's made. And yet he's still wrong. Isn't he? "Listen, we're going to all be stuck together for three months. Trust me, I've been a counselor for a long time. And I understand, this is your first time working at a camp so I'll let you in on a little secret." I lower my voice. "Camp romances can be really messy. I know better than to get involved with someone I work with and you should, too." I hope he doesn't push me on that, because having only been at Girl Scout camp, I've heard that piece of advice secondhand. I have no actual experience with it. "So let's not get into this, okay?"

He nods furiously, looking hurt. "I wasn't trying to come on to you. It was just a simple observation." He looks down at his tightly clasped hands and I feel terrible again. Like I've kicked a defenseless puppy, then laughed about it afterward.

I reach over and give him a playful punch on the arm. "We're fine! It's no big deal. And thank you again. Seriously, I needed a little bit of confidence today and your compliment gave it to me. I really appreciate that. Truly, I do."

He smiles big, looking relieved. His eyes play along my face, seeming to take every inch of me in. As he stares, a warmth radiates over me that feels so good. I don't mean to be pompous, but I can tell he likes me. The silly boy doesn't even try to hide it. I almost regret reprimanding him now. Maybe it wouldn't be so bad if he followed me around and told me how pretty I am all summer long. He's so young and sweet. And he's certainly not boring, that's for sure. I can already tell he's going to be a great friend to have around for these next three months. As long as I can get him to tone down all his infernal optimism.

CHAPTER FOUR

THEO

"YOU COMING?" MY bunkmate Wendell asks from the doorway of our staff quarters. "Everyone's meeting outside."

I quickly hide the paper in my hand, guilt washing over me for some stupid reason. "Yeah. I'll be there in a minute."

I wait until he's gone and go back to what I was doing before: staring out the window…at her.

Her name is Annie. A giddy feeling bubbles in my throat as I repeat the beautiful word inside my head. *Annie. Annie. Annie.* I can't believe after three long years of waiting, I now know her name. I can't believe after three long years of waiting, she's finally here.

I told you I'd take care of it. The voice lilts sweetly inside my head.

Yeah, but I thought I wouldn't have to wait this long, I chide back.

Such impatience! Did you forget what the word eternity *means?*

I laugh out loud. Then glance around sheepishly, hoping no one has caught me acting so strange. I've gotten used to my Angel Guide making me look like a fool, so it doesn't bother me anymore. But I probably should be more careful now, so I don't screw this up.

I unfold the paper in my hand and read over the words again.

Hair like spun gold.

Freckles on her nose.
She frowns, but I smile.
I can't believe it. It's her!
But I know not to say anything. She won't understand.
Not yet.
A flash of green. A thin band. A rope maybe? A string?
She's reaching out. Touching me.
A jolt goes through me. It feels so good.
Does she feel it too?
I think about asking. But no, I should wait.

They're the words I'd written afterwards. When I was lying in the hospital bed, trying to remember every detail of the flash of a moment I'd been shown when I was with my Angel. I'd tried to capture every detail, every emotion, every nuance I saw so I would recognize the mystery girl when I met her again.

It wasn't much to go on. I'd forgotten so many bits of that night since then. Which was why I was beginning to doubt if we were ever going to find each other. The odds were against us. Even with the help of all those pulling for us from beyond.

But now we've done it! We're here, together at last. She's right there in flesh and blood, outside my window. Laughing with Greta. Swatting flies off her neck. Flipping those adorable braids behind her shoulders every two seconds. She's oblivious to what we're here to do. But that's okay. We have time. At least a little of it.

When Annie and I met in the dining hall yesterday, I'd waited for her to have the same recognition I had, and for a split second I swore I saw something in her eyes. A flash of knowing. A flash of her wanting to leap into my arms, just as I wanted to pull her into mine. But then she covered it up so quickly. And looked at me like I was crazy. Which, yeah, is a reaction I'm used to getting by now. But I was hoping that she, of all people, would know me better than that.

So, this is how it's going to be, huh? I mutter inside my head.

May I remind you, You didn't want it to be too easy. You literally said 'where would be the fun in that?'

Yeah, you're right. We both like a bit of a challenge. But still… my time is getting a little short, don't you think?

Again. Look in the mirror, buddy. This is all on you.

You'd think Angel Guides would be all stuffy and reverent. Leave it to me to get the one who thinks she's a comedian.

Hey, I heard that. Plus, I have to be silly. You humans take this life stuff way too seriously!

Again, I laugh out loud and don't even stifle it this time. Outside, the group is preparing to walk to breakfast. Annie hesitates, looking at my cabin with a hopeful expression, almost as if she's waiting for me to come join her.

It all makes sense now. How I got here in the first place. When I'd interviewed with Miles, I wasn't sure coming to Camp Boundless was the right move for me. But when he'd asked if I wanted the job I'd blurted out *Yes!* as if someone else had control of my vocal cords.

Sorry if I got a little pushy there. Like you, I'm also under a time crunch.

Even though I hadn't known at the time that this is where I'd finally meet her, I'd had a hunch. I was praying that fate (aka my Angel Guide) would bring us together. Good thing I believe in things like that. Of course, it's easy for me because, unlike most people, I've seen how these things work firsthand.

I stuff the paper back in my duffel and head toward the door to meet Annie, nervous about what to do next. I was up half the night wondering if I should just tell her everything. Show her the paper and get it all out in the open and ask her what she thinks we should do. And then there's the matter of the postcards I got in the mail right before I left for camp, in the envelope with the odd return address with the note inside. I feel like they have to be connected to Annie and the reason we've been brought together like this. But how?

I need to move carefully. Even I'm overwhelmed and I've had three years of living with this knowing. Is three months of camp going to be enough to get Annie to listen to me? She doesn't know me. And from what I've gathered so far, she doesn't seem like one to throw caution to the wind and believe such a wild story as mine. How am I going to convince her to listen, much less get all the way to the place where it might change both our lives?

Are you sure you can't give me any more information? I prod my Angel, as I step outside the cabin.

That's the fun part, remember? If you knew everything ahead of time, where would be the challenge in that? The voice reminds me sweetly. *Besides, there's no need to get all worked up about it. I said I'd help.*

I smile. She's right. I need to just relax, follow my instincts, and take life as it comes. It's the message I keep getting, and so far it hasn't let me down. No. Now is not the time to dump everything on Annie. I need to go slow. Get to know her better first. See if we can have some fun together. Then maybe she'll remember on her own.

Annie's blue eyes light up when she sees me walking toward her. My stomach drops to the ground at the sight. Yeah, I think we can do this. I think we're going to be alright.

If all I have to do is get to know her better, have some fun with the most beautiful girl I've ever laid eyes on… well, that's an assignment I don't mind one bit. Because even if she thinks I'm a bit weird right now, I can change that. And as for me? After three years of dreaming about Annie…I'm already in love.

CHAPTER FIVE

ANNIE

FOUR DAYS GO by in the blink of an eye. We spend almost every minute in class, learning the details of the diagnoses we'll encounter this summer. Our campers will have cerebral palsy, spina bifida, cystic fibrosis, Down's Syndrome, kidney disease, various forms of childhood cancers, and some diseases I've never even heard of before.

Dottie leads lectures on feeding tube care and wheelchair transfers and subcutaneous injections. And the big one: Pressure sores (otherwise known as bed sores to laypeople like me).

Based on the amount of time Dottie spends on skin care it seems like pressure sores are going to be my biggest nemesis this summer. *Pressure sores. Pressure sores. Pressure sores.* The thought of the little buggers fills my every waking moment and haunts my dreams. From how serious Dottie becomes when she talks about them, I'm pretty sure if a camper is caught with even the hint of a red mark on their skin, their counselor will be marched out at dawn and executed in front of a firing squad.

We've barely been out in the woods at all, which makes my body physically ache. I'm used to spending a lot of time outdoors. I often feel trapped when I'm inside four walls, caged like a zoo animal whose choices have been reduced to moving from one lackluster space to another. Whereas the expansiveness of the outdoors gives me options. It's comforting to know I can always run if I need to. That with one decision, I can disappear and leave everything that scares me behind.

But I'll have to wait for training on the ropes course, touring the nature center and trails, visiting the lake. Dottie has her priorities, you know. How can a kid learn about wildlife camouflage if they're sitting in their wheelchair with a festering ulceration on their hip? (She didn't actually say that, I merely inferred it from her tone.)

Looking around the classroom at all the serious faces, nodding like they understand every word Dottie says, I feel even more out of my element. There are a few other Outdoor Recreation students here but, because of the type of camp this is, we're in the minority. I study hard every night, and feel like I understand the material, but how will I know until I practice it? These medical students, with their years of training and hands on experience, are light years ahead of me. I've never been around counselors as smart as this group. Even goofy Theo is a walking encyclopedia of knowledge.

Case in point: one day at lunch I was lamenting about an upcoming class on catheterization. (Catheterization! How the hell am I qualified to do that to a kid?! I used to get squeamish when one of my Girl Scouts asked me to rub sunscreen on her back, for God's sake!)

"You guys are lucky," I'd grumbled to Theo and the rest of his cabin mates at the table. Since we live next to each other, the eight of us do pretty much everything together now.

There's Adam, the Cabin Leader, a super tall anesthesiology student with a dark brown mullet.

Wendell, a handsome dark-skinned pre-med student with a halo of curly hair.

And Juan, a skinny Puerto Rican nursing student with short, perfectly gelled locks.

The four of them look like models in one of those books of haircuts at the salon you look at when you can't make up your mind about what style you want. They're each so different it's comical. But I already love every one of them. Because having succumbed to the Law of Residential Summer Camps (whereby stress and proximity intensify relationships at nine times the rate that occurs in the natural world) these boys are now my lifelong best friends.

"Why are we lucky?" Adam had asked at the table, looking perplexed.

"Because shoving a straw up a penis is way easier than catheterizing a girl," I'd haughtily informed him.

Once all the boys had stopped wincing, Theo chimed in. "Yeah, I'll admit the penis is way easier to locate." He stabbed a glob of macaroni and cheese on his fork. "But a female urethra isn't that hard to find. You just spread the labia folds, locate the vagina, and look up."

Hearing that, I'd nearly spit out my Kool Aid, fully expecting everyone else at the table to do the same. But they'd all simply murmured their agreement without even cracking a smile. As if what Theo had just said wasn't scandalous at all. I couldn't believe how blasé they were, talking about *spreading labia folds* as if it was normal lunchtime conversation. Nursing students are so fucking weird.

That day I'd nodded along with them, just to fit in. But even now, I can't help thinking of how disturbing it is that Theo knows more about my anatomy than I do.

∞

We're in the infirmary practicing our patient transfers, two metal folding chairs standing in for what is supposed to be a wheelchair and a toilet bowl.

All the girls in our cabin have practiced transferring each other. Honey Bear practically flinging Greta, Susan, and me from chair to chair as easily as if we were feather dusters. But when it came time for us to transfer her, she'd staunchly refused.

"No way in hell I'm letting you lightweights have a go at all this puffy goodness!" she'd crooned, waving a hand down her body. She'd pointed at me first. "Freckles here is the size of a damn twelve-year-old... and you," she'd whirled to Greta, "with your measly arm and a quarter. You'll drop me on the floor like a splat of pancake batter. No way I'm going to even let you try."

I'd been relieved when Greta laughed at Honey Bear's jab. I'd noticed how she'd struggled with the transfers. Because of her prosthesis, she couldn't get a good enough grip to move someone safely by herself. I'd heard Dottie quietly tell her she'd always need to ask for help when she was working with the campers. Greta had acted like it hadn't bothered her, but I'd seen the frustration on her face when she rejoined our group. She's fiercely independent and never asks for help unless it's a last resort.

Now Dottie barks at us to rotate and find new people to transfer. Theo lurches in front of my chair before I can even look around. "Pick me! Pick me!" he says, waving his hand in the air like a five-year-old.

"Fine," I relent, rolling my eyes like he's a royal pain in my ass. Actually, I'm kind of relieved. He definitely doesn't weigh as much as some of the other choices around here.

I stand square in front of where he sits in the chair grinning up at me. Yeah, this is going to be interesting.

To transfer a patient alone, you have to wrap your arms around their shoulders and basically bear hug them really tight to your chest, then lean back using your own weight as a counterbalance to lift them off the chair. After that comes the pivot and the controlled lowering onto the other chair. It's quite an intimate procedure and from the look on Theo's face, he can't wait for it to begin.

"Stop looking so happy," I snap, but I can't help but smile, too. Theo has that effect on everyone. He's like a Golden Retriever puppy. You'd have to have a heart of stone to not feel at least a little bit of glee when he's around. "Remember, you're about to piss your pants," I remind him. "You need to play the part."

He squeezes his legs together, feigns a pained expression which cracks me up. As I giggle, he reaches up and tugs one of my braids.

"Stop it!" I slap his hand away. "Why do you always do that?" He's always playing with my hair, pretending to use the end of my braid as a paintbrush, or draping it across his lip like a mustache, or tugging it like he's turning out a light. Seriously, the guy would make a really great street mime.

"I can't help it. It's so pretty. So shiny and gold," he says, reaching up to finger the end again. "It reminds me of what Rumpelstiltskin spun out of straw."

I shake my head. "Can you please stop being weird for like two seconds?"

He shrugs again, smiling big. "I'll try. But I can't promise anything. Weird is just who I am."

This kid is literally going to be the death of me.

Taking a deep breath, I lean into him in the most professional manner I can muster. Which is hard considering I can still see him smiling with sheer delight out of the corner of my eye as I press my chest against his. When I wrap my arms around his back, I'm keenly aware of his face pressed into my hair.

"If you tell me I smell good, I swear to God I'm going to punch you," I grumble in his ear.

"Oh, don't worry, I won't," he says matter-of-factly. "Because you stink."

I burst out laughing so hard I have to let go of him. It's funny because it's true.

"I know! I do stink, don't I?!" I cry, bracing one hand on his shoulder as I laugh. He shrugs like it doesn't bother him. The guy's training to be a nurse. I'm sure he's smelled much worse than my clammy pits. "My deodorant can't keep up in this heat!"

This is another of Theo's quirks. He's painfully honest…like a little boy with no filter who tells an old lady she needs to iron out the wrinkles on her face. I think it's because of the homeschooling. No one has ever taught him how to lie.

"And by the way." I lean closer so our noses are practically touching. "You stink too!"

"I know!" He says chuckling along. "We all do! It's the tie that binds us all!"

That cracks me up even more. "Body Odor: The tie that binds us all!" I declare, sweeping a hand through the air. "That's going to be the title of our memoir about this summer."

The grueling pace of this week of training must be catching up to us because we both giggle maniacally, even though I'm pretty sure this joke isn't all that funny. And yet we can't seem to stop.

I'm almost collapsed in Theo's lap in hysterics when Dottie calls from across the room. "Concentrate people! Learning how to lift patients safely is no laughing matter!"

"Okay…okay…we can do this," I say, taking a deep breath and lining myself up in front of him again. "Just don't make eye contact with me, okay?"

Theo nods and stares stone faced ahead. I straddle his long legs and lean into him, trying not to notice how soft his hair feels on my cheek. It actually smells good, like soap and fresh air. Which is not something I should be thinking about as I haul him up on his supposedly non-functioning legs, shift him over, and ungracefully dump him on his fake throne. I hesitate a moment, taking in the feeling of his cheek pressed against mine before I stumble away, disoriented.

"There. You can piss now," I say, trying to catch my breath. Why am I so out of breath after touching him, anyway? I didn't feel this way when I transferred anyone else.

"You did great," Theo tells me, leaping to his feet beside me.

"Well, you helped me, so it was kind of cheating." I'd noticed he stood up a little as I'd pivoted him.

"No, it's not. A lot of the kids have some strength in their legs, so they'll be able to partially support their weight. In fact, it's good if you make them do a little bit on their own."

I nod, feeling relieved that it might not be as hard as I expect. Although Theo's comment only highlights the fact that he knows so much more about these kids than I do.

"Okay, your turn," he says, motioning me to the seat.

When I sit, I don't look at him towering over me because I know I'll start laughing again and Dottie will come over and kick us both in the shins.

When he bends down and wraps his arms around me something terrible happens. My entire body flushes with heat and I get this really intense impulse to wrap my arms around his neck and hug him back hard. Which is completely crazy, because I do not like him like *that*. I'm so discombobulated by my traitorous body that I end up stiffening like a block of cement in my chair. When Theo lifts me in the air, I'm so rigid my body stays folded in the sitting position like I've just come down with the world's worst case of rigor mortis.

"What the hell, Annie," Theo grunts into my ear, as my bent knees slam into his groin. "Can you relax a little?"

"Oh, yeah, yeah," I say, flattening my body against his, which only makes the damn hugging impulse rage back again. What the hell is happening to me? I know I haven't gotten laid in a few weeks, but this blushing and flushing stuff that keeps happening around Theo is really getting out of hand. The kid is only nineteen. And I never get turned on by younger guys, or guys with long hair, or guys who are nice. It has to be something else. Maybe I'm allergic to his damn shampoo or something.

I feel how red my face is when he lets go of me so I desperately try to distract him so he doesn't notice.

"Did you just curse when you were lifting me, Theo?"

"I curse sometimes. I just try to keep it to a minimum."

"I think I'm corrupting you."

"Greta's my best friend. I'm kind of incorruptible now."

I start to say, "Is that a challenge?" with my best devilish smile. But then I realize that would be flirting and I don't want to undo all the work I'd done the first day when I'd insisted that nothing is ever going to happen between us.

Turns out I don't have to even figure out a comeback because the next second Dottie orders us to find new partners and before I can even open my mouth, a cute little brunette appears at Theo's side and ushers him away. I watch as he throws his arm around her shoulder and whispers something in her ear that makes her giggle. I hate the twinge of jealousy that runs through me. For all I know he could be telling her she's pretty too. In fact, for all I know, Theo could have a crush on every single girl at this camp, not just me.

Why does that thought bother me so much?

Before he gets too far away, Theo whirls around and calls back to me, "Goodbye, my love!" with one of his floppy-armed waves.

I stand there smiling big, shaking my head in exasperation as he disappears into the crowd.

CHAPTER SIX

"YOU'RE FUCKING KIDDING me!" Greta wails from the bunk across from mine. "That's not really true, is it?!"

It's late at night and the four of us are tucked into our beds in the staff quarters. It's one of the last nights we'll all be together like this because once the campers come in two days, one of us will always have to sleep in the main room in case anything goes wrong during the night.

The thought of having to take a night shift, of being in charge of so many sick kids all alone, scares the shit out of me. Which is why I've distracted myself by asking everyone to tell me the story of how they lost their virginity. Of course, I've graciously gone first, because... well not many people can top the story of my first time.

"Yeah, it's true," I say, trying not to look too proud. "I was fifteen and he was twenty. He was one of my sister's friends in college."

Both Greta and Honey Bear have now pulled themselves up to sitting positions on their beds and are gawking at me with a mixture of shock and awe. It's the reaction my story always gets. Which is why I like to tell it. I figure I might as well be transparent about how messed up I am. That way, I won't mislead anyone into thinking I'm normal.

Susan's eyes bulge, and her mouth hangs open. She's clearly horrified.

"Don't worry, it was consensual," I say to her, and she relaxes just a bit. Then I add, "I was the one who seduced him," and she seizes up once more.

"Tell us all the gory details!" Greta calls excitedly. The huge EXIT sign over the door outside the room coats her cheeks in an eerie red glow, making her look like she's blushing. But I've heard enough of Greta's filthy jokes to know my story hasn't fazed her.

"Well, as you might expect from a first bang, it wasn't very good," I say, and everyone murmurs their understanding. Except for Susan, who looks a little worried. Yup. She's definitely a virgin. "But we kept practicing, and it got better."

"I bet it did!" Greta says, wagging her eyebrows. "You little minx, you!" She claws the air, growling like a wild animal.

"More like you little slut, you!" Honey Bear calls from the other side of the room. We all burst out laughing. I'm not offended because I know she means it affectionately. Honey Bear always calls us sluts and whores and bitches and assholes. They're terms of endearment to her. Although she's been working hard to clean up her language before the kids get here.

"I know. I kinda was, wasn't I?" I muse, thinking back on that time in my life. "I just wanted to get it over with. Find out for myself what all the fuss was about." I pause for a second, then add thoughtfully. "I was always a very curious child."

Everyone giggles again, Greta still gawking at me with admiration. "Wow. You are so cool."

I roll my eyes and pretend to be embarrassed. I don't correct her, even though I should, since what I'd done was about the furthest thing from cool there could be. In truth, it was an act of complete and utter selfishness.

At the time I'd been trying to get away from my mom, like I guess every teenager does. (Although now I regret all the time I wasted that I could've spent with her.) I'd hitchhike to Caroline's apartment at college on the weekends, timing it perfectly so I arrived when everyone was already too drunk to give me a ride home. That way she'd have to let me stay.

My appearance on her doorstep became such a routine that her friends just expected Caroline's little sister to show up and party with them every weekend. Which no one minded because I was a helluva lot more fun than uptight Caroline. I ended up spending hours drunkenly debating the meaning of life with her friend Todd, a brooding business major who barely ever cracked a smile for anyone but me. We'd become pretty good friends by the time I'd convinced him to have sex with me, so the act wasn't completely meaningless. And like I said, it got better the more we practiced. It might have even gotten great if Caroline hadn't found out and banned both me and Todd from ever coming to one of her parties again.

After telling them the whole sordid story, I point to Greta. "Okay, your turn. Tell us how you got your cherry popped."

Susan winces at my terminology but leans closer, like she can't wait to hear all the details. I'm surprised she hasn't gotten out her binder and started taking notes.

"This is a great story, so gather 'round children," Greta says, big brown eyes dancing with mischief. "It was from a very sexy relationship I had with a Tampax tampon. He and I would meet up every three weeks and just get it on!!" She makes a jabbing motion at her crotch. "For like five days straight! I'm not kidding. That guy was all up in there from morning till night! I couldn't get rid of him."

We all laugh along. No matter how serious the situation, you can always count on Greta to come up with a good joke.

I'm not letting her off the hook that easily though. "Seriously. Tell us the real details."

When I notice Susan looking green around the gills, I add. "But only if you want to, of course." I mean, I'm kind of an asshole sometimes, but I'm not callused enough to force anyone to reveal something they're not comfortable sharing.

"Alright, but it's not as exciting as yours," Greta says. "In fact, it's pretty boring. It was just some guy on the basketball team in high school. I had a major crush on him and he'd been flirting with me for most of the school year. So one day he asked me to go to his house during our lunch break. We screwed on his bed and were back to school in time to make fourth period." She shrugs, scanning our faces. "See, pretty boring."

"Did it hurt?" Susan pipes up out of nowhere.

"The actual act?" Greta asks, and Susan nods. "Not really…" Greta stares off into the distance, like she's conjuring back the memory. No one else can probably see it in the dim light, but I swear I notice a faint quiver in her bottom lip.

When she speaks again, her voice has lost all its normal buoyancy. "What really hurt was when I found out he'd only had sex with me because his buddies had dared him to. They all wanted to know what it was like to screw the deformed girl. They challenged him. Bet him he'd never be able to get it up for a girl with a disgusting half arm and half leg like me." She lifts her arm nub and wiggles her leg under the sheet, eyes glistening.

Silence swells in the small space as we all sit frozen, not knowing what to say. Then Greta shudders and in the next instant she's back to her old self again, her voice bubbly as she goes on. "But he proved them wrong. He got his little pencil dick hard. So it turned out to be a win-win for us both. He won the bet, and I lost my virginity and barely even felt a pinch. What more could a girl ask for?"

She slaps her leg, laughing like it's the funniest story she's ever told. I grin big, because I know how much Greta hates to be pitied. Even though my heart is breaking a little by what I just heard.

After Greta's honesty, Susan flat out admits to everyone she's a virgin, explaining that she's saving herself for her long-time boyfriend who she's planning on marrying next year. We all commend her for her commitment to her values. Then, when the silence doesn't get filled in by the next logical storyteller, we level Honey Bear under a collective stare.

"Oh no, no, no!" Honey Bear waves her hands in the air like she's putting up her own little force field against us. "You bitches ain't getting nothing on me!"

We all beg and plead, but she doesn't waver. "No way. When I become a famous singer I can't risk you underlings coming out of the woodwork to blackmail me with some humiliating story from when I was sixteen!"

Greta claps furiously. "Oh!! So it was when you were sixteen, then? Who was it with? A guy from your improv troupe?"

"Your brother's friend?" Susan chimes in, uncharacteristically giddy. I knew we'd corrupt her eventually.

"I bet it was a guy from your church choir!" I offer. Honey Bear rolls her eyes, but I ignore her. "A baritone…a guy that can go real *loooow*…" I wag my tongue like Gene Simmons.

Honey Bear crosses her arms over her chest and glares, looking like a bouncer at a bar. She's clearly not budging. I've noticed how, during our nightly pow wows, she reveals very little about herself. I understand her position. I'm careful about how much information I share too, so I can hardly blame her for wanting to keep her own secrets.

Wanting to let Honey Bear off the hook, I turn to Greta. "So, are there any guys here this summer you have the hots for?"

I expect Greta to deflect the question instantly, but to my surprise, she gives a coy shrug. Taking that as an outright confession, we all start squealing.

"It's Adam, isn't it!" I shout.

"Would you shut the fuck up?" Greta hisses. "They're going to hear you next door! And I'm not telling you guys anything. You'll just embarrass me if you know who it is."

"I've seen you and Adam talking a lot," I push on. "I think he's really into you. He was practically fighting to push your wheelchair the other day."

We've all been taking turns pushing each other up the hill from the lake so we can get in shape for when the kids get here. And Adam was very eager to push Greta. Everyone noticed it.

Greta makes a face. "Yeah, because it was between me and Louie who weighs almost two hundred pounds!"

"Yeah but, still…"

Greta insists it's not Adam, so we start throwing names at her.

"Tom, the dialysis nurse from Brook Cabin?" Honey Bear offers.

"I said I'm not telling you."

"A.J., the lifeguard who just graduated high school?" I try.

"I said I'm not telling you."

"Bill, the guy studying to be a gynecologist?" Susan volleys.

"Really? You think I want to date a guy whose job is looking at hootchies all day? I said I'm not telling you."

We list basically every boy in camp. (Leaving out the ones who are obviously gay.) Yet Greta remains stoic, refusing to give us even the smallest crumb.

"Well, whoever it might be. I'm sure you'll reveal your Mystery Man to us in time," I finally give in, knowing we're beat.

"I seriously doubt that. Not with your big mouths," she says, then flops down on her bed and pulls the covers over her head. "Now all of you shut up. I need my beauty sleep."

We all comply, mostly because we know Greta will throw her shoe at our heads if we don't. But as I drift off to sleep all I can think of is how awful it must have felt for her to be treated like a freak by those boys in high school. And I'm sure that's only one of many encounters with thoughtless people she's had to endure in her lifetime. Yet she still stays so upbeat, so undeterred by the challenges life has thrown at her.

Damn, that girl is tough. I've never met anyone as resilient as she is. I swear, if I could glean just a quarter of her moxie over this summer I might be able to walk out of this place a better person than when I came in.

CHAPTER SEVEN

I STEP OUTSIDE the cabin, shutting the door gently behind me so I don't wake anyone up. It's God-awful early in the morning, the sun just beginning to crack through the trees, but it's pointless to stay in bed anymore. I tossed and turned most of the night. The campers finally arrive today and I'm too anxious to sleep, so I decided to escape the stuffy air inside the cabin and come outside, hoping the breeze and the dawning sky will help calm my nerves.

I wander to the fire ring and settle on a log. Above me a melee of birds chatter. They flitter from branch to branch for no apparent reason, blabbering on relentlessly about how excited they are to start the new day. I'm glad someone's excited about what's about to come, because I'm certainly not.

The fire circle sits in the middle of two facing cabins. One for the boys and one for girls. The structures are unlike anything I've ever seen at a camp before. They're long single-story buildings that have ramps leading to every door, with wide walkways inside, vast shower bays, beds the exact height for easy transfers from wheelchairs, doorknobs levered so those with limited mobility can easily open them.

But the biggest difference between these cabins and the ones at Girl Scout camp is they each have a phone on the wall that not only goes to the camp nurse but to the local ambulance unit. A stark reminder of how high the stakes here might one day be, if someone makes a mistake.

I just want to get this day over with. I'm tired of worrying if I have what it takes to do this job. I want whatever's in store for me to hurry up and happen so I can finally stop dreading it once and for all.

Dread. That's a feeling I know all too well. It nearly suffocated me in those last months when my mom was dying. Haunted me like a ghost through endless days when we didn't know how long it would take, how much pain she'd be in, how much more her body would waste away until her organs finally gave out. It was all the uncertainty that got to me. It was all the not knowing that eventually made me run away.

I lift my eyes upward, to the smeared pastel streaks that make the sky look like a real-life watercolor painting. Again, I'm reminded of my mom. She was known for her landscape paintings, which I've noticed this past week resemble a lot of the vistas around here. Wooded forest paths. Shadowed cave entrances. The lake rippling on the sandy beach at the waterfront.

I was only nine years old when my dad left us. Although technically maybe we left him. When he took his dream job at Yale just as they'd planned, my mom refused to follow him like she'd promised. Instead, we'd stayed behind in Indiana where, according to her, the "three of us would get along just fine without him." Dad didn't have much recourse against her since they'd never married; a source of great embarrassment to me at school.

"Why don't you have your Dad's last name?" the kids would ask. It was too embarrassing to tell them the truth. That my mom was a hippie who didn't believe in the concept of binding herself to a man through an outdated contract that had nothing to do with real, free love. So, I just said it was because my mom was a famous artist, and famous artists didn't need to get married like normal people did.

It was a little bit of an exaggeration at the time. Mom wasn't quite famous yet. But not long afterward she began putting on her own exhibitions, selling her paintings for hefty prices to art collectors who claimed she was the next big thing. Her work eventually becoming lauded enough by the supposed experts that she became well known, at least in our regional art world.

Last night when I couldn't sleep, I'd gotten out the little postcard-sized watercolors of hers I carry with me everywhere I go. They always distract me when my thoughts start racing out of control. To me, those tiny paintings represent both beauty and mystery.

When Mom's will was read after she died, the lawyer had given me a manila envelope bearing my name, shakily written in Mom's handwriting. Inside were two small landscapes, painted loosely on rough edged paper. I immediately recognized them as studies; what my mom always created as a precursor to one of her larger paintings. She liked to do little practice layouts so she could become "more intimate" (as she so cringingly put it) with her subject. She'd lightly penciled the date onto the back of the paintings. *September 1967*. Which meant she had painted them when she was pregnant with me.

"She was very clear that she wanted you to have those," the lawyer had said, which only baffled me further. They were lovely renderings, my mom's immense talent shining forth even though I knew she probably had spent little time on either of them. Collectors praised her for the way she could capture the minute details of nature, using such an unforgiving medium as watercolor.

I remember her explaining the nuances of the paint to me when I was little. "Watercolors are the hardest to work with," she'd told me. "When the paint and the water combine, they tend to have a life of their own. Which is why you can never get too attached to how you *think* it should be. Instead, you always have to stay open to the flow. Let the color show you where it wants to go."

Her words came back to me when I read the little slip of paper she'd included with the two studies.

When the time comes, you'll understand, she'd scrawled on a torn scrap of art paper, her normally perfect handwriting shaky and crooked, the way it had devolved the last days of her life. *And remember, stay open to life, Buttercup. Let it show you where it wants you to go.*

Sitting on this log now, surrounded by the beauty she devoted her life to capturing, guilt weighs heavy in my chest. Because I haven't followed her advice, have I? In fact, I've done just the opposite. Every day, I add some kind of new fear, new worry to my life; my perspective shrinking, not staying open and expansive as she wished for me. And as far as her promise that one day I'll understand what her note means, I've failed at that too. Because those two postcards and their underlying message still remain a complete mystery to me.

Suddenly, I'm jarred back to reality by the sound of footsteps thudding from the woods. I whirl, half expecting a deer to leap out from the trail. But instead, Theo jogs into the clearing. He's shirtless and sweaty, his hair pulled up into a messy bun. When he sees me, his face brightens and he slows to a walk, pressing a button on his black watch, smiling at whatever he sees there.

I stand as he comes closer, trying to ignore how happy I am to see him. "What are you doing up this early?" I ask, even though it's pretty obvious.

"I run every morning. It helps me get ready for the day." He walks a big loop around me, cooling down. He's breathing hard, and I notice that although he's slender, his smooth chest is nicely muscled, his stomach chiseled enough so that each ab is clearly defined as he sucks in gulps of air.

I shake my head, stupefied by his answer. We all make fun of Theo's boundless energy. But starting his already grueling day with a workout? Now that's taking it too far. Why would he do such a thing? I ask him as much as he lopes circles around me.

He shrugs like it's nothing. "What can I say? I like how good my body feels when it's healthy. So, I work out to savor that feeling."

I make a face. What a strange answer. My body is healthy but I barely notice it…until something goes wrong, that is. Like when I'm tired or have period cramps or a headache. Who the hell notices when their body's working properly?

Of course, Theo would. He notices everything. He's the one who saw the wooly bear caterpillar crossing the path and stopped to stand guard so no one would step on it. He's the one who leaps up from the table and refills our drinks when we're two sips away from being empty. He's the one who sweeps in and gives someone a hug just when they're beginning to feel down. (A gesture that Juan seems to enjoy a bit more than the rest of us. I'm pretty sure he has a crush on Theo from the way he stares at him googly-eyed all the time.)

It's as if Theo is more finely tuned to the world than the rest of us. Although why he'd want to be so sensitive to a world as rough as this one is a mystery to me. Maybe it's because he's young and inexperienced. His life has probably been so sheltered, so privileged, that hardest thing he's ever had to face is getting a C on an English paper or having a girl turn him down for a date. That's the only reason I can think of to explain why he sees the best in everything. He must not know any better, yet.

He points off in the distance. "I usually run the Whippoorwill Loop down by the lake. But sometimes I take the Cardinal Trail, then meet up with Bluebird Way and do that twice, then catch the Owl Point trail back to here."

It always shocks me how well he already knows the camp. I'm supposed to be the nature expert here with all my training in the outdoors, and I've barely had time to explore more than the path from our cabin to the dining hall. Yet here Theo is, running circles all over the place like it's as familiar as his backyard.

The other day I heard him explaining the schedule to Juan and Adam, telling Greta about some of the special events Camp Boundless runs every year: a talent show, the parade, and fireworks they put on every 4th of July. He must have done some serious research before he started this job. How else would he know so much about this place?

"You run all those hills?" I ask in disbelief.

"Yeah. I didn't only do track in high school. I ran cross country too."

"Let me guess. State Championship senior year?"

"No, I placed third. I was favored to win. All the newspapers were saying I was a shoo-in, but I got knocked down at the start and lost one of my shoes and then someone spiked me in the calf so I was bleeding the entire race. Yeah, things didn't go as I planned. I ended up needing three stitches afterward. But hey, at least I finished."

He grins big, as if the story is hilarious and not kind of heartbreaking. Alright, so maybe his life hasn't been a bed of roses after all.

"Geez, that's awful."

He shrugs. "Makes for a good story." He stops right in front of me. Too close, only a foot away. His glasses are tinted from the sun, so I can't see his eyes clearly. I'm curious about what color they are. Maybe brown? Possibly blue?

"Why do you have your shirt off?" I grumble, taking a step back, not liking that I'm kind of enjoying the heat radiating off his bare chest.

"Uh, maybe because it's like a hundred degrees already," he says. I have to make a concerted effort not to stare at the beads of sweat rolling down the ridge between his pecs. What the hell is wrong with me? It's Theo, for goodness sakes. I can't be attracted to him.

"Still, I don't think it's fair that boys get to take their shirts off and girls don't."

He gives me a devilish smile. "Girls can take their shirts off too. They just choose not to."

"Ugh," I huff. "Don't even start with me right now! It's too early to argue with you."

"I know, I know. You haven't had your coffee yet."

I've already trained Theo to not speak to me until after I've had my morning coffee. Even though we've only been here a week, he and I already have a routine down: Every morning when I walk through the doorway of the dining hall, he hands me a cup of coffee he's prepared just the way I like (a quarter milk, the rest coffee). Then, after I take at least three full swallows, I give him a little nod and he bubbles over with every little detail he's thought of since he's seen me the night before. All while I roll my eyes and try to act disinterested, which is kind of hard because by that time I'm always laughing really hard at his antics.

Theo furrows his brows. "Why are you up so early anyway?"

I consider telling him I've spent most of the night having nightmares of accidentally dropping a camper on her head and having the police come and haul me off to jail for negligence. But Theo's heard all my worries before. I know how he'll respond. He'll just tell me how wonderful I am and that I have nothing to worry about, and I'm not sure I can take his sweetness so early in the morning.

Instead, I blurt out what I was thinking right before he crashed out of the woods. "I was looking at the sunrise." I point to the break in the trees where the sky is muddled in gentle shades of pinks and oranges. "It made me think of my mom."

He cocks an eyebrow, inviting me to say more. And to my surprise, I do. "She was an artist. She loved painting landscapes. Her favorite part was painting the backgrounds like that. Blending all the colors together so they look just like they do right now."

I lift a chin to the horizon and he turns to take it in with me. Seeing the wash of color framed in the V of the trees, I can almost hear my mom's voice. "The broad strokes are always the easiest Annie," she'd say, sweeping her brush confidently across a pristine piece of watercolor paper. "It's when you get to the details. Now that's when things get a lot more difficult."

Yeah Mom, I know. Details make everything so much harder. Which is why I avoid them as much as possible.

"She *was* an artist?" Theo says, picking up on how I used the past tense.

"Yeah. She's dead now."

He startles from my bluntness, exactly the way I'd wanted him to. Blurting it out like that tends to fluster people and I get a sick satisfaction watching them struggle for what to say next. I brace myself for the predictable questions that always come. "How did she die?" "What kind of cancer was it?" I brace myself for the pity to pool in Theo's eyes. For him to reach out and give me a patronizing pat on the arm as he gently probes me for more lurid details of her final days.

"I'm so sorry, Annie," he says. And yet I see no pity on his face. Instead, he simply says, "Tell me about her."

I blink at him in surprise. Now I'm the one who's flustered. *Tell me about her.* No one has ever asked me that before. Usually, people only want to know all the details of her diagnosis, her decline, her death. But not Theo. He wants to know about her *life*.

The sincerity on his face makes a prickling feeling begin behind my eyes. I realize now he hasn't even asked a question. Instead, it was more of a command. *Tell me about her*, he'd said. For some reason I like the firmness in his tone. His voice is like a hand on the small of my back leading me somewhere. Somewhere that feels safe to go with him there beside me.

"Um. Like I said, she was an artist…" I start off slowly, not giving too much away. But the more Theo listens, the more I reveal. I tell him about how Mom won a state-wide contest in high school for a watercolor painting she'd done. Later she was awarded a scholarship to the Rhode Island School of Design, where she'd studied under some of the best art teachers in the country. To help pay her college expenses, she'd worked as a nanny for a wealthy family and ended up loving the kids so much she'd stayed in touch with them for the rest of her life.

"She was always so good with kids," I muse. "I had such a great childhood. She taught college classes for a while. Sold some of her paintings here and there. But she gave that up for a while when Caroline and I were little." As I speak, I look at Theo's chest instead of his eyes. For some reason his gradually slowing breath settles me, seems to slow down my own heartbeat too, making it easy for me to say more. "She was a great mom, always making up games for us and letting us play in all her art supplies and taking us on field trips to zoos and museums. She was the kind of mom that made everything so much fun."

"She was good with kids, huh?" he says. "You must have inherited that from her."

"Yeah. I guess," I say, so engrossed in my memories I forget to brush off the compliment like I normally would. "She used to make up games for me to play to help calm my nerves. I was always a rambunctious child. And anxious too. As you might have guessed." He gives a little shrug, like he just might have noticed a few of my, uh…idiosyncrasies. "So, my mom got good at coming up with clever ways to keep me occupied. My favorites were the Treasure Hunts she used to set up for me."

"Treasure Hunts? You mean with maps and clues and stuff like that?"

"Yeah. All of that. It was crazy what she did." I think back on my mom's elaborate multi-stage adventures. "When I was really small, the clues were easy to find. Just simple riddles scattered under couch cushions or propped in the hand of one of my stuffed animals. The treasures at the end were usually little trinkets or art supplies I'd covet for weeks. Sometimes she'd even plant a big "X" cut out of construction on top of the surprise to make the hunt more like pirate stories I used to love as a kid." Saying that, I remember exactly what it felt like to be cuddled on her lap with a book spread before us; her breath tickling my cheek as she read aloud to me about quests for buried treasure.

"But as I got older the searches became more elaborate," I say. "She expanded the boundaries from the house to our entire five-acre lot, and her clues became so convoluted it would take me hours to decipher. Those hunts ended with more grown-up gifts like lip smackers and new journals. You know, stuff a cool teenager like me would like. And there was no easy to find paper X anymore. No, she left it all up me, with only my wits and instincts to go by. Which made finding the ending spot so much more thrilling. "

I grin big, thinking of how I used to insist I'd outgrown her game and didn't want to play it anymore. Unperturbed, she'd say, "That's fine. You don't have to play if you don't want to. I understand." Then she'd casually leave a folded up piece of paper on the end of my bed and say in a tinkly voice, "But here's the first clue. You know, just in case you're curious" and that would be it. I'd be off and running in seconds flat.

Theo nods, like he's scared to interrupt in case it might make me suddenly clam up.

Although he doesn't need to worry because it seems I can't stop myself. "But one time the last clue led to our barn," I ramble on. "And there waiting for me was the new horse I'd been begging for all year." I let out a strangled laugh, the thrill of that day rushing back with almost the same force as when I'd turned the corner and seen Velvet's beautiful black eyes staring at me from her stall. That was the day I stupidly started believing in miracles. And a few years later, I stopped believing in miracles just as suddenly, when my prayers to save my beloved mom went unanswered.

"Yeah, she had scrimped and saved for months to pull off that surprise," I tell a wide-eyed Theo. "She said, 'Don't expect me to ever replicate that again, Annie.' And afterward, just like she'd promised, the treasure hunts went back to little trinkets again. But I didn't mind, because by that time I'd realized it wasn't really the treasure at the end that mattered. It was more about the fun I had along the way."

Theo bounces on his toes, like there's a million things he wants to say. But he stops himself, noticing how my cheeks are burning from all I've over shared. He seems to recalculate himself, going on in a measured tone. "She sounds like a wonderful mother. You were very lucky to have her for the time you did."

A voice barks from inside the cabin. Honey Bear yelling at Greta to get her ass out of bed. The sound shocks me even further back to reality. To Theo, staring deep into my eyes, as if he's sharing every emotion I'm feeling.

The sensation from when we first met in the dining hall comes flooding back. The odd notion that I've known him for a long time. That he's no stranger to me. But that's impossible. Theo and I have already compared notes about our pasts and determined our paths have never crossed before.

"Anyway. That's that." I clap my hands, needing to put an end to this exchange. I was already confused enough when I came out here this morning. I don't need Theo and his strange familiarity making it even worse.

"Thanks for sharing all of that with me, Annie," he says. "I'm really close to my mom and I know I'd be devastated if anything happened to her." He hesitates, seeming to fight with himself about what he wants to say next. "But I want you to know that death doesn't separate us from the people we love. Your mom may be gone physically, but she's still always with you… never too far away."

"Oh my God!" I throw my palms up, backing away in horror. "You're not one of *those* kind of people are you?"

"What kind of people?"

"The kind of people who come up to you at your mom's funeral to tell you your dead mother is still looking down on you. That you're lucky because you'll always have a Guardian Angel watching out for you now."

He chuckles a little, tipping his head back and forth as if he's weighing his words carefully. "I might not say it at the *funeral*, but…"

I can't believe he's actually laughing. Acting like this is nothing. Acting like dying is no big deal. I would've preferred his pity to this nonchalant attitude.

I shake my head, backing further away. "Listen, you can think whatever you want to about death. Just do me a favor and keep it to yourself, Buster."

"Buster?"

"It's the name I give to people who need to keep their big traps shut."

"Duly noted," he says, unruffled by my inane outburst. "But about your mom…"

"Watch it," I warn. "Or I'll Buster you again."

He ignores me. "I don't just think she's still near you, Annie. I *know* she is."

The conviction in his voice freezes me in place. What the hell does he mean by that? I can tell he's baiting me. Wanting me to ask him how he knows something that's clearly unknowable. But I'm not falling for his trick. He's probably going to start spouting a bunch of bullshit like my Aunt Lydia did at the gravesite when she said my mom was still by my side, even though I can't physically see her anymore. Typical crazy Aunt Lydia stuff. Ever since she was a girl, Mom's sister has claimed to have some kind of hot line to the other side. Always sensing auras and hearing whispers in her head that supposedly give her real-time guidance in her life. You know, outrageous, impossible stuff like that.

"Like I said, you can believe whatever you want," I snap, wishing my voice didn't sound so shaky. "I'm not stopping you. I just don't want to hear it myself, okay?"

He furrows his brow at me, a little smile playing on his lips like he's thinking, "*The lady doth protest too much*." And maybe he's right. Why does this topic always make me so damn mad?

"Listen, I'm going to take a shower now." I say, desperate to escape Theo's smug grin. "And you, sir," I point to his bare chest. "You need to put on a damn shirt."

Again, he laughs, like we've been talking about the weather, not heavy important stuff like whether or not my mom still gives a shit about me. Which pisses me off even more. I want to storm back to the cabin and slam the door behind me, I'm so aggravated. But I don't want Theo to know he's gotten to me, so instead I make a point of leisurely strolling away. And not looking back once.

I'm so riled up that it takes me until I'm halfway through my shower to realize something. Theo never did ask me how my mom died.

CHAPTER EIGHT

A STEADY STREAM of cars pours into the parking lot next to the dining hall. So far, arrival day has run like clockwork. Miles stands at the edge of the parking lot welcoming families, giving out the kids' cabin assignments, then directing each group to the lawn of the dining hall where we counselors complete the check-in process.

As Cabin Head, Susan sits at our Franklin Cabin table recording care instructions from the parents while Honey Bear, Greta, and I greet the campers. I'm trying my hardest to act normal; to muster the same energy I'd always had on opening day of Girl Scout camp. But inside I feel like an actor playing a stilted, incredibly cringe-worthy version of myself.

I'd tried to conjure back the old me this morning; gathering our cabin with the boys next door and forcing everyone to touch their friendship bracelets together in a circle. Then I'd shouted a rallying cheer for us to have the best summer of our lives. But no matter how excited I might appear on the outside, inside I feel like an imposter. My heart keeps leaping into my throat every time a new girl arrives, wondering if it's Jenny, the seventeen-year-old with cerebral palsy who will be my primary charge for the session. And that's certainly not how an over-qualified, veteran camp counselor like me is supposed to be feeling right now. And yet here I am. Scared of a freaking kid.

Of course, Theo and Greta are in their glory, yucking it up like two Vaudeville performers on the lawn in front of me. Theo is juggling (not just three balls but six) and Greta is high-fiving every camper that walks by with her prosthetic arm. A gesture which had earned a sheepish smile from a teenaged boy who'd whacked her back with his own matching prosthetic arm as he'd taken his place in line a few moments ago.

Watching the exchange, I thought of how the boy probably doesn't get to see many people like himself in his everyday life. The poignancy of the simple act hit me hard and for a split second I forgot to be nervous. Maybe that's what I need to do to settle down. Stop thinking of my own damn self for once.

I test out my theory by searching for the boy again. He's at the table next to ours looking bored while Adam talks to his parents. He keeps glancing back at Greta every two seconds. I can tell he's already smitten. Whether by her beauty or the way she brashly flaunts her supposed disability, I can't tell. Miles had told us in training this was another reason a camp like this is so important. It gives kids the chance to see other people who look just like them.

Juan sidles up next to me and together we watch Theo and Greta's antics. He launches into a rant about Theo's shaggy hair and terrible fashion sense, a topic that's bonded us this past week.

"If I could just get my hands on him, style that hair, get rid of those glasses, those horrible clothes," he whispers to me. "Mmmmm. That boy could be gorgeous."

I laugh, agreeing with his assessment. Although we're all wearing our green Camp Boundless polos, Theo has accessorized his in his typical bizarre way; wearing a folded red bandana as a headband, garishly striped shorts, and two different colored tube socks pulled all the way up to his knees. He looks like the love child of Axel Rose and Bozo the Clown. I've noticed a few of the parents giving him the side eye as they walk by. But those odd glances are nothing compared to the number of kids he's made smile so far today.

My nerves must have shown earlier, because Theo had found me before the kids arrived, slung an arm over my shoulder and hugged me roughly to his side. His hair was still damp from the shower and he smelled really soapy and clean. I hoped it was early enough in the day that I still smelled good, too.

"Everything's going to be alright," he'd reassured me. "Just remember. Kids are all alike. They just want to play and have fun and get the hell away from their parents for a little while. It doesn't need to be anything more than that."

I'd hugged him back, grateful for the way he always makes hard things seem so easy. Although, it still annoys me how relaxed he is. As the veteran here, I'm the one who is supposed to be reassuring him, not the other way around.

Now, at the entrance of the parking lot, a long line of parents and kids line up in front of Miles. He's especially brilliant today, so handsome and charismatic, oozing his Aussie charm all over the place. Sometimes, to help myself fall asleep at night, I think what it would be like to kiss him, touch him…do other things with him. He's older, off limits, and would be a scandalous choice of a man. Which makes him even more tantalizing to me.

Honey Bear sits at the end of our table, talking with the girl who will be her primary charge. Although I'm not sure I'd call it a conversation, since I don't think Honey Bear has gotten a word in edge wise since Lisa rolled up in her wheelchair a few minutes ago. She's a fifteen-year-old with Spina Bifida, and from what I've gather from her loud monologue, she has a crush on Johnny Depp, a stash of makeup in her backpack that her parents won't let her wear at home, and a fierce determination to have "the time of her life" this week. Yeah, she's going to be a handful.

Just like the two boys who keep drifting away from their group in order to check out cute girls. Wendell and Juan have had to corral them back three times already. Each session we'll either have a cabin of able-bodied kids or a cabin of kids who use wheelchairs. Miles says the rotation will prevent us from getting too burned out from the physical demands of taking care of the higher needs kids.

When my eyes swing back to Miles, he's pointing straight at me. The man and woman he's talking to give me a little wave, and although I can't see her yet, I immediately know they're Jenny's parents. I wave back, smiling so big my cheeks cramp.

As the group makes their way toward me, Jenny comes into view and my smile relaxes into one that feels a hundred times more genuine. She's adorable. Her brown hair is pulled back into a high ponytail and she's dressed head to toe in pink. She's decorated her electric wheelchair with sparkly streamers and glittery stars on the wheel spokes.

I have to remind myself she's seventeen because she looks so much younger. She seems so small, so fragile. The bones of her skinny arms contort at odd angles; her legs wound so tightly around each other I'm not sure which foot is the right and which is the left. I swear, she looks like she's made of matchsticks. My stomach flips imagining what would happen if I accidentally let her slip through my hands in the bathroom stall. From the looks of her I think she'd splinter into a million pieces.

Her parents flank her sides, looking tired and anxious. As they come closer her dad leans down and whispers something in Jenny's ear. Jenny's eyes shoot upward and she groans at what appears to have been a bad Dad joke. I'm shocked by what a normal teenaged reaction it is. Hearing myself, I cringe. After an entire week of training, I'm supposed to know better than to judge these kids as normal or abnormal anymore.

Susan greets the parents and introduces me as Jenny's lead counselor. As the parents take me in, my heart hammers so hard in my chest I struggle to catch my breath.

"So great to meet you all!" My voice sails up way too high at the end. "I'm Annie!!" It's a stupid thing to say since Susan just told them that. I hold out my hand for Jenny to shake and immediately know it's a very, very wrong thing to do. Jenny has spastic cerebral palsy with very limited control of her limbs, so she can't shake my hand. Trying to cover my flub, I swing my hand over to her dad, who shakes it, then to her mom who does the same. Although she's a bit distracted because she's busy showing Susan a notebook full of instructions on how to keep Jenny alive this week.

I smile wanly down at Jenny, trying to think of something to say. She's in constant motion, body rocking and head waving from side to side, seemingly out of her control. Her mouth opens wide, lips pulled all the way back to show her gums, then closes again. A tiny strand of saliva escapes out of the corner of her mouth and dangles down her cheek. Her dad takes a cloth from the bag on the side of the wheelchair and gently wipes it away, barely taking his attention away from his wife who is now reading each bullet point to Susan in a drill sergeant voice that rivals Nurse Dottie's.

"Are you happy to be here Jenny?!" I shout it so loudly both her parents stop and give me an odd look, then return to what they were doing. I cringe again. What's wrong with me? Jenny doesn't have a hearing problem. In fact, she doesn't have any problem other than her uncooperative body. When we'd poured over her chart yesterday, Dottie had drilled that fact into my brain. Jenny has no intellectual disabilities, which means she's just as smart as any other seventeen-year-old. And I have to remember to treat her that way.

Her head tilts backwards as she peers up at me. She grunts something I can't understand, but since she appears to be smiling, I assume she's saying that Yes, she is glad to be here.

"Good to hear that! I'm happy to be here too," I chime back woodenly. Her smile fades a little and I have the distinct impression I've said the wrong thing. She slides one hand erratically around on the tray attached to her wheelchair. A large alphabet is printed in bold letters on the middle of the board, with brightly colored symbols along each side. Dottie taught us that communication boards like this are how non-verbal kids express themselves. Although Jenny's chart said she also speaks. But I have a sinking feeling that if the grunts I'd just heard are her way of speaking, I'm never going to understand a word she says.

The more Jenny's hand darts around the board, the faster my heart ratchets in my chest. Out of the corner of my eye, I see her parents watching me but I still can't make out what Jenny is trying to spell. The harder I try, the more my mind goes blank. It reminds me of the panic that used to come over me in school whenever I'd get called up to do a math problem on the chalkboard in front of the class. From the safety of my seat I'd know how to solve it, but up there with everyone watching, all I could think of was how badly I was failing, how stupid I was, how everyone was laughing at me. Then everything I logically knew only moments before would dissolve out of my mind like it was made of mist. And the more I desperately tried to grab it back, the further it slipped away.

The same thing is happening now. But instead of a room full of schoolkids staring at me, the only eyes on me are an adorable girl dressed in pink and her increasingly worried-looking parents.

Trying to save myself, I whirl to Jenny's mom and dad. "I saw that Jenny's been coming to camp for a long time. Uh, how many years has it been?"

They exchange a concerned glance. "Yes, she's been coming since she was little." Her mom motions to her daughter. "But you can ask her yourself how many years it's been."

I swallow hard, turning back to Jenny. The noonday sun beats down on me, making me feel like a hunk of meat roasting on a spit. She jerks in her seat, and I have the distinct impression she's fighting to keep herself from rolling her eyes at her mom. I focus on the hand that has now swung over to the number pad on board. It's not as jerky as before, but it's moving enough that I can't quite make out which number she's pointing to.

Still, I figure I better at least give it a try. "Umm…three years?"

She grunts something loudly and I know my guess is wrong. Her parents watch over my shoulder as she struggles valiantly to still her hand. The effort looks so frustrating I want to yell, "Can someone please just tell me so this poor girl doesn't have to work so hard?!" But then I remember another of Dottie's lessons: Don't do too much for the kids. It's important to support the campers' independence.

I guess another wrong answer, and the panic mounts higher. What if I never get it right? What if I just start shouting random numbers and her parents realize I'm never going to understand Jenny and they ask Miles to reassign her to another cabin because I'm obviously too incompetent to take care of their daughter? Oh my God, I should have never come here. I'm not strong enough to do this. I'm only going to mess everything up.

Finally, her mom comes over and pulls me closer to her daughter. "You see how this one knuckle points out a little more than the others?" Although Jenny's hands are clenched in a fist, I see that one finger protrudes more than the others. "That's how she points. That's how you can make out which symbol she's trying to show you."

"Ahhh! Yeah, I got it." I take a deep breath, feeling just the slightest bit better. Then I try again. "Six! You've been coming here for six years!"

Jenny careens back and forth in her chair, laughter pouring forth, a universal sound that doesn't need any interpretation at all. I pump a fist in the air. Her parents clap and look just the slightest bit relieved. Maybe they won't rat me out to Miles after all.

They return to Susan and I notice a bit of drool escaping the side of Jenny's mouth. Her dad is distracted, so I do what he did earlier, grabbing the cloth out of the backpack and mopping her mouth with it. But I must not do it right because she jerks back in her chair, whipping her head away from me, grunting like I've somehow insulted her. I mean, yeah, I probably should've folded the cloth up a bit so it didn't flop into her eyes so much, but I don't think I did it all that differently than her dad. What did I do wrong?

Jenny's parents head to drop her medication off at the infirmary, leaving Jenny and me alone. I feel like I should try to talk to her again, but I'm terrified I won't be able to understand what she says. So, I stand stiffly beside her chair as she looks out on the busy scene unfolding around us, a huge smile dancing along her face.

An unbridled joy radiates from her; a vibration of energy that doesn't need words for me to understand. She beams and grunts softly, clearly excited to be here with kids her own age. What was I doing at seventeen, anyway? Drinking too much, having too much sex with anonymous boys to numb the pain of losing my mom.

As hard as that time was, at least I'd had my freedom. Which is probably something Jenny rarely experiences. She has to rely on her parents to feed her, dress her, take her to the bathroom. She's never away from them, except for this one week of the year when she gets to come to camp and be a teenager like everyone else. The rarity of this time makes me feel even more responsible for making this week special for her. I hope I don't let her down.

One thing's for sure though. It's going to be awfully hard to know if Jenny's having fun if I can't even make out a Yes or a No answer when I ask her a question. I decide I have to try talking to her again. I wait until her head bobs back in my direction and catch her eye.

"What are you excited about doing this week?" Again, my voice is way too loud, but at least it doesn't sound as babyish as before. I used to ask the girls at my other camp the same thing when they arrived on the first day, so I don't think the question is too patronizing.

She responds with a string of garbled noises. When I stand there frozen, she repeats the exact same garbled noises. Alright, that means it's a full sentence. She says it again. This time I make out six syllables and I definitely heard an "I" at the beginning, so that's something. But everything after that is just gibberish. My armpits prickle as she says it again and I still can't make it out. Desperate to end this pointless struggle, I consider just faking like I understand and say, "Oh that sounds like fun!" But from the knowing glint in Jenny's eye, I have a feeling she's not going to let me off the hook so easily.

Suddenly, Jenny starts convulsing wildly in her chair; arms flailing, upper body straining against the straps that hold her upright. Panicked, I whirl to Susan for help, but she's busy checking in another family so she doesn't notice Jenny's distress. Right when I'm about to shout for the nurse because my camper is having a seizure, I hear a voice call out Jenny's name behind me and whirl to find Theo running at her with his arms outstretched, a huge smile on his face. That's when I realize that Jenny's not having a seizure, she just excited to see him.

"How are you, my friend?" Theo asks, swooping in to give Jenny a big hug, which she welcomes with an enormous grin. Then Theo does the craziest thing: he kneels down in front of her wheelchair so they're both eye to eye. From that vantage point, Jenny doesn't have to wrench her neck back to see him, which makes her look a thousand times more comfortable than when I was trying to talk to her. Wow. Bending down to her level. Why didn't I think of that?

Still, their joyous reunion confuses me. How could they know each other if Theo has never been a counselor here before? He did mention that he's already done rotations at the Children's Hospital in Indianapolis for school. Maybe that's where they met.

Jenny calms down, but her body still jerks with excitement. Theo holds her clenched fist in his hands, gently stroking the back of it to soothe her. "Oh, sorry to interrupt," he says, looking up at me. "What were you two talking about, anyway?"

When I meet his eyes, I have the distinct impression he's aware of my predicament and has swooped in to soothe me, too.

"Uh, I was just asking Jenny what activity she's excited about doing this week," I say stiffly.

Jenny looks directly at Theo and repeats the same six syllable sentence I couldn't understand before.

He nods vigorously, hair flapping around his red headband like a lion's mane. "I know! Me too. It's so hot." He glances pointedly at me. "I can't wait to go swimming, too."

Oh! So that's what she was saying. *I want to go swimming*. Now I hear it.

The next thing I know, something strange begins to happen. Theo and Jenny start having a conversation. Like a real, normal, back-and-forth conversation. He asks questions. She answers them. She asks questions. He answers them. He teases her. She apparently teases him back. At least that's what it seems like by the way they're both laughing. I stand there watching the scene unfold completely dumbfounded.

It takes me a while to notice that Theo is repeating all of Jenny's responses out loud. "You're going to miss your dog huh?" "Of course I'll play my guitar for you…" "You can't wait for pizza night…" I realize he's interpreting for me so I can learn to understand her. And he's definitely on to something because the more I listen, the more her grunts begin sounding like words.

I study how Theo interacts with her. Sometimes if he can't make out an answer, he asks her to use her communication board. He seems adept at catching what her various symbol combinations mean. (A heart tapped after spelling out the words trees meant she wants to go on a hike; and X after spelling out the word ants…well that one's pretty obvious).

He waits patiently as she fights her contracting muscles, trying to wrestle her arm where she wants it to go. And if he doesn't understand what she's trying to spell on the first try he doesn't panic, he simply says "Again," and waits for her to start over. And when a line of saliva falls down from her mouth, Theo doesn't even break the conversation. He just finds the cloth and subtly dots her mouth in such an unobtrusive motion it's almost like a sleight of hand. Jenny doesn't even notice he's done it, unlike when I engulfed her entire face with the cloth and nearly smothered her.

It really is quite beautiful, this gentle dance going on between the two of them. I marvel at Theo's sureness, wondering if he really is some sort of magician. Because right now he truly seems like a man with mystical powers I'll never possess.

After a few more minutes, Theo tells Jenny he better get back to his kids and stands up tall again. He gives me a reassuring "you got this" look and I have the odd urge to clutch onto his arm and beg him not to leave.

"Oh man, you're so lucky, Jenny," Theo says before he goes. "Annie's the best counselor in the whole entire camp! You guys are going to have so much fun together."

I touch his arm, silently thanking him for his kindness once again. He gives me a little wink and heads off. And when I turn back to Jenny, I swear she gives me a wink, too.

∞

Jenny's parents return soon afterward, and we spent the next hour at the campsite, unpacking and meeting the other girls in our cabin.

Being old hats at drop off day, Jenny's parents are one of the first to leave. So, Jenny and I wait by the fire ring while the rest of the girls say their tearful goodbyes inside.

Many of the parents are leaving their kids for the first time in their lives. Miles said that for most of the parents the week their child comes to camp is the only break they get for the entire year. Which makes me feel pretty wimpy for wondering if I have the stamina to make it through a few measly months of being a camp counselor.

I sit on a log next to Jenny's wheelchair, watching Theo a few feet away. He's smiling mildly at two boys having a contest over who can snap the biggest stick over their leg in the fastest time. I'm not used to boys, so I don't know if breaking things then grunting like cavemen afterward is normal behavior. But Theo doesn't seem too bothered, so apparently it is.

Jenny already knows a lot of the campers assigned to our two cabins from previous years. In fact, I noticed how she blushed when Sean, a cute boy with Hodgkin's Lymphoma, had stopped by to catch up what she'd been up to since they'd last seen each other.

With a cabin full of girls in wheelchairs, I didn't think I'd have to worry about one of my campers slipping off to have a make out session in the woods with a boy. But maybe I'd been wrong to make that assumption. I guess I shouldn't underestimate the power of hormones. And hey, if our goal here is for the kids to have as normal a camp experience as possible, then maybe I can look the other way if Jenny just so happens to get a kiss here and there. She is seventeen, after all.

"So, what do you want to do while we wait, Jenny?" It's a pretty specific question, but I'm emboldened by the fact that Theo's nearby if I need help interpreting her answer.

She says a word, then repeats it. When I furrow my brows at her, she slides her hand to a symbol on the side of her board. It's a bright yellow face with its mouth open wide. She points her knuckle at it then lets out a long, "*Ahhhhhh,*" her voice rising and falling as she drags out the sound.

"You want to eat?" When she shakes her head, I'm confused. I thought that's what that symbol meant?

She tries again. Open mouth face symbol. "*Ahhhhhh!*"

Out of the corner of my eye, I see Theo come closer, but he doesn't butt in. He lets me keep trying to figure it out. Although I can tell by his little grin, he already knows what Jenny's saying.

When I still don't understand after Jenny does it again, she and Theo both crack up at how I'm struggling.

"Don't laugh at me!" I wail, giggling along with them. "I'm trying so hard here!"

Jenny laughs even louder at my admission. I figure I might as well just be truthful about it. Something tells me Jenny respects honesty way more than people blowing smoke up her ass; something she probably gets a lot of.

Theo works hard to wrench down his smirk. "Try doing it yourself," he suggests. "Do what the symbol is doing and then make the sound like she is."

I make my mouth into an exaggerated O shape just like the yellow face on the board, hamming it up to make Jenny laugh harder, then mimic her long *Ahhhhhh* sound. As soon as the sound comes out, I know exactly what she's trying to tell me.

"You want to sing!"

Theo claps and Jenny rocks back and forth violently, both excited I've finally figured it out. Hearing our commotion, the boys stop their cavemen reenactment and come over to see what's going on.

"I'm glad you guys got such a kick out of my stupidity," I grumble, then shoot Jenny a sly wink. I feel so much more relaxed around her now that I'm not pretending to be someone I'm not.

"Alright, singing camp songs is one thing I know how to do," I tell her. "So, what song do you want to sing?" Even as I say it, I wonder how this is going to work. So far I've only heard Jenny grunt and groan a bunch of odd sounds. Is she even capable of singing a song?

Theo and I both draw closer, bending over her board as her hand whirls over the alphabet. After a few letters, she looks up at us expectantly, but neither one of us has caught what she spelled. "Again," I say, and as she starts over, I realize my heart isn't pounding like a jackhammer because I didn't get it the first time. I'm too busy trying to decipher what she's trying to say to waste time beating up on myself.

In my calmness, my focus becomes sharper and I'm able to make out exactly where each knuckle is pointing.

"D-E-R" I spell slowly along with her. "B-Y." She hesitates and I clasp my hands together in sudden realization. "Derby Town! You want to sing Derby Town?"

She nods furiously and Theo elbows me, acknowledging my new prowess. I'm so excited it takes me a moment to remember something. "Hey, wait a minute. They banned that song at my old camp."

I blink around at all their smiling faces. The boys look especially intrigued by the word banned. Derby Town is an old song passed down through generations. Each stanza ends with a dirty word that you never actually say out loud, even though the rhyme makes it clear which word is implied. That's why parents weren't so happy when their little kids came home singing it at the top of their lungs.

"Yeah, that song is outlawed at Camp Boundless, too." Theo lifts an eyebrow at me, almost like he's daring me to sing it.

"Well, let's give this girl what she wants!" I say, and the three kids cheer.

I start singing and everyone chimes in.

"In Derby Town, in Derby Town the streets are made of glass. And if you tend to slip and fall you'll fall right on your…"

The rest of us hesitate like we're supposed to, but to my complete surprise Jenny shouts out with perfect clarity, "ASS!"

We all dissolve into laughter, Jenny the loudest, and I go on.

"Hocus Pocus, domino-cus, two men digging a ditch. One is a son of a millionaire, the other's a son of a…"

"BITCH!" Jenny bellows.

I clutch my stomach, laughing hard, catching eyes with Theo as he laughs just as hard. Jenny doesn't hold back as we keep singing. No, the little rascal might look like an innocent fourteen-year-old, but she's definitely every bit of seventeen. And when she yells out the next curse word, I can't help but think about how Theo is right. Kids really *are* all alike.

CHAPTER NINE

THREE DAYS LATER I'm lying on the couch in the staff lounge cabin, a fan blowing directly on my face, determined to meet only one goal: spending my entire free period not moving one single muscle in my body.

So far, the first session of camp has gone better than I expected. I can now make out roughly seventy percent of what Jenny and Lily, the other girl with spastic cerebral palsy in our cabin, have to say. I'm nearly an expert on female catheterization and have only spilled the contents of my collection on the bed once. (And on the floor another time, but that clean up was easy, so it barely counted.) And I've given Jenny not one but two enemas using the Dawn dish soap container her parents left behind filled with the exact ratios they instructed (a tablespoon of dish soap, the rest warm water). Which was not at all how I was taught to perform an enema in training. But since Dottie said we always follow the parents' instructions, I did what I was told and everything came out all right in the end. Pun intended.

Yet even with all my success, there's still been the exhaustion to contend with. Now I know what Miles was trying to prepare us for. Not only is there the physical toll of lifting and dressing and bathing the girls along with pushing wheelchairs up and down hills in the relentless heat of June. There's also the mental toll of worrying about pressure sores and brewing low-grade infections and testing blood sugars and urine samples, the results of which can turn life-threatening if something is inadvertently missed. Add to that the strain of constantly trying to communicate with the campers while staying patient and calm amid a tightly structured schedule. Even after only three days here, I'm quite certain this is going to be the hardest (and quite possibly the most rewarding) three months of my life.

I've decided the only way I'm going to get through this marathon is by taking it day by day. Hour by hour. Minute by minute. And for the next 60 minutes of this day all I want is cool air blowing on my skin and a brief moment of not worrying about anyone other than myself.

The screen door slams and footsteps come closer, but I'm too tired to even open my eyes to see who it is. I feel a presence looming over me, but instead of acknowledging them, I silently scream inside my mind for whoever it is to leave me the hell alone. Don't they recognize a person in a state of complete and total collapse when they see one?

"What are you doing?" Theo asks.

I groan. Of course it's him here to bother me. I swear to God, I can't get a moment's peace from this guy.

"Isn't it obvious? I'm solving the world famine crisis," I snap, sarcastically. "Shhhhh...I'm just on the verge of ending drought in Africa. Don't interrupt me."

He huffs a laugh. There's no point in opening my eyes. I already know what I'll see; him grinning down at me, wearing that damn red headband again over his wild hair, practically glowing with energy.

When I'd complained about his enthusiasm the other day, he'd explained that the word enthusiasm originally meant '*inspired by theos*' the Greek word for God, so that was the reason he was the way he was. He was simply living up to his namesake. Sometimes I wish he wasn't so smart. He'd be a lot easier to argue with if he really was as dumb as he looked.

"So you're spending your time off in here?" The tone of his voice makes me crack one eye open. Surprisingly, he's not smiling at me like

I'd predicted. Instead, his face is all scrunched up like I've completely lost my mind.

"Yeah. It's the staff lounge, isn't it? The name kind of implies that this is the place where we, the staff, do in fact *lounge*."

"But it's so hot in here."

I let out a heavy breath. He's right. The cabin sits in a field with the sun beating down on its roof. Even with its two tiny windows open and the fan blowing directly on me I still feel like I'm being baked alive.

"It's hot everywhere," I counter, not wanting him to be right again.

He goes to the old-fashioned refrigerator in the corner and slings the door open wide. "I know a place that's way cooler than this." He bends to look inside. "I'm going there now. You should come with me."

He retrieves a shiny glass bottle of Coke and pops the top off with the bottle opener nailed to the wall. My mouth waters, hearing the bubbles hiss and fizzle.

"Would I have to move my body to get to this place?" I ask.

"Yeah. There might be a little bit of movement involved." He takes a long swallow of the Coke. I can almost taste its icy sweetness running down my throat. God, I want a drink of it so badly. "But I promise, you'll like it when you get there," he says.

He grabs another bottle of Coke from the fridge, opens it, then comes to the couch and dangles it above me, just out of my reach. Damn the bastard. I swear he can read my mind.

"Come on. Let's go." His mouth is cocked up on one side like he knows he's got me hooked.

I'm going to have to sit up to get the damn Coke. And once I'm up, I might as well follow him to this supposedly much cooler place, which he claims I'm going to like. And which, from his past record of knowing me, he's probably right about.

"Alright, alright." I groan, feeling every aching muscle as I slowly make my way to my feet. I snatch the bottle out of his hand, grumbling as I follow him out the door. "But this better be good."

CHAPTER TEN

THEO

ANNIE PLODS BEHIND me, slower than I've ever seen her walk before. She must really be as tired as she looks. But when I get to the path to the lake, she stops dead in her tracks.

"Oh, no. I'm not going down there. Then I'll only have to climb back up. And that's way more movement than I agreed to."

She glowers at me, arms crossed, blue eyes narrowed; her golden braids all askew. It takes everything I have not to burst out laughing. I find it funny how she pretends to be so tough. I'm not sure who she thinks she's fooling. I've seen her with the kids. I know how hard she works to make sure they have fun. How concerned she is about their comfort. How she wants to make their week so special. She's a big softie pretending to be a hardass.

She's even sweet with me although she tries to cover it up with sarcastic jokes.

"You look a little haggard today, Theo," she'll say. "Are you sure you're sleeping okay?"

"Here, let me run and get that lunch tray for you. You obviously need to conserve your energy because you have so very little of it."

I don't know why she tries so hard to hide who she really is. Maybe she truly doesn't know how good she is yet. But I do. Which is why, standing here in this forest with her all alone, I not only want to laugh at her, I want to sweep her in my arms and kiss that adorable little pout right off her lips. But I can't do that. At least not yet.

She tips her head, waiting for my response. There's only one path before us and yet I still feel like I'm at a crossroads. When I'd asked her to join me I'd known exactly where I wanted to take her. But now I'm not so sure.

I already know the questions this place will bring up. How will I answer them? Should I tell her the entire truth of what's going on between us or just part of it? She still seems so skittish, like she's fighting with herself all the time. So defensive and wary about trusting anyone. Although I can feel her loosening up around me. I've noticed how she always seeks me out in a crowd, like she actually enjoys being near me. Our bond is clearly snapping into place. Slowly. Very slowly. Still, I feel like it all might be too much, telling her how I already know her. I'm afraid instead of drawing her closer, it might do just the opposite and push her away.

She closes the space between us. Stands so near I can see the little smattering of freckles on her nose. Dammit. I want to kiss those too.

"Where are you taking me?" She's slipped and accidentally let her angry facade down. My stomach flips at the way she looks at me with this tiny, almost flirtatious smile on her face. Yes, she clearly wants to be here with me, no matter how much she pretends otherwise. Something lifts in my chest at that realization and in that instant the voice slips in.

Show her, she says.

God, I'm lucky I can hear my Angel. Sometimes it's sad to think that other people hear theirs but actually choose not to listen. Or, like Annie, mistakenly believe they're here all alone and abandoned with no guidance at all.

"Just trust me, Annie," I tell her.

Then I step off the path, holding my breath, waiting for what she's going to do next.

And without another word, she follows.

CHAPTER ELEVEN

ANNIE

I'M SHOCKED WHEN Theo steps off the trail and starts crashing through the woods.

"Where are we going?" I ask.

"Just trust me, Annie," he says, not even looking back.

"Fine." I begrudgingly follow, prattling on about all the ways I'm going to make him pay if he's wrong about this place in between slugs of my Coke.

"So, when are we going to get there?" I whine a while later, sounding worse than a kid in the back seat of a car.

"Like I said before, Annie…"

"I know, I know. Trust you." I stop to wrestle away a branch that's become snagged in my braid.

We only have to bushwhack for a little while before Theo steps out onto another clear trail which angles upwards, not down. It's lined with weathered boards, some broken, some completely missing in places so you can see the mud underneath. But even in its current state of disrepair, I can tell it once was a path meant for wheelchairs.

My mind rifles back over the maps I've seen in the Nature Center. "What is this trail? I don't remember seeing it on any of the maps."

The forest is dense and overgrown, the only sound now the

rhythmic slap of our sneakers on wood, the occasional whir and click of a cricket. The umbrella of trees only allows in thin smudges of sunlight, making the air cooler and easier to breathe in here. Already I'm glad I came. But I'm not about to admit that to Theo.

"This is an old trail," he calls over his shoulder. "Which, as you can tell, needs a lot of work. That's why they don't want anyone knowing about it."

He lopes easily in front of me, his stride so long I have to jog to keep up. I stay quiet, watching the light strobe on his flowing hair, wondering how he knows about this trail if it isn't on any map.

As we walk, I consider complaining about the fact we're going uphill, which is clearly against my wishes. But the angle of the climb is subtle, the forest so hushed and peaceful I can't muster up the energy to bitch at him like usual. I already feel so much better than when I was in that stuffy cabin. Even if this destination turns out to be a disappointment, just knowing about this abandoned trail will be worth the trip.

After walking a little further, an opening in the woods appears in the distance; a brightness in the archway of the trees that hints at some kind of open expanse beyond. As we get closer, I make out a platform at the trail's end made of the same weathered boards we're walking on, with railings along three of its sides. We've obviously reached our destination.

Theo takes a step up on the deck and waves one hand around the space with a dramatic flourish. "Behold. Bluff Point Lookout!"

Walking out on the platform I'm stunned by what I see before me. The deck is perched up high on the edge of a cliff looking out on the glittering lake below. From this vantage point you can see the water's entirety; its elongated kidney shape curving far off in the distance, edged by trees that look so tiny they remind me of something you'd buy at a craft store to decorate a school diorama.

The vista is so beautiful it takes a few seconds before I can catch my breath to speak.

"This is amazing," I whisper reverently. I feel like I've stepped inside an ancient church cathedral, the turquoise lake and cloudless blue sky and variegated green trees glittering like stained glass windows all around us.

"Be careful," Theo says gently, coming up behind me. He points out where some boards are cracked and rotted. "Don't lean on the railing. It might give way."

"Yeah," I say, noticing a spot on one side where a fallen board has left a gap between land and air. "I can see why they don't want anyone coming here."

Even though the structure juts out over the lake, the trees shade most of it; the breeze blowing up from the water cool and refreshing, laced with the loamy smell of mud and rocks.

All of a sudden, a rush of emotion hits me like a punch in the gut. My chest aches and eyes well, as if I'm about to cry. But out of happiness, not sadness, like usual. It feels like I'm meant to be here… like I'm coming home to a place that's important to me. Although I have no idea why.

I turn to Theo, now standing beside me, soaking in the view too. "You were right. This place is way better than the staff lounge." I fight to get my equilibrium back. "Thanks for bringing me here."

I'm bewildered by my strange reaction to this place. It's not like this is the first time I've ever seen a breathtaking view. So why am I getting all choked up like this?

Theo doesn't take his eyes from the lake. "Thanks for trusting me, Annie."

I'm glad he convinced me to come. Yet, as I stand here, remembering how hidden the trail was and how this Bluff Point Lookout isn't on any maps, I can't help but wonder something.

"How in the world do you know about this place?"

He tips his head at me. "We used to come here past summers when I was younger. Back when it wasn't so run down."

I furrow my brow. "Past summers? But you said you've never been a counselor here before."

"That's right. I haven't been a counselor here before." He walks to the other side of the platform and leans his back on an oak tree. He says nothing more, just crosses his arms, watching me pensively.

I still don't understand. "So then, why were you here other summers?"

He cocks an eyebrow, like he wants me to put two and two together.

"You've been at camp before…" I say, trying to work it out. He nods, urging me on. "But you weren't a counselor…"

His eyebrows shoot higher. I'm obviously close. What is it? What is it? Suddenly, it hits me.

"You were a *camper*?!" Even as I say it, it sounds ridiculous. Theo, a camper at camp for disabled kids? He's the strongest, healthiest person in this whole entire place. That can't possibly be right.

"Ding, ding, ding, you got it!" He breaks into a huge smile.

Taking in my shocked expression, he goes on. "I had childhood leukemia. I was diagnosed when I was fourteen. So, I came to Camp Boundless for two summers before I went into remission."

Something sharp stabs at my chest. "Remission?"

He tips his head back and forth. "Remission. Cured. They can't really say for sure until I get older. The only thing I know is I don't have cancer now. Which is all that really matters, right?"

My stomach plummets at the horrible word. *Cancer*. No. No. *No.* Not Theo, too.

I blink at him, so stunned I can barely find words. "Wow. It's just…I don't know…you don't seem very…"

"Sick?" he says with a laugh. "That's because I'm not sick anymore, Annie. I'm very, very healthy, as you can see." He waves a hand down his body. His very strong, very muscular body. The response he'd given me when I'd asked why he ran in the morning comes back to me. *I like how my body feels when it's healthy*. Now it makes sense. The reason Theo takes such pleasure in his body feeling good is because there was a time when it didn't.

"When I was younger I was really, really sick," he goes on. "Like so sick I nearly died."

I swallow hard, not wanting to think of a world where someone as special, as loving and good as Theo didn't exist. Of course, I know all too well of a world where special, loving, good people are taken away too soon. A nonsensical world which steals away good people and leaves selfish people like me behind.

He stares over my shoulder, eyes going distant as he speaks. "I spent a lot of time in hospitals. A lot of time not having the strength to get out of bed. That's why my mom had to homeschool me for part of high school. I wasn't allowed to go to school because I was too sick. And because of the fear of infections. A simple cold that a normal kid could kick in a week would be life-threatening to me and my non-existent immune system."

I cringe, thinking of how I'd so quickly categorized him as a freak for being homeschooled. Typical of me to be so judgmental. To jump to conclusions before I have all the facts.

"You wouldn't even recognize me if you saw pictures of me from back then," he scoffs. "My face was all swollen up from the drugs. And my hair had all fallen out. God, I was so ugly."

I suck in a sharp breath. "You mean you didn't have this?" I point to his wild mane. It seemed impossible. Theo's abundance of hair is his most defining feature.

"Yeah. It was terrible. I hated it. I was at that awkward teenage stage where I was so self-conscious. I felt like such a freak, being bald. I used to pray every day that if I beat the cancer, God would give me my hair back. And I swore if it ever did grow back I would never, ever cut it." He tosses his head, making his beautiful, thick waves dance along his shoulders. "And I kept that promise. I haven't cut it since."

"Oh Theo," I murmur, hating myself even worse than before. How many times had I made fun of his hair? Told him how stupid it looked and how he should cut it if he ever wanted to get a girl? I had no idea what it meant to him. *My long hair has nothing to do with the music I like.* He'd told me that the day we met, but I'd never asked him more. I'd just assumed he was some rock star wannabe. But his hair had never been about trying to prove something or impress a girl. His hair was a reminder that he'd endured a battle no kid should have to face and lived to tell the story.

He holds his palms up at me. "Hey, don't look at me like that. No pity, okay? I might've said that not much bothers me, but pity. Yeah, that's something I really can't stand."

"Oh I get it," I say. "I know a thing or two about pity myself. I know how much it sucks when people think they're being nice and don't realize they're only making everything so much worse."

We nod at each other, and even though we're standing several feet apart, the same electricity I'd felt the first day we'd met sparks tantalizingly in the space between us. There's something about being with Theo I can't explain. There's some kind of connection between us. Some kind of kinship that doesn't make any logical sense. He's so unlike any guy I've ever dated before. I still hold firm that I cannot be physically attracted to him. And yet the more moments like this—the more times I feel that delicious buzz on my skin when he's near—the more I begin to wonder if I've made another snap judgement that might turn out to be untrue.

"I'm not pitying you." I step closer to where he leans back on the tree, hoping so much I can make him understand. "I'm mad at myself for being such an asshole to you about your hair! I'm sorry. God, I feel so stupid. Can you please forgive me for every horrible insult I've ever made about it? I feel like such a bitch right now."

He reaches out and grabs my hand, gives it a little squeeze. My heart races in response to his touch. "You're not a bitch, Annie. You could never be anything but perfect to me." He looks deep into my eyes and I have the distinct feeling he's fighting with himself. That he wants to tug on my hand, pull me close until our bodies press together, but he knows he can't do that. I almost wish he would just go ahead and try. With the way I feel right now, my reaction might not be what either of us expects.

"Does everyone else know you had cancer?" I ask, casually extracting my hand from his, scared of what might happen if we keep touching this way.

What I'm really asking is, "Have I had my head so far up my ass that I'd missed you telling us?" It would be just like me to be so self-involved I hadn't paid attention to something he'd said.

"No. I mean Greta knows. But the guys in my cabin don't. It's not like I keep it a secret. It just hasn't come up in conversation, so I haven't mentioned it. Plus, I'm not really one to dwell in the past. I'd much rather use the time I have to enjoy myself now."

"Yeah, of course." I say quickly, as if enjoying the Now is my philosophy too. But I'm full of shit. Every time my mind has a chance to wander there's only one place it goes: Racing back to the past to rehash everything that's ever gone wrong in my life.

I return to the edge of The Lookout, squinting a little because the light bouncing off the lake is so bright it hurts my eyes. Theo comes to stand beside me. He has no trouble looking at the surface of the lake because his glasses are now tinted so dark I can't see what's beneath them.

"I hope you're not going to treat me differently now." He nudges me with his elbow. "I hope you're not going to go easy on me because I'm some kind of fragile cancer survivor."

I nudge him playfully back. "Oh, don't worry, I'll never go easy on you. What fun would that be?"

He lets out a long breath. I give him a funny look, wondering to myself why he seems so relieved.

"It's just…I wasn't sure if I should…" he starts, as if he's actually heard the question I haven't spoken out loud. "Part of me wasn't sure if I should tell you all that. But I had this really strong urge to let you know about my cancer. And I think I was right. You see, I get these feelings right here." He points to his chest. "These impulses to say things…and do things. And I always try my best to follow them. Even when I'm not sure exactly what they mean. I try to listen and trust that they're right. Do you ever get impulses like that?"

My mouth goes dry as he gazes down on me with such an earnest expression, I already know I'm going to reveal way too much to him again. But I have to be careful not to tell him everything. I can't tell him about the strongest impulse I've ever felt. The one that made me stay home and not go to the hospital the night my mom died. The impulse I'll regret for the rest of my life.

I swallow hard. "Uh, yeah, I get impulses sometimes. Of course, unlike yours, mine always turn out to be very, very *wrong* impulses." I honk a hollow laugh. "But the funny thing is, even though they seem wrong at the time, I still listen to them. Crazy, I know. I guess I have some kind of sick desire to screw up my life."

I glance over at him for the briefest of moments, stomach turning at the concern I see in his eyes. He opens his mouth, most likely to spew some kind of encouragement which I've heard too many times before, so I cut him off quickly. "Listen, I'm fine. You don't need to try to figure out a way to fix me. I really don't need that from you, okay?" It comes out sharper than I'd intended, but at least it works. Theo shuts his mouth.

I turn away from the edge, feeling dizzy, but not from the height. My rational mind is telling me that coming here with him wasn't a good idea. But the other, fainter voice in my head is telling me it never wants to leave.

It's no surprise which one wins out. "Umm, I better head back now. I forgot I was supposed to meet Lizzy at the Nature Center to help her plan a hike for her girls."

"Oh right, right. No problem," he says as if it's nothing, but I see the disappointment flicker across his face.

As I watch him turn to go, more realizations about him being a camper here flood in. Now I understand why he was so familiar with all the trails here at Camp Boundless. And how he knew there was a talent show at the end of each session…and that the Derby Town song had been banned. And that's also why he knew…

"Jenny," I say out loud and he whirls back to me.

Again, I don't have to explain my train of thought to him. "Yeah, she and I were campers together for a couple of years."

I remember the words he'd used when he saw her. *"Hello my friend!"* It hadn't been a cast-off greeting. Theo and Jenny were friends. He was once just like her, arriving for check-in day, eager to get away from his parents and escape his real life for a while to simply have fun. It's still so hard for me to imagine him sick, and yet his history explains the compassion he has for the kids here at camp.

I head toward the path but just before stepping off the platform, I turn to take in the view one last time. Theo watches the clear awe on my face. "You probably shouldn't come here by yourself," he says. "It's not safe to be here alone."

I give him a wry smile, already knowing what he's angling at. He returns the same wry smile, acknowledging his clear intent. "You should only come here with me."

"Oh really? Is that what I should do?" I tease. "Because you're so concerned about my safety, huh?"

"Yes. I'm extremely concerned about your safety, Annie." He grins big and something swells in my chest at the sight of it. "We could arrange it so our free periods are the same every day and come here together."

I pretend to agonize over the decision. "It *is* awfully pretty here," I offer lightly.

He nods with all his namesake enthusiasm.

"And it's much cooler here too," I add.

"So, so very, very cool." He nods even more vehemently.

"I guess that could be fun…coming here together," I finally relent.

He pumps both fists in the air, jumping up and down on the balls of his feet like Rocky on top of the stairs, just to crack me up.

As we walk side-by-side back down the trail I remember how he'd said he didn't want me to treat him any differently now that I knew he'd been sick.

"So, your glasses then?" I ask. "Do they have anything to do with your cancer?"

"Nope. I got those a couple of years before I was diagnosed."

"Oh, thank God." I wipe my brow dramatically. "At least I can still make fun of those!"

CHAPTER TWELVE

"I'VE DECIDED TO help you get a girl this summer," I announce to Theo.

We're at The Lookout, lying in two hammocks I found in the closet of the Nature Center. Theo hung them in a cluster of trees near the edge of the platform where we can still see the view but are close enough to talk without shouting.

"What about your moratorium on camp romances?" He's stretched out, arms propped leisurely behind his head, dirty running shoes spilling off the end of the netting.

"I've decided to suspend my rules since this is a special case and you obviously need to make up some time in the romance department. You know, after growing up inside a plastic bubble and all."

"Hey. Don't make me regret confiding in you about my past," he mumbles, sounding half-asleep like me.

"I won't. As long as you don't make me regret confiding to you about my past, either."

"Deal." He extends a hand across the small space dividing us. I clasp it, then tug hard as I let go, making us both rock in our makeshift cradles.

It's near the end of the second session of camp and we've been coming here every day since Theo first showed me the place. It's become our refuge. A sacred space where we lie quietly together, enjoying the breeze off the lake, and simply talk.

Maybe it's because I don't have to look him in the eye when I'm in the hammock. Or because I know I'll never see him again after this summer. Or because the light-dappled branches swaying overhead hypnotize me into some strange, altered state. But over these past weeks I've revealed things to Theo I've never told anyone before.

I've rambled on in great detail about how scary it was when my mom got sick with her stomach cancer. Revealed how we'd found out too late because she'd hidden how often she threw up; how she could barely keep any food down at all.

I was the only one living with her at the time, but I'd been so wrapped up in my own life I hadn't noticed her drastic weight loss. It wasn't until Aunt Lydia visited from Montana and freaked out about Mom looking like a walking skeleton that I paused and really saw how much my mom had changed.

I'd been a surly teenager back then, moping around the house, sequestering myself in my room to marinate in my fears and anxiety. Nevertheless, it was no excuse. She was my mother, the person closest to me in the world. And yet I'd been blind to what she was going through. I think finding out the truth about her cancer was when I first started losing confidence in myself and my decision making. And it only got worse after that.

But I haven't had the guts yet to tell Theo *that* story yet.

Now, in the hammocks, Theo props up on his elbow and peers over at me. "I don't need you to set me up with some random girl when you know there's only *one* girl at this camp I want." He gives me a loaded wink, in case I don't get that he's talking about me. I guess he's never heard of the age-old dating game: playing hard to get.

"Oh, Theo, Theo, Theo," I say, sighing in exasperation. "Dear sweet, wonderful Theo. I've told you before you deserve someone much better than me."

He shakes his head, lying back down to stare up into the trees again. I haven't been the only one revealing things in our forest confessional box. Theo has told me about his childhood and his time battling cancer. About how his mom and dad got divorced in the middle of his treatment and he still blames himself for their breakup. It had killed me to see the rare flash of pain in his eyes. I'd tried to cheer him up by telling him that at least it meant we have one thing in common. We both have asshole dads.

Across from me, Theo huffs. "I don't deserve someone better than you. Why do you always say that?"

I struggle to sit up so I can argue with him face to face. "Because I've told you before…there's something seriously wrong with me. I am *not* a good person."

"What are you talking about? You're the best person I've ever met!"

"Oh, you would say that. You think everyone is amazing, and wonderful…the best person you ever met!" I mock his cheerful voice.

"Yeah, I happen to like people. So sue me." When I don't respond he goes on. "Besides, I think you, Annie, are the very best of all the best people I've ever met."

"Uh, when I figure out what that sentence means I'll get back to you."

"You're the bestest of the best!" he declares loudly, making me giggle.

We both don't speak for a while. The only sounds around us are the rustle of the leaves above, the distant call and response of two sad-sounding mourning doves. Their forlorn song tugs at something deep inside me.

"I seriously think I'm a sociopath," I mumble without thinking. Once it's out I cringe, hoping maybe he won't have heard me.

He scoffs loudly. "A sociopath?! Why the hell would you say that?"

"Because I saw it in one of Caroline's psychology books once," I say. Caroline had been studying to be a therapist before she got pregnant with Jack and put her degree on hold. "A sociopath is a person who has no regard for right or wrong. Who ignores the feelings of others." I repeat the words that had frozen me with recognition the day I'd read them. "That's exactly me. I'm cold…I don't feel emotions the way normal people do. The way I'm *supposed* to feel them."

Theo props himself up on one elbow, glaring over at me in abject horror. "You're not a sociopath! I've seen you with the kids. You're so loving and sweet with them. They all adore you."

"They have to," I deadpan. "Otherwise they have to sit in their own piss all day long."

He ignores me. "And you're really nice to me."

"Am I? Really?"

"Well…most of the time," he admits. "Really. You're too hard on yourself. You're a kind, loving person. Not a sociopath."

"You don't know. You don't know some of the terrible things I've done. You wouldn't like me so much if you knew who I really am."

His brows pinch with determination. "Annie, there's nothing you could say that could make me not like you."

His righteousness rankles me. Makes me want to prove him wrong. I want to tell him the truth and knock that smug smile right off his face. This guy needs to wake up out of his fairy tale and realize how the real world works. That most of the time life sucks and people disappoint you. I'm a living example of that.

I carefully sit up, swinging my legs over the side to perch on the edge of my hammock. "Is that a challenge?" I narrow my eyes at him.

He sits up too. Planting himself on the edge of his hammock and narrowing his eyes back at me. "I think it is."

"Fine. Then I'll tell you the worst thing I've ever done." My heart speeds at just the thought of talking about my terrible behavior three years ago. I've never shared this with anyone before. Can I really do it now?

"It happened the night my mom died," I start off shakily. Warning bells clang in my ears telling me to shut the fuck up. *Now*. But something pushes me on. "It was near the end, when things were getting worse and worse and we were staying with her around the clock. I'd gone home to take a shower and get a few hours of sleep and Caroline had stayed in case…you know… the time came." Funny how suddenly it's hard for me to say the word *died*. "The phone had rung in the middle of the night. It was Caroline telling me to come in, that this was it. It was time to say goodbye." I choke on the last word. The pain searing through my chest almost as sharp as when I'd held the receiver to my ear and heard the awful news for the first time.

I survey Theo's face, hoping to remember the way he looks at me now, so I can remember it after his opinion of me changes. "But you know what I did? Cold-hearted me? Instead of racing to my mom's side…my sweet loving mom who I loved more than anyone in the entire Universe…I locked myself in the bathroom and had a complete breakdown like a damn coward. Then I fell asleep on the floor and missed saying goodbye."

When I finally get the courage to look at Theo, there's only understanding in his eyes. "Annie, it's okay," he says softly, reaching out as if to hold my hand, but I slap him away.

"Don't you get it, Theo?!" I yell breathlessly. "I wasn't there when my mom died! I deliberately refused to be by her side when she needed me the most. My God, it doesn't get any more selfish than that!"

When I finish my heart is racing so fast it's hard to breathe. *Oh, no. It's happening again. No. No. No. This can't be happening now. I knew I shouldn't have talked about this.*

I struggle out of the hammock and lurch to the nearest tree. Once there, I press my palm into its trunk, forcing myself to take some deep breaths; concentrating on the tree's sturdiness, the whirls in its bark, to help me calm myself down.

Theo joins me, his face masked with compassion. Which, for some reason, instantly pisses me off.

Didn't he hear what I just said? I showed him who I really am. All my stunted emotions are out in the open for him to see. There's no way he can still like me now.

"See? I'm a sociopath," I say, feeling strangely victorious. At least he can't argue with me anymore, now that he knows the truth about me.

Yet when I survey his face more closely, I noticed his expression hasn't changed one bit. How can that be?

"Annie, there was nothing wrong with what you did," he says gently, as if he truly believes it. But…but…how can he believe that?

He goes on. "It's completely understandable you wouldn't want to see someone you love die right in front of you. Everyone has different ways of dealing with death. And they're all valid and reasonable. There's no *right* way to face something as painful as losing your mom. "

"Really?" I say bitterly. "Because I'm not sure my sister would agree with that."

I can still hear all the horrible things she'd said to me when she came home from the hospital and found me curled up on the bathroom rug. She'd called me the most self-centered, uncaring person she'd ever met. And yeah, she's since apologized, blaming her grief for making her fly off the handle like that. But her accusations are hard to forget. Probably because I know they're true.

"Again, everyone has their own ways of dealing with pain," he says. "What you really need to know is your mom doesn't blame you for not being there. She's not holding any grudges against you or thinking about that moment at all. Because where she is now, the only thing she can feel for you is love."

When he finishes his sentence, a wave of relief floods my body, as if a heavy armor I've carried for years has been lifted from my shoulders, leaving behind a lightness I haven't felt in a long time.

But despite how good Theo has just made me feel, I can't give in that easily. "Right, because you can know that for sure," I snap, thinking back to the morning after his run when he'd made a similar claim. *I don't just think it Annie. I know it.* I still can't understand how he can be so adamant about something as unknown as what happens after death.

"I do…I know it for sure," he says voice rising in his vehemence. Then he stops himself, recalculating as if he's said too much. "And I also know that this is all just a misunderstanding. You've taken this one experience…not going to your mom's bedside as she died…and twisted it to mean something it's not. That you're a bad person. A sociopath. That you've done something wrong."

He pauses for a moment, letting it sink in. "If anything, it doesn't mean you care too little. It's the exact opposite. To me, it means you care an awful lot."

A shudder passes through me, his words spreading like a balm over my aching heart. Could what he's saying be true? Could I really not be as horrible as I think I am? No. That doesn't seem right. Forgiving myself shouldn't be that easy.

Theo waits, lips parted slightly, face full of a kind of tender sincerity I'm not sure I've ever witnessed in a person before. Why does he always seem so sure of himself? Again, I have the urge to close the small space between us and nestle myself in his arms. It would feel so good to be held by him. I just know it would. But how? How do I know that? I can't be right. Lord knows I rarely am.

So instead, I roll my eyes and give him a rough shove. "You're only saying all these nice things to me because you want me to go out with you."

He stumbles backwards, laughing. His smile is big; even more adoring than before. Dammit. Operation Make-Theo-Hate-Me clearly hasn't worked. I'm surprised by how happy that makes me.

"So I haven't scared you off yet?" I ask, fighting the urge to reach up and smooth a rogue strand of his hair back into place. Why do I always feel like I want to touch him?

"On the contrary. You've only made me like you more."

"Oh Theo," I say, sighing heavily. "That's just the nurse in you coming out. You only like me because you want to fix me."

He chuckles, wearing that little smirk that always makes me feel like he knows so much more about me than I even know about myself.

"No Annie, that's where you're wrong. I don't feel like I need to fix you," he says, looking deep into my eyes. "Because I don't think you're broken."

CHAPTER THIRTEEN

THE ENTIRE CAMP is gathered at the waterfront for Fisherman Day, a tradition that's been going on for decades at Camp Boundless. Apparently, years ago, the local fishermen agreed to give our campers rides in their motorboats in exchange for fishing privileges on Lake Henry. Now here we are at nine o'clock in the morning, sucking in gas fumes and getting leered at by forty-year-old men in multi-pocketed vests and lunchboxes full of worms. Good times.

This week the girls in our cabin are all ambulatory. So Susan and I sit on the dock, dangling our feet in the water as we watch our campers, now clustered together on the sand, furiously whispering to each other, as teenage girls do. Honey Bear is in the water, splashing and creating a ruckus with the few girls who aren't too cool to actually get in the lake. And Greta is playing beach volleyball with Theo, Adam, Wendell, and a few of their campers.

I watch over my shoulder as Theo and Greta roughhouse with each other, shoving and wrestling for the ball like two puppies fighting over a rawhide chew. (Shenanigans I know they're only putting on to make the kids laugh.)

I found out Greta has three older brothers, which explains why she's such a tomboy. Now, as I watch her loping around with such grace, I can't help but feel a little jealous of how at home she seems in her own skin. Greta is the kind of girl who has no idea how beautiful she is. Which—in one of the great paradoxes of life—only makes her that much more beautiful.

Boats drone in the distance, their wake making the water lap rhythmically against the shore of the little man-made beach. The sounds blend, lulling me into a pleasant daze, and I close my eyes and tip my head up, letting the gentle morning sun warm my bare shoulders and heat my cheeks. For once, feeling recharged by its rays, not fried to a crisp like I normally do.

With my eyes closed, I can just make out the campers behind me whispering.

"Isn't he gorgeous?" one girl purrs.

"Mmmmm, so yummy," another agrees.

I smile to myself, knowing without even looking who they're drooling over. Miles is out on the dock helping load and unload kids. And like the girls behind me, I too noticed how particularly Adonis-like he looks today. With his golden blonde hair and impossibly blue eyes. (One of which, if I'm not mistaken, winked at me when I walked by in my bathing suit earlier.)

"Oh my God. And that tan," a third girl adds. "And those muscles. I dream about them at night."

"Yeah. And his hair. It looks so soft, so silky. I just want to run my fingers through it!" They all burst out in trills of giggles. "I love how long it is!"

Instantly, my eyes fly open. I whirl to see where they're looking and when I trace the trajectory of their stares, my mouth drops open. Wait a minute. They're not lusting over Miles. They're lusting over *Theo*.

What the hell?

After my shock subsides, I stare at Theo, trying to see him through the teenagers' eyes. I mean, I've always known Theo is cute, in a sweet 'boy-next-door' kind of way. But the sheer desire in the girls' voices is beyond anything I would've ever attributed to him before.

Alright, I can kind of see what's going on. Theo has his damn shirt off again. And, okay…I will admit he does look kind of athletic when he leaps up to spike the ball like that. And yeah, there might be some sweat glistening on his hard pecs, which is a bit…uh…*alluring,* I guess you would say. And the sun has bleached his hair out a bit, so it has these really cool blonde stripes tousled in with the brown, that makes him look more like a surfer than even Miles. And his skin. It is quite flawless…creamy and brown and…

Oh my God, what am I thinking? It's *Theo,* for Christ's sake. I feel like I'm leering at my girlfriend's kid brother!

Luckily, Greta appears before my thoughts can dip even further in the gutter. As she plops down beside me I squeeze my thighs together, not wanting to acknowledge the tingly feeling now flickering between my legs.

"Hey you freak," she bumps her shoulder hard into mine and for a second I think she's caught me ogling Theo.

"I'm not a freak," I shoot back. "They were the ones who said it, not me!" I point to the girls behind me, my face going hot.

She gives me a funny look. "What are you talking about? Who said what?"

Realizing my misunderstanding I stammer, "Nothing, nothing. Hey, you were doing great over there." I hook a thumb to the volleyball court, hoping to distract her. "It looked like you were uh…like…" I motion as if I'm serving ball. "Hitting that ball really good! It was like going over the net and everything! Good game…or set…or match… or whatever you call it!"

Geez, I need to just stop talking. What's wrong with me, anyway? Why does my brain feel like it's made of scrambled eggs?

"It's called a match," she says, wrinkling her brow. "And yes, getting the ball over the net is kinda the point, Annie."

I'm relieved when she doesn't address my manic behavior any further. "I got sand in my leg," she says, wrestling off the lower half of her leg and tipping the prosthetic up to brush out the sand. Then she takes off the sock thingy that covers her stump so she can dip her leg into the lake water.

She lets out a groan when the cool water washes over her skin. "Ah, that feels so good."

Every time I've opened my mouth to complain about something these past few weeks—like how hard it is to push the campers up the steep switchback from the lake—I've stopped myself. Because I've seen the welts on Greta's leg stump at night. I've watched how hard it is for her to keep the wheelchairs on the path with only one arm. I've seen how the sweat breaks the suction of her leg prosthetic and makes it fall off at the worst possible moment. And she never, ever complains. So, I've decided that, if she can do it with her "Discount Den" body (as she likes to call it) then I can too.

"Hey, I got a question for you," I whisper to Greta, still not wanting to think about why I'm so out of breath after looking at Theo.

"Lay it on me, Annie Freckles."

"Is your Mystery Man here now? Can we try to guess who it is?"

Greta looks skyward, clearly regretting what she'd divulged to us the other night.

On my other side, Susan squeals excitedly, leaning forward to get in on the gossip. "Yeah, give us a clue, Greta!"

Hearing the commotion, Honey Bear sloshes over to see what's going on.

"Alright, alright," Greta says. "I'll give you one clue. Yes. He's here right now."

We all burst out in cheers, Honey Bear splashing water up in the air in delight.

"Would you all stop it!" Greta grabs my clapping hands, wrenching them down into my lap. "This is why I don't tell you guys anything. You need to be more discreet!"

"Yes, discreet," I agree. "We need to be more discreet."

The three of us turn and frantically scan the waterfront with absolutely no discretion at all.

"Stop it! You're going to make an ass out of me." Greta smacks my shoulder, but she's laughing. Of course, I know why she gave us that clue when she's normally so tight-lipped about her Mystery Man.

"My God, the entire camp is here," I mutter, taking in the crowd. "We'll never figure it out."

"Oh, what a shame," Greta smirks.

"But we can still guess, right?" Susan asks.

Greta shrugs cooly. "Go ahead, give it a try. I'm not stopping you."

"Adam!" The three of us say in unison, which makes it come out as a shout. It feels like every person on the beach stops to stare at us. Adam whirls from playing volleyball and gives us a funny look.

"You guys need something?" he calls over.

"Yeah, Greta needs your big dick inside of her," Honey Bear mutters, making us all dissolve into hysterics. Even Susan.

"No! We weren't talking about you," Greta shouts to Adam, kicking Honey Bear in the shin at the same time. "We were talking about my friend Adam from back home."

Once Adam turns back around, Greta hisses, "Now do you see why I don't tell you anything, you fucking assholes?!"

"Well, I think Adam's cute," I say. "And he obviously really likes you."

Greta makes a face. "Why would you say that? Because he didn't make me re-stack the firewood to his exact specifications the other day?"

It's true that Adam approaches everything he does at camp with meticulous attention to detail. But he's studying to be an anesthesiologist. It's kind of his job to be precise about details. But Greta always makes him laugh. (Which, believe me, isn't easy. I've tried.) And I've seen them kind of awkwardly flirting with each other. And from the way she just blushed, I think we might be on to something. Why else would she eat her lunch at the guys' table every day?

"Adam complimented you on how quickly you converted ounces into grams the other day, remember that?" Susan offers.

"Oh right. Makes sense that the marriage proposal is coming any day," Greta deadpans.

We try naming a few more guys to see if we can get a reaction out of her, but she remains stone-faced.

"You can guess all you want. I'm not telling." She scans the entire waterfront area slowly and we all follow her eyes as if she might give us a clue. There are boys everywhere. I know she's trying to confuse us and it works. Any of the guys here could be her crush.

"I will tell you one thing, though," she says with a coy smile. We all lean close and she whispers. "I'm thinking about maybe letting Mystery Man know how I feel about him soon."

The group explodes in whoops, Honey Bear whirling and splashing like a lawn sprinkler gone wild.

After I wipe the water out of my eyes, I reach over and hug Greta to my side, hoping she'll forgive us for our ribbing. She deserves a hot camp romance. She deserves to find someone who treats her better than those horrible boys from high school.

Miles shouts for our campers to get on the boat, so Susan and Honey Bear run to help while I wait with Greta as she replaces her leg. She sheepishly glances behind her at the volleyball court, where Adam is serving to Wendell; Theo now cheering them on from the sideline.

I bump her on the shoulder. "Hey, Mystery Man is going to be all over you when you let him know how you feel."

"Really? You think?" I'm surprised to see doubt in her eyes. Greta always seems so damn sure of herself.

"I don't think. I *know*." After it's out I realize how much I sound like Theo. Man, he's really getting to me isn't he?

Greta lets out a heavy breath, seeming relieved at the possibility of things working out for her. Then suddenly her smile drops as if she just remembered something important.

It's subtle, but I notice her body go rigid beside me. "You know I just said that stuff about telling my crush how I feel to get you guys off my back, right?" She says in a clipped tone. "I'm not *really* going to say anything to him."

"You're not?"

"Naw. Boys? Relationships?" She makes a face like she's about to get sick. "I've tried it before. And it might be fun for a while, but it's never worth all the effort in the end."

She brusquely pats non-existent sand off her leg, then stands, hauling me up by the arm beside her. I can tell she's lying. That she's trying to make me think she doesn't care when she clearly cares an awful lot.

She starts to walk away, but without thinking, I catch her wrist and pull her back. I need to tell her how important it is to be honest about what she wants. To take risks and keep putting herself out there. To not let one isolated experience shape the rest of her life. But then I realize how hypocritical that would be, coming from me.

Greta stares at me, waiting for what I was going to say. I simply give her a curt nod. "You're right about boys. They really aren't worth all the effort."

CHAPTER FOURTEEN

I SIT ON the floor of the metal rowboat, my back propped up against the seat, watching Theo row us across the lake.

He's taking me to another of his secret spots today. A shaded cove where the stream that feeds the lake trickles in, making the water much cooler than at the beach. At least that's what he'd claimed earlier, when he'd lured me away from my beloved hammock. I'd offered to help him row, but he'd insisted I sit back and enjoy the ride. And since I don't have the energy to argue (or to row) I've let him have his way.

The sun is high in the sky, making the surface of the lake look like a bolt of undulating green fabric studded with a million glittering diamonds. With my eyes hidden by my sunglasses, I can stare openly at Theo as he rows. His chestnut hair is loose and blowing back in the breeze (for once he's not wearing his stupid red headband) and he doesn't look quite as goofy as he normally does.

I've tried to forget the girls' comments from yesterday. But they've burrowed themselves into my brain. Now I keep noticing things about Theo I wish I wouldn't. Like what a distinctive profile he has as he stares out over the water—like something you might find on some ancient Roman coin—and how good his carved biceps look every time he tugs on the oars.

I wonder how would I feel if Theo decided to show his special places to someone else instead of me? What would happen if I got to

The Lookout one day and he was there with another girl? I hate to admit it, but I'd be jealous as hell. Which doesn't make sense. I don't want Theo for myself. So why do I still feel so possessive of him? I'm not sure I've ever been as confused by a boy in my life.

When we get to the cove it's even better than Theo described. It has a tiny sandy beach, an umbrella of trees overhead, and a wide stream trickling in at its mouth. As our boat floats closer, the picturesque scene makes me think of one of the watercolor scenes on the postcards my mom left me. Just this morning, I'd taken out the two studies to look at. They always seem to ground me when my racing thoughts begin to feel out of control.

Seeing the strokes of her brush, the faint pencil marks she left behind, the wash of colors she picked for each blade of grass makes me feel close to her. It's comforting to hold something in my hand she once touched. Lately, I've been thinking of how much she would've liked Theo. The two of them are so much alike. My God, if they'd ever gotten together they would've driven me crazy with all their airy-fairy views on life. It's too bad they never got to meet.

As soon as he docks the boat, Theo shucks his shirt off and wades in to swim. I think maybe he'll take off his darkened glasses and I'll finally see the color of his eyes. But he just holds them over his head as he dunks under, then puts them back on. He claims to be blind without them. And no matter how many times Juan and I try to berate him into wearing his contacts, he says he doesn't have time to put them on in the morning. Which is a pretty valid excuse, given the schedule we keep around here.

I undress down to my utilitarian, one-piece Speedo and follow him in, moaning out loud when the water hits my skin. It's swirled with currents so cold and refreshing all I want to do is lay back in it and fall asleep like I do in my hammock.

The only problem is every time I try to float, the current pushes me into shore, so I can only relax for a little while before I have to get up and walk back out in the deeper part and start all over. Seeing my dilemma, Theo comes to my side.

"Here, I'll hold you in place so you can relax," he says, unfolding his arms like he wants me to lie down on top of them.

I make a face. "Why would you do that?"

"Like I just said…so you can relax and float for a little while."

"And what? You're just going to stand there and hold me?" When he nods I go on. "Won't that be boring for you?"

"No. I want to. C'mon, just try it."

I stretch out in the water, but when he comes closer I clamor back up to my feet. "You're not just trying to cop a feel, are you?" I'm just teasing. I know Theo would never do that.

He looks horrified. "No! See." He motions for me to lie back again. "I'll just put one hand really lightly on your back and one under your legs. You'll hardly even feel it."

It's true. When I stretch out again he holds me so gently I can barely tell he's there. I try my best to relax, but it still feels too weird. Once again, I ungracefully flail to my feet. "Seriously Theo. You shouldn't have to just stand there, holding me while I relax. That's not fair to you."

"I told you I want to!"

"You do?" I don't understand him. What's in it for him if I'm the only one who gets to have a good time?

I try it once more, but I'm still too self-conscious. All I can think about is how I'm taking advantage of him. And how selfish it is to once again let him do all the work while I lay back and enjoy myself, just like in the boat. Only a few seconds later I splash all crazily and stand up again.

"Annie," he holds my upper arms and gives me a little shake. "Why won't you let me take care of you?"

Hearing him say it that way makes something shudder inside me. *Take care of me?* It's been so long since anyone offered such a thing. Ever since my mom died I feel like I've been on my own, forced to rely on no one but myself. Yeah, my sister is around if I need her, but she has her own life. I don't want to burden her. I don't want to be a burden to anyone, really. And now Theo is here actually asking me to be a burden to him. Wanting to literally hold on to me and keep me from floating away? I'm not used to being offered such a selfless act.

He must read the hesitation on my face because his voice drops to a soothing purr. "You can trust me, Annie. Really. I want to do this for you."

He's so sincere I have no choice but to believe him. Something tight releases in my chest as I slowly lower myself down, tipping my face upward, and stretching out in front of him. As he holds me in the water, I imagine my body becoming light and porous, floating on the surface like a cloud in the sky. My ears are underwater, so when I hear the muffled sound of Theo's voice— "That's it. I got you, Annie"—it's like the words are coming from the earth below, radiating into my bones, fusing with the blood pulsing through my skin. Maybe I *can* do this. Maybe I can give myself over to him. Just for a little while.

Once I truly let myself relax, the freedom of floating begins to feel like ecstasy. It's what I imagine being inside the womb might feel like, where everything I need is taken care of and there's nothing I have to worry about anymore. The more I give in to the lightness, the more I lose track of where my body ends and the water begins. Until it's almost like I don't exist anymore. Like my edges have all melted away and I've become one with the lake.

After a while I become vaguely aware of Theo easing me from side to side, so the water brushes over my skin in a really soft, sensual way. I take in every nuance of the delicious feelings, letting them expand inside me until it feels like my heart might burst from the sheer pleasure of it all.

I let him hold me, let him take care of me, until I eventually become so disconnected I lose track of time. And when I get the impulse to stand up again, I don't struggle or splash. I simply slip out of his arms and gradually rise on my feet in one fluid motion, like what we've just done together was the most natural thing in the world.

His smile is bright as he stares down at me. "How was it?"

For some strange reason, my nose prickles and I have to blink a few times to keep the tears at bay. "It was amazing," I tell him, truthfully. "Really, really amazing."

I can't believe how honest I'm being with him. Usually, I'd be trying to shrug off this strange encounter with some kind of stupid joke.

"Good. I'm glad," he says.

It's so odd, how genuinely happy he is for me. I have to fight the urge to go to him. To cross the space between us and lay my head on his sun-warmed chest. Then wrap my arms around his waist and press the full length of my body against his. I can't do that though, because I don't want to lead him on. If I touched him like that he might think I like him. Which I don't. I mean, I don't *think* I like him. I shouldn't. I can't. And yet, still…

I tamp some cold water on my burning cheeks, trying to shock myself back to real life. "Here, I'll do you now," I offer, holding my arms out the same way he did to me.

"No, that's okay. I'm good."

"But that's not fair to you."

"I told you. I wanted to do it. I got as much pleasure out of it as you did."

At the sound of the word pleasure, heat explodes deep in my belly. It scares me, how primal it feels. It's so wild, so strong…like something that, if I ever gave in to it, I might not be able to control.

And if there's one thing I hate most in the world, it's losing control.

"We should get back," I snap, startling not only Theo but myself with the harshness of my voice.

"Alright…if that's what you want," he says, looking confused.

No. It's not what I want. It's not what I want at all.

And yet I still rush to the boat, acting as if nothing out of the ordinary has happened. But my denial has trouble finding its normal traction. Because no matter how hard I keep telling myself otherwise, I already know I'm going to remember this experience with Theo for the rest of my life.

∞

In the boat on the way back to camp, I covertly stare at Theo again. He looks even more different to me now. Like what we shared back at the cove has changed something between us that runs deeper than the surface of our friendship.

But that's not to say Theo's surface isn't awfully nice too.

"Do runners lift weights?" I ask idly.

He rows one stroke. Then another. "Yeah. Not too much because you don't want to get too bulky. It can cut into your speed, your stamina. But developing your upper body can help drive your stride. So, I do lift weights."

"Hmmmm." I lean over the boat's edge, letting my fingers trail in the water as if his answer means nothing to me. The question had slipped out before I could stop it and now I'm hoping he'll let it drop.

"Why do you ask?"

Dammit. I knew I couldn't get out of it that easily. Oh, what the hell.

I tip my head at him coyly. "Because you have nice arms."

He startles, surprised by my rare flattery. That makes two of us. "Oh. Okay… Well, thanks."

I try to go back to looking disinterested, but the shit-eating grin now spreading across Theo's face has to be addressed.

"What? Why are you smiling like that?" I ask, annoyed.

"No reason," he says, fighting to wrench down the corners of his mouth.

"Tell me!"

He shrugs, his smirk growing wider. Then he leans forward, leveling me under an unflinching stare. "You like me," he says plainly.

I huff and sputter for a few beats too long. "Stop it! I do not!"

"Yes, you do."

"I swear to God, I give you *one* compliment and you blow it all out of proportion!"

Again, he just shrugs nonchalantly, like he's happy to sit back and let me dig my own grave. Which I promptly do.

"So I think you have nice arms?! That doesn't mean anything! I was just trying to be nice!" The shrillness of my voice is not helping my argument one bit.

He cooly looks away, ignoring my rant. "You like me," he repeats with complete sureness.

"Ughhhh! Remind me to never give you a compliment ever again!" I reach down into the lake and splash a huge handful of water right at his gloating face. "You are so fucking annoying!"

"You like me!" He provokes me again, splashing back. We go back and forth that way—*You like me!...No I don't!*—splashing and teasing, accusing and denying, until my stomach hurts from laughing so hard.

After we've nearly exhausted ourselves arguing, Theo finally picks up the oars again and calls a truce; promising he'll stop teasing me. But the funny thing is, I think if he had made his claim one more time, I just might've told him he's right.

CHAPTER FIFTEEN

"HOW'S THIS?" GRETA asks, turning from the mirror to show me her face. "Do I look more like a sexy vixen or drunk raccoon?"

I survey the eyeliner in question. "Um. Maybe a sexy raccoon?"

"Ugh!" she groans.

"Drunk vixen?" I try again.

She tosses the eye pencil in the sink in a huff. "I told you I'm not good at this make up stuff."

"Well, unfortunately neither am I." I grab a square of toilet paper and hand it to her. "Maybe just make the line…uh…not quite so…*fat*."

We're going to a party tonight so we're trying to look a little fancier than we normally do. Of course it's a camp party, so we'll still have to wear sneakers, douse ourselves in bug spray, hike there, and take our flashlights so we can find our way home in the dark. But at least it's something different than our usual routine.

Normally all the counselors except the international staff go home on our days off. But Tim, the camp handyman who lives here all year round—the man I saw the first day who has no arms—is throwing his annual bash this weekend, so most of the staff stayed over.

Susan went home to see her boyfriend, but Honey Bear, Greta, and I weren't about to say no to a kegger. I, for one need to let off a little steam after weeks of playing the part of patient, caring, morally upright camp counselor. A girl can only be good for so long. And a wild night of drinking and dancing is just what I need to help muster up the energy to do this all over again on Monday.

"Hey, don't look at me for help," Honey Bear calls from the shower bench where she's lounging behind us. "I don't use all that slop on my face, either. I don't have time to pretend. What you see is what you get from me!"

"And believe me, we see quite a lot of you," Greta deadpans and we crack up. Honey Bear has a habit of walking around naked after her showers. She claims she has to air dry because the scratchy towels irritate her sensitive skin.

"I gotta warn you, girls," Greta says seriously. "I'm a mean drunk." She lets out a growl, which only makes her look more like a sexy raccoon.

"Well, I'm an affectionate drunk, so watch out!" I chase Greta around the room, arms open wide, smacking my lips like I'm going to kiss her. She screams, racing around the open shower stalls to get away from me.

"This is not a good combination." Honey Bear warns, pointing a finger back and forth between us. "I'm gonna stay in the middle of y'all all night to make sure a fight doesn't break out. I don't need you turning that damn arm of yours into a weapon now, child." She glares at Greta, who's told us too many stories of the torture she'd inflicted on her brothers with her prosthetics. "That's gonna get too ugly. Even for me."

Greta chuckles, then primps some more in front of the mirror, wiping away some of the makeup and fluffing her hair. She looks gorgeous, her brown eyes huge in her perfectly angled face; her body sleek and tan in jean shorts and cropped shirt. It's so unlike her to spend any time in front of the mirror. Honey Bear catches my eye behind Greta's back and mouths, "Mystery Man" to me. I nod discreetly, not wanting Greta to catch us whispering. After I'd seen how much this guy means to her I'd stopped giving her a hard time about her crush. I hope she changes her mind and takes a chance on telling him how she really feels. From the way she's primping, I think there's still a chance she might go through with it.

Before we leave, I take a second to check myself out in the mirror, too. I've managed a few subtle swipes of blush; a little eyeliner to hopefully make my eyes look more blue. Although I'm wearing boring old jeans, I opted for a sleeveless white blouse with some lace details on the front that shows off the faint tan that's finally taken hold after my multiple sunburns faded away. I have half my hair pulled up and the other half falling over my shoulders. No one will probably recognize me without my signature braids since I haven't let my hair down the entire summer. It's kind of exciting to think of how different everyone is going to look all cleaned up, with no sweaty armpit circles or food stains on their clothes.

As we walk down the dim trails to the party, my mind drifts to Theo again.

I don't want to think about him so much, but lately I can't help it. He's like a puzzle I can't figure out, no matter how hard I try. I don't understand how he can be so excited about life all the time. So self-assured and unconcerned about all the things that could possibly go wrong in his future. So accepting of whatever the hell comes his way.

In other words: How can he be so opposite of me?

At The Lookout the other day, he'd given me a peek into why he's so damn trusting of life.

I'd been listing off all my anxieties about my senior year of college. Worrying about whether my roommate Darcy and I would get along sharing our new apartment. Wondering if I'll ever get a job when I graduate. And if that job will ever pay me enough money so that one day I'd be able to fulfill my dream of starting my own camp. (I still can't believe I'd told him about that. I've never admitted that pipe dream to anyone before.)

He'd let me vent for a while, whining on and on about how hard it was going to be to figure everything out. Then he'd seemingly changed the subject.

"Want to know one of my favorite quotes from Albert Einstein?" He'd shifted sideways in his hammock so he could meet my eyes.

"Uh…yeah, I guess," I'd muttered, a little miffed that he clearly hadn't been listening to me at all. What did Albert Einstein have to do with all my problems?

"I'm paraphrasing here a little, but basically he said the most important question a person should ask themselves is whether or not they believe the Universe is friendly."

Immediately I'd tensed, suspecting where this conversation was going.

He'd gone on. "When you're able to answer that for yourself, you begin to see the foundation upon which all your beliefs are built. If you think the world is unfriendly, then you'll build up defenses in order to protect yourself against it. But if you believe the world is friendly, you'll remain open and let it have its way with you."

The first thing I thought of was my mom's note. *Remember, stay open to life Buttercup*, she'd written. *Let it show you where it wants you to go.* It was like Theo was repeating the same thing she'd told me. But how the hell could he have known? It's almost like the two of them are in cahoots somehow. Which I know is completely and utterly impossible.

That day at The Lookout, I'd gritted my teeth and waited for him to ask me exactly what I believed. But he didn't. He just laid back and stared up at the trees, letting the silence take it from there.

After the quiet swelled too loud for my comfort, I'd grumbled, "I bet I know which side you come down on."

He'd chuckled. "Yeah, I'm pretty clear on what I believe."

When I didn't say more, he went on. "This world is friendly, Annie. You don't have to do all the work. You can trust it to take care of you."

Hearing that, my body had hummed like a tuning fork that had just been struck. Which flustered me so badly I'd made a jab about him being a hopeless Pollyanna and then changed the subject.

But even now, as I walk through the dark trails to the party, I still can't forget how good Theo's words made me feel. How the resonance in my body made it seem like, for the briefest moment, I'd remembered something…something I'd always known but had simply forgotten for a while. That, just like that day floating in the water at the cove, I was being held…supported…taken care of. And that no matter what happened in my future, I would always, *always* be okay.

∞

When we get to the party, I see a group of counselors standing around the fire pit talking. As I fill my cup at the keg, my eyes immediately search for Theo. I find him in the circle, standing with back his to me, which means I can openly stare.

He's wearing faded Levi's (the tight denim making his ass look oh, so inviting) and a fitted pale blue t-shirt, with his hair hanging in silky, sun-kissed waves just past his shoulders.

All week Juan has been begging Theo to let him fix him up for the party. And from how neat and styled Theo's hair looks, it seems he may have finally given in. I gulp a few swigs of the icy beer, surprised by how nervous I am to see him. My God, it's just Theo…why is my stomach doing flips like this?

Ignoring my odd emotions, I join the group at the fire, pushing in to stand beside him.

"So, you finally let Juan give you a makeover, huh?" I tease, elbowing him in the ribs.

He turns and smiles down at me. "Yeah, I did."

I suck in a sharp breath. "Oh my God. You're not wearing your glasses!"

Everyone laughs at my reaction, Theo the hardest. It was a stupid thing to say, since it's pretty obvious he's not wearing his glasses. But I can't seem to find any other words right now. His eyes are beautiful;

a crystal pale green with long dark lashes. Eyes that, for the first time ever, are staring directly into mine with nothing to shield their gaze. And as we blink at each other, I can't help but feel like he's looking not just at the surface of me, but deep into my soul.

"Damn, you look good."

I pray I've only thought the words, but when Juan pipes up, "He does, doesn't he?" I know I've blown my cool.

Juan gushes on, "I told you I could do wonders with him! A little hair gel, some scrunching…get rid of those glasses…those awful clothes. I swear this boy could be on the runway in Milan right now!"

Theo looks mortified by the attention, but Juan is right. Theo does have the exotic beauty of a runway model. Still, I can't help but think back on the moment at the cove when I'd come out of the water and wanted so badly to touch him. That feeling was primal, like something pulling at the very core of me. It had nothing to do with what he looked like on the outside. Although that doesn't mean I still can't appreciate what I'm gazing upon right now.

"Why didn't you ditch the glasses before now?" I ask him.

He shrugs, giving me a crooked smile. "Because I wanted you to fall in love with my charming personality before I hit you with my stunning good looks."

I laugh like I'm supposed to. Theo clearly doesn't see what all the fuss is about. He's told me before that he's always felt ugly and awkward. That he still sees himself as that bald, bloated kid in the hospital whenever he looks in the mirror. I want to tell him he might want to take a second glance at his reflection because that little boy is long gone. Replaced by the incredibly handsome man standing next to me now.

Greta shoves in on the other side of Theo. "What's with all this?" She flips his hair roughly, frowns at where his glasses normally sit on his nose. "Do you actually have *product* in your hair? What are you? Some kind of pussy?!" Sometimes it's really apparent that Greta was raised in a house full of boys.

"Oh, yeah?" Theo gives her a little push. "Would a pussy be able to beat you down to that apple tree with a five second head start?"

Without another word, Greta bursts through the circle in a full speed sprint, knocking two people aside on her way out the other side. Theo casually hands me his beer, then explodes after her, while the rest of us simply stare after them, dazed by their sudden outburst.

Juan comes to stand next to me, watching as Theo overtakes Greta as she's almost to the tree. But before he can pass her, Greta trips him and they both go tumbling. Then the two of them belly crawl and tackle their way like two war heroes trying to make it to the safety of their bunker while we all cheer them on from the fire ring.

"He's going to undo all my hard work," Juan grumbles as Theo leaps in the air—shirt untucked and hair disheveled—to celebrate his victory.

"Yeah, but what are you going to do?" I say. "Theo's going to be Theo. No one's going to change that."

I wait until Juan walks to whisper the rest of my thought. "And that's what I love about him the most."

CHAPTER SIXTEEN

MUSIC THUMPS LOUDLY off the wood-paneled walls as Honey Bear, Greta, and I dance in Tim's cramped living room.

With each beer I've drunk tonight, the idea of having a summer romance with Theo is sounding better and better. *What would be the harm in it?* I reason as I gyrate with the pounding beat of the song. *I can let myself have some fun with him. Then once camp is over I'll end it and we'll go our separate ways and I'll never see him again. We'll have a tiny, encapsulated fling with its ending already planned at its start. It's the perfect setup. No expectations, no commitment. Three months of fun and then Goodbye Theo. It'll be easy.*

Honey Bear shouts at Greta over the music. "Adam keeps staring at you!"

Greta rolls her eyes. "Of course he's staring! How could he not when I'm such a wonderful dancer?" She thrashes and jerks like she's having a seizure, then tops it off with the world's most exaggerated chicken dance. She looks ridiculous, but being Greta, she doesn't even care.

I motion to Adam and Wendell to come join us. Adam shakes his head no, but Wen bops over and squeezes in next to me, laughing at our wild moves. I love being around Wen because although he's quiet (I'm not sure I've ever heard him say more than 2 sentences in a row) he has a warmth about him that's hard to explain. He always wears this barely-there grin, like he finds everything he encounters slightly amusing. Which seems like a great tactic to get through life. Even if I can't seem to master that light-heartedness myself.

Wen copies Greta's dance moves, the two of them laughing hard, challenging each other to see who can look more ridiculous. I vote for Greta because Wen (with his super hot body) somehow still looks cool thrashing around like an out-of-control garden hose.

"There's too many people out here now," I say to Greta when I get bumped in the back for the umpteenth time. "Go over and talk to Adam."

Wen nods furiously, like he's got some insider information. Which only confirms my suspicion that Adam likes Greta but is just too shy to make the first move.

Greta stops dancing, opening her mouth as if she's going to give us some kind of lame excuse as to why she can't leave. Then, after scrutinizing Honey Bear and me, she seems to think better of it.

"Fine, I'll go," Greta relents, then lowers her voice so only Honey Bear and I can hear. "But one eyebrow wag or *woo hoo* from you two and I'm out of there faster than you can say Cootchie McGregor."

We burst out laughing at the nickname Honey Bear uses for her private parts.

Once Greta is gone, I slip back to furiously scanning the house for Theo. I haven't seen him in over an hour. The logical part of me hopes he's already gone home. That way I can sober up before I let anything slip about how his crush isn't so one-side anymore. Then he'll be safe. He'll escape my clutches and not get hurt like everyone else who's ever cared about me has.

But the drunk part of me wants to track him down, pull him into a dark corner, and ask him if he wants to make out. Oh my God, I want to kiss him so badly. To see what those luscious lips of his taste like…to slip my hand up his shirt and feel that hard stomach under my fingers…to reach down between his legs and feel…

"You know what?" I yell to Wen and Honey Bear, trying to put an end to all my lurid thoughts. "I'm going to get another beer!"

I shove through the crowd, toward the door, the drunk part of me in full control now.

As soon as I step outside, I see Theo standing by the garage with Tim and a few other guys. As I get closer a waft of sweet smoke hits me and I realize they're smoking pot. Hmmm. That's interesting.

When I get to him, Theo throws an arm over my shoulder and pulls me roughly to his side.

"Annie, Annie, Annie. Where have you been all my life?" he purrs in his velvet voice, making my stomach drop out from under me. Being this close to him only makes me want him more. Which the nasty voice in my head keeps insisting is a terrible idea. But for the life of me, I can't remember why.

"I've missed you so much," he goes on, kissing the top of my head like we're reuniting lovers instead of mere friends.

I struggle away from him, the voice of reason finally gaining a little traction inside my head. *You're going to regret this in the morning,* it warns. That damn voice is such a party pooper. Why won't it ever let me have a good time?

"You're obviously high," I snap at Theo, pretending to be disgusted as I wipe his kiss from my hair. He usually tries hard to respect my boundaries. Probably because I'm always drilling into him how we'll never be more than just friends. But he's a touchy-feely kind of guy, and I know it kills him to hold back his affection. After that weird head kiss, it's clear that I'm not the only one whose inhibitions are in tatters tonight.

"Yeah, I might be just a teeny tiny bit high." He grins down on me, eyes half mast, lashes batting slowly. I can't help but think of how he looks even sweeter than normal, if that's even possible, since he's already the sweetest boy I've ever met. The way he's looking at me makes me want to crawl back into his arms and hug him tight. But I try to hang onto my last shred of reason, since apparently one of us has to.

Tim takes a toke on the joint he has wedged in the little nub on the end of his half arm, then offers it to Theo. Tim is the oldest person here, probably in his late thirties, although I can't really tell because he has the haggard face and skeleton body of someone who's lived a hard life and has the stories to prove it. Apparently, he's worked at Camp Boundless forever. I'm ceaselessly amazed by all he can do with just his feet and a quarter of an arm. He zips around the place in his golf cart—accelerating with one bare foot and steering with the other—delivering medicine, distributing lunches, collecting the trash, basically being the gofer for whatever anyone needs. And it's only now, as he tells a story of when Theo threw up inside the rowboat back when he was a camper, that I realize the two of them have known each other for a while.

Tim nudges Theo with his shoulder. "My God, I wouldn't have recognized you if you hadn't introduced yourself on the first day. You certainly look a lot different than you did back then."

"Yeah," Theo says a bit sheepishly. "I've come a long way."

"That you have, man. That you have," Tim says, sounding almost like a proud father. "To Theo!" He calls out to the surrounding group. "Let's take a toke to his good long life!"

Everyone laughs at the irony of smoking being equated to a long life. But as Theo takes a drag on the joint, I notice how uncomfortable he looks. How he gazes off into the darkened woods as everyone cheers, a hint of sadness in his eyes. But the next second his smile reappears in full force, making me wonder if I'd misinterpreted his flash of emotion.

Lowering my voice so the other guys can't hear, I hiss, "I can't believe you smoke pot."

I've been partying since I was fifteen years old, but I've always stuck to alcohol, categorizing the kids who smoked pot as the loser druggies. In high school, they'd taught us that marijuana was the gateway to hard core drugs. But the words *hard core* and *Theo* just don't fit together in the same sentence.

"I don't do it that often," he says. "Just when I want to let my hair down." He flicks his hair behind his shoulder, laughing so long and hard at his joke that I can't help but join in. He's swaying a little, so I take the opportunity to snake my arm around his waist to steady him, enjoying having a reason to touch him again.

"It was actually my mom who got me weed for the first time," he says.

My eyes go wide and he explains more. "It helped with the nausea from the chemo. I was only fifteen at the time and she had to run around doing some shady back-alley shit to get it. I know…crazy, huh? But you know how moms are. They'll do anything for their kids."

"Yeah, moms are pretty fierce when it comes to their children," I agree, wishing my mom was still around to champion me from the sidelines the way she always did when she was alive.

Theo levels me under a serious stare. "You're right. Moms are relentless when it comes to supporting their kids. Even death can't stop them from being there for you, Annie. Really. I'm serious about that."

I can tell he wants to say more, but I shoot him a warning look before he can explain how my mom is still with me, even though I have hard evidence to prove that she's not.

"You surprised me tonight, Theo," I say, wanting to change the subject. "You seem too good to do something as bad as using illegal drugs."

He grins and totters a bit in my arms, contemplating my words. Then he bends down and nuzzles his face in my hair, lingering purposely for a few seconds to breathe me in before he speaks.

"I've got a little secret for you, Annie," he whispers, his voice so seductive my legs go weak. "I'm not as good as you think I am."

∞

"And that's why you have to be really good friends to party with me," Tim says, taking a drag on a regular cigarette as he leans against the kitchen counter. "Because by the end of the night, you just might be the one who has to wipe my ass!"

He laughs uproariously and I join in just as loud. At the beginning of the summer, the thought of wiping this grown man's ass would've horrified me. But after all I've done these past months, not much makes me squeamish anymore. Greta and I even have our own motto: "With a good pair of gloves, we can do anything!"

"I like you and all, Tim," I deadpan. "But I'm fine if we stay as mere acquaintances after hearing that."

He laughs even harder, which triggers a coughing fit, and he stumbles off to the keg to find some relief.

I'm hiding out in the kitchen, drinking water, and trying to sober up. I know Theo's in the living room, but I've been trying to stay away from him before my most base instincts have me climbing him like a tree in front of the entire camp. But now that I'm alone, I tiptoe to the edge of the doorway and slyly peek at where he's sitting on the couch with Greta. The two of them have their matching brown heads bowed close, talking intensely about something. Knowing them, they're probably organizing another arm-wrestling tournament, best three out of five, like they challenged each other to last week.

I'm just about to go in there and squeeze on the couch in between them when Theo stands and motions outside while Greta nods. He must be getting her another beer. I watch as he walks off, Greta's gaze trailing him all the way until he disappears out the door. She has a little smile playing on her lips, a wistful look on her face that I've never seen before. And, as she stares at the blank space where Theo's just been, that dreamy smile doesn't fade. It's like she's thinking of something really pleasant. Something she really, really loves.

Hearing my own words, everything inside of me freezes. And all the pieces that have been staring me in the face these past weeks suddenly fall into place, one by one. Greta's adoring look. The way she's always hanging out with the guys. How she and Theo spend so much time together. Oh my God. Why haven't I seen it before? Adam isn't Greta's Mystery Man. Theo is.

CHAPTER SEVENTEEN

I RACE THROUGH the boys' cabin screaming at the top of my lungs, a gaggle of middle school girls following closely behind.

"Here, like this," I tell them, riffling through some poor kid's drawers, throwing handfuls of his bundled socks all over the floor. "Remember. Nothing too destructive. You just want to make a bit of a mess."

The girls fan out around the room, rumpling covers, emptying drawers, messing up dresser tops, just as I've instructed them to. Greta strings toilet paper from bed to bed. Honey Bear and another pack of girls squeeze into the bathroom to write silly messages on the mirrors in soap, while Susan waits outside, acting as our lookout. She'd eventually given in to my plan when I'd told her my logic.

"Didn't they tell us in training that our goal was to give the campers as normal a camp experience as possible?" I'd reasoned. "And what could be more normal than a good old-fashioned raid of the boys' cabin?"

Susan couldn't come up with any argument, so now here she is, our begrudging accomplice.

I pause for a moment to take in the glee on the girls' faces as they wreak havoc on the space. Out of an entire week's full of carefully scheduled activities, this spontaneous melee will probably be the moment they remember the most when they return home. They're so overjoyed it makes me wonder how often they're allowed to be reckless and naughty like this. I've never thought of what being sheltered and constantly supervised robs from a kid. Yeah, I've stirred up a lot of trouble in my life. But at least I've had the opportunity to make my own dumb mistakes. I'm not sure these girls have been afforded the same luxury.

We've told the campers that staff quarters are off limits, but as the chaos unfolds around me I find myself standing in the doorway of the boys' room, once again feeling the unexplainable pull toward Theo… or in this case, toward his belongings. It's wrong, I know, but I want to rifle through his clothes, see what he keeps on his bedside table, search for prescriptions, maybe even find his private journal. I want to know everything about him. Actually, I could distill that sentence down and make it even more true: I just want *him*.

I can't stop thinking of how he'd whispered that seductive innuendo in my ear at the party. Of course, right behind that memory always comes the stark realization that Greta's in love with him. She's my best friend. I could never interfere with her relationship with Theo. She's known him so much longer than I have. And they're so close… and have so much in common, both of them being nurses and all. And with as loyal as Greta is, I know she'll never run away and break his heart. Which is something I can't say about myself.

The day after the party, I'd tried my best to act casual as I asked Greta whether she told her Mystery Man how she felt.

"Of course not," she'd huffed. "I told you it's not worth it. Especially since we're such good friends now." That last part had only confirmed my suspicions about her feelings for Theo. But despite how relieved I was that she hadn't told Theo the truth, I still know Greta is much better for him than I am. That's why the kindest thing I can do is to back off and not let my silly infatuation mess things up between them. And yet…

I walk into his room.

Immediately I can tell which bed belongs to him. His clothes are strewn everywhere, multiple pairs of worn running sneakers tossed willy-nilly under his bed, which is unmade. Adam and Juan are always complaining about what a slob he is, which kind of makes me happy. It's nice to know Mr. Perfect has his faults, just like the rest of us.

The green duffle he carries back and forth from home is open, lying on the floor at the end of his bed. I peer inside, heart leaping when I see a folded piece of paper sitting on top of a pile of clothes. Now this is interesting. I wonder if it's a letter to a friend telling them about his summer. Has he told this person about me? And if so, what did he say? I look over my shoulder to make sure no one's watching, then crouch down beside his bag and open the paper.

The writing inside is messy, almost illegible in fact, slanting at a sharp angle across the page. Short lines stack up, forming a jagged tower, in what looks like some kind of free form poem.

Hair like spun gold.
Freckles on her nose.
She frowns, but I smile.
I can't believe it. It's her!
But I know not to say anything. She won't understand.
Not yet.
A flash of green. A thin band. A rope maybe? A string?
She's reaching out. Touching me.
A jolt goes through me. It feels so good.
Does she feel it too?
I think about asking. But no, I should wait.

I frown down at the page as the girls' screams from the other room swell loudly. I should go check what's going on, but I'm too transfixed by the letter to move.

Theo said he sometimes writes songs, but this doesn't seem like lyrics. There's no rhyme, no rhythm to them. And the words feel so familiar to me. As I read them again, it suddenly becomes hard to catch my breath. Wait a minute. I know what he's describing. It's the moment we first touched, when I tied the friendship bracelet on him in the dining hall. A simple snapshot in time that, for some reason, now feels really important. Like the words mean more to me than the sum of their parts. But why? What is it about these sentences that feel so special to me?

"I see you've taken to snooping now, huh?" Theo's voice calls from the doorway.

I'm so shocked I scream and fall backward on my ass; landing in a heap with the paper flailing in my hand, making it impossible to deny his accusations.

"Oh, I…um…was…just…" I awkwardly scramble to my feet.

"Going through my things?" He leans against the door frame with his arms crossed and, to my relief, he's smiling.

"One girl grabbed this. I was just putting it back." Good God, why am I even trying to lie to him? Haven't I learned the futility in that by now?

"It's okay," he says. But he doesn't come closer, which is weird for him. If I'm around, Theo always makes a point of being close to me. His expression is hard to read. He seems almost worried. Maybe a bit embarrassed, too. "Did you read it?" he asks quietly.

"Yeah. It's a good poem, but a bit rough." I laugh uneasily, trying to lighten the mood, which has suddenly become as heavy as a lead brick. "And you might want to work on your descriptions. This is all you could come up with for me? Surely you could do better than *hair of gold, freckles on nose*' to describe me."

He shrugs. "Oh, I don't know. I think I did a pretty good job with the details, considering I hadn't even met you yet when I wrote it."

A faint humming swells in my ears…the feeling of time screeching to a world-tilting halt.

"What are you talking about? This whole thing is about the moment we met, just a few weeks ago." I wave the paper in the air for emphasis. *Flash of green. A thin band. A rope maybe? A string?* The part about touching him. It perfectly described when I'd tied the friendship bracelet on his wrist the day Greta introduced us.

"Which I wrote three years ago," he says plainly. "When I was sixteen years old."

I shake my head, the ringing in my ears growing louder. "But… but…that's impossible."

He finally comes into the room. Ever so gently takes the paper out of my hand. "Annie, we need to talk."

CHAPTER EIGHTEEN

Somewhere *else*...

HE'S MADE HIS decision.

He's leaving here to return to his physical body still waiting in that hospital bed, and giving his old life another try.

All because of her. All because of that beautiful, Intertwined Path full of love. A path that there's a one in a billion chance they just might find. Together.

I want to tell him he won't regret going. But he wouldn't regret staying either, so the point is moot. Regret is only possible in the physical realm. It doesn't exist here. When all choices are equally loved, judgement just isn't possible anymore.

He turns to make last-minute plans with her, startling when he sees her fading form. He's still connected, however thinly, back into the physical world, which limits the amount he's able to understand. The longer a soul's here, the more it dawns on them how the experience of Life really works. Which is why—if these two want this game to be fun and not a total cinch—I need to get them back there as soon as possible.

"Hey...why is she so, so...misty?" he asks, pointing next to him.

"She didn't come here the same way that you did. So her experience is different from yours," I explain.

"Which means?" he asks, looking suspicious.

"Which means," I turn to her. "You, my love, will not remember the rest of what happens here, at least not at first. And you're also not going to remember him either." I point to her companion.

"Not at all?" she asks.

I tip my head back and forth, feeling into the connection I have with her. It's stronger than I'd expected at this point in her life…so maybe…just maybe, she might let some of this through. "Not until just the right time. If you two happen to get to that point, that is."

"So, I'm going into this completely blind?" she asks excitedly. Funny how, back on Earth, she considers herself so meek and mild. When what lies beneath is a soul as fierce and fiery as any I've ever known.

"You'll remember a little. But whether or not you listen to it… well that's another story."

She laughs hard, turning to her partner beside her. "Looks like you're going to have to do all the heavy lifting this time around." She tries to nudge him, but since they're not physical, their two forms merge into one, making everything around us surge brighter for a moment, like two live wires sparking at their union point.

"I'm up for it," he says, rising to the challenge. "But the fact that you're going to forget all of this is definitely going to make things a lot more interesting."

"Which is the way you two always want it, if I remember correctly," I remind them.

They grin fondly at each other, as if they're thinking back over their eternities together. They have done well as a team, I'll give them that. But this time…well, we've upped the stakes a notch or two. Upon their own request, of course. But that's the part that neither of them can remember now.

"There is only one thing you have to do," I tell her.

"Yeah? What's that?"

"When he comes…believe him."

She breaks into a grin almost as bright as mine as she looks up at him in adoration. "I think I can do that. He's always been pretty trustworthy in the past."

He waves her off, pretending to be embarrassed, and they dissolve into giggles again. These two. They know how to have a good time together. Which is really what this whole life adventure is about.

"And don't worry," I reassure her. "I'll give you a few more instructions before you leave. The memories should pop up at just the right time. But the rest will be up to you."

I turn to him. "And remember…when and if. And it's a big *if*…the time comes. You'll have to take it slow with her. It's going to be a little shocking, so you'll have to be careful not to overwhelm her all at once."

"Slow and steady wins the race!" he chimes. Then drops his voice, adding wryly, "Although it's really not a race because it has no beginning or ending and just keeps going around and around forever."

"Too bad no one remembers that part," I say. "Everyone in the physical world is always in such a damn rush to get things done!"

He sighs heavily, closing his eyes, clearly wanting to soak in the ecstasy a little longer before he leaves. I can't blame him. The pleasure must feel so heightened compared to the pain he just left. But soon his glow fades too, then comes back up, like the signal at the theater that intermission is just about over. While her glow stays faded, limited by the manner by which she's come.

Realizing he doesn't have long, he asks, "And if we don't complete it…whatever the heck this purpose we're supposed to do together?"

Deep down he already knows the answer, but those pesky human veils he still wears block so much. So, I remind him of the truth, sing-singing cheerfully, "No worries! You'll just give it another try the next time around!" I make it sound like an advertising slogan. Which it kind of is.

He chuckles, always so good-natured this one.

"What do you say?" he asks, holding out an upturned palm to her. "Do you want to give it a try?"

"Sure. Why not? Sounds like fun." She tries to slap his hand but again, their forms just pass right through each other. They laugh and laugh, then try again, blending their hands together in an embrace that makes the air spark and snap around us.

Then they chant their promise together, like they do every time.

Across time and distance, lifetimes and eternities, always together, forevermore.

For a moment everything goes white in an explosion of pure love.

When we all return to our vague forms, he sobers…looking down at himself, his glow now dimming in earnest this time. As for her, only a wisp remains. Just enough presence so that one day, if she so chooses, she'll be able to remember all of what happened here.

"It's happening now, isn't it? We're going back aren't we…" she asks.

"Yes. We'll have you both back in your bodies in no time flat. Especially you," I point to him. "We don't want to torture your poor mom for too long."

"Thanks for that." Suddenly he frowns, looking out over the darkness before us, noticing something about the myriad of geometrical facets of his possible lifetimes for the first time. Ahhhh. I wondered when that little detail would register with him.

"Wait a minute," he says. I feel his human emotions seeping back. Doubt, worry, and the worst one: fear. In him, they're much fainter than most people. But here, where only pure love exists, even the slightest trace of its opposite sticks out like a sore thumb. "Why do all my life trajectories end at that one spot?"

Oh boy, they're going to love this twist. "Oh yeah…about that…"

CHAPTER NINETEEN

THEO

FOR THE FIRST time ever, we walk in complete silence to The Lookout. We'd had to wait through all of lunch and the next period before we could get away to talk. And even though I'm eager to explain to Annie what I'd written on that piece of paper, a part of me is glad I had a little time to recalibrate before I take this next leap.

When I'd seen her holding the paper, I'd panicked, sure that I ruined everything by her finding out that way. I was certain the shock of seeing my writing about her would freak her out, making her too closed off to ever listen to my explanation.

But then I felt like I was whisked up in the air and could see everything that lead up to that moment from a bird's eye view. Last night, I'd had the impulse to read the letter when I couldn't sleep. Then, when I'd finally started dozing off, instead of putting it away in my sock drawer like I usually do, I'd set it on top of my duffle bag in plain sight. Standing in that doorway, I'd realized there was a reason I'd done something so out of character. Nothing had gone wrong. Annie was supposed to find that letter.

But even with that knowing, I'm still not sure what comes next. All I know is I have to stay relaxed. Stay trusting. Not let the doubt creep in like it has in the past. Otherwise, I won't be able to hear my guidance. Annie is just starting to open up to me and let her guard down. I need to respect where she is. And remember what I was told. To take it slowly. To not try to drag her kicking and screaming to a place she's not ready for yet.

Annie gives me a weak smile as we step up on the deck. She's nervous, I can tell. Who wouldn't be when some crazy person has just told you they'd met you in a vision three years before they'd actually met you in real life? It's hard for me to fathom too, and I'm the one who's lived it. I just hope I can find the right words to help her understand.

I brought some old beach chairs to The Lookout last week and now Annie settles herself in one, waiting for me to join her. When I don't sit across from her, she looks disappointed.

"Sorry," I say, pacing by the railing. "I need to keep moving in order to get my thoughts organized."

She cracks a smile. "Is that why you're constantly moving? All your brain power comes from your feet?" She's clearly trying to put me at ease. Looking down on her, sitting there with her beautiful blue eyes wide, my heart aches to touch her. But that would only frazzle my brain even further and I need to be clear minded to get through this.

I pause in front of her chair. "Can I ask you a favor before I start?" When she nods, I go on. "I know you can be a little…uh… skeptical sometimes…"

She laughs. "Most people would say cynical and judgmental but thank you for choosing a kinder word."

Her lit-up face relaxes me a little. "I wondered if maybe you could just keep an open mind as I tell you my story? Just entertain the possibility that what I'm about to tell you is true."

A quick shadow of worry flashes across her expression, but she covers it quickly, slipping into an old-lady voice to tease me. "I can't promise you anything, Sonnie. But I'll try to crank open this rusty old trap of a mind," she taps her temple. "And try to let some of you kids' new-fangled ideas in."

"Thank you for that." I go back to pacing, gazing out over the lake as she waits. Where to start? Where to start? I've only told this story two times before. Once to my mom and once to my doctor. Only one of them believed me. Whose side will Annie come down on?

And if she really remembers nothing from before, like we agreed to...well, what I'm about to say is going to be a tough sell.

"So, you know I had cancer." That seems like a good beginning. Start with something she already accepts as true.

"Yeah."

"Well, what you don't know is that when I had cancer...I died."

Her eyes go wide. Okay, maybe I dove in a little too deep there.

"I mean, I died for four minutes. Then I came back. I mean, obviously." I wave a hand down my very much alive body, then rush on. "I got sepsis from an infection, and they were trying everything to treat it, but my organs started shutting down. And long story short, I went into cardiac arrest and they weren't able to get my heartbeat back for four minutes."

Annie's mouth hangs open. It takes her a moment to finally speak. "Oh my God, Theo. That's horrible."

"What? No crack about how the oxygen deprivation affected my brain, and that's why I'm so weird?" I chide. "I'm disappointed in you, Annie."

"I'm trying to be good, like you asked. But yeah, that thought did arise." She gives me a little wink. "It would explain a lot of things."

I take a deep breath and go on. "So, during that time I was technically dead, I went somewhere. Somewhere not of this world. Have you ever heard of a Near-Death Experience?"

She looks off in the distance. "Yeah. I think so. My mom had a book about how some guy supposedly died and saw a bright tunnel of light and all that stuff and then came back to tell about it."

"That's what happened to me. I experienced what happens after you die."

She sits very still, clearly at a loss for words. I plow on, looking out on the vista instead of her face. It will be easier that way. I need to get this out all at once. Then I can worry about her reaction later.

"So my Near-Death Experience was a lot like what you've probably read about. At the beginning, I was walking through what felt like a long tunnel. It was dark at first but it got lighter and lighter as I went along until I was surrounded by this dazzling white light that led to this...like...center place up ahead where I could sense there were people waiting for me. And it all felt so, so good. My body had been in such pain only moments before, but as I walked it became light and healthy, kind of blurry at the edges, pulsing with this all-encompassing energy that felt like it wasn't only inside me but humming around me too. I felt blended into every single particle of life. Like it was me, and I was it...no differentiation at all." I shake my head, hating how I can never find the right words to describe the magnitude of what I experienced. "It's so hard to explain how wonderful it felt. This feeling of complete and overwhelming love and well-being. It was the best feeling I've ever known."

I risk a glance at her as I walk by. She's sitting up in her chair, arms wrapped around her knees, listening intently. That seems like a good sign.

"As I went further down the path, things around me began to take shape. There were trees to the side and then a clearing. In it, I saw a woman smiling at me, her arms open wide like she was calling me to her. And behind her there were other people who I couldn't quite make out as clearly, but they all felt familiar, like they were my family welcoming me home." I smile as the beatific face of the woman flashes back in my mind. She was so beautiful, even though the details of her face have become blurred in my memory in the years since my NDE happened.

I stop my pacing to search for any sign of recognition on Annie's face; any sense she's remembering what I've just described, too. But her features remain schooled. Although, I get a sense from the slight tick in her jaw that holding back judgement is taking some effort for her.

I continue my story. "I remember they were all so excited to see me. Giddy almost. The woman wrapped her arms around me and everyone else joined in and they were all saying how proud they were of me and telling me what a good job I'd done and how much they loved me…" I have to stop because my throat has closed up and I can't push out any more paltry words. The tears come the way they always do when I remember that moment of complete and utter love and acceptance. Beautiful, joyful tears that feel like liquid love turned into physical form.

"Sorry," I finally choke out, motioning to the tears now streaming down my face. "I always get really overwhelmed at that part. I can't really control this. And honestly, I don't really want to because… although it may not look like it…it feels really good."

In the next instant, Annie's on her feet, catching my hand, pulling me close. "Is it really that beautiful?" she asks softly. I'm surprised to see her eyes glistening, too.

"Oh yes, Annie. More beautiful than anything you could ever imagine."

She struggles to get out her next words. "Do you think it's that way for everyone?" As soon as I hear the pleading tone in her voice, I know what she's asking.

"Yes. For everyone. It's what your mom is feeling right now, too."

Her face contorts with emotion. She fights so hard against it, it breaks my heart. I know how she's feeling because I've felt it myself. A tidal wave of relief so forceful there's no way to hold it back.

"Come here," I say, wrapping her up in my arms and squeezing her tight.

As soon as her body presses into mine, her resolve crumbles and she sobs into my chest, somehow both pushing against me and pulling me close at the same time. I know it's killing her to cry in front of me, to let herself be vulnerable like this. I know how hard it is for her to believe that the peace I've described is possible. And yet she cries. Which is how I know that, deep down under all those layers of anger and hurt and bitterness, there's a chance she believes what I'm saying is true.

She finally struggles out of my arms, practically shoving me away. I wouldn't have expected anything less from her and her predictability makes me laugh. She laughs too, knowing I can see right through her. We both mop our wet faces and she retreats to her chair as I resume my march back and forth across the deck.

"Sorry for the interruption there," she mumbles, looking embarrassed. "Go ahead. Get on with the rest of your story. You've obviously pried something open in here." She points to her head again. "You might as well keep going."

I take a moment to think of what part of my story I want to include next. Which pieces she might be able to absorb now and which need to wait for her beliefs to become a bit more porous before I spill them at her feet.

"So, I felt like the woman in the middle was like some kind of guide or…or…"

"Guardian Angel?" she offers.

I take a second to consider the moniker before going on. "An Angel, for sure. But I wouldn't use the word guardian, because life doesn't feel that way when you're there. Because there's nothing to guard against, Annie. That's the part that most people don't understand."

She tips her head, trying to let what I've said sink in. I know she wants to argue with me and I don't blame her, considering what she's already faced in her short life.

I move on quickly, not wanting to get sidetracked. "Let's just call her my Angel Guide, okay? Anyway, she wasn't at all what I expected. She wasn't all stoic and serious, handing down verdicts and judgements. She was cheerful and bubbly. Fun, even. She had on this brightly colored coat and big dangly earrings and tinkling jewelry. And she was just gushing love all over me. She felt like the most accepting, doting mother you could ever imagine. And I began to recognize some people standing behind her. I saw my grandfather and my grandmother, both of whom had died when I was younger. They were just as I remembered them, except more vibrant. Even more alive than when they were alive, if that makes any sense."

She nods. It surprises me that she's not fighting everything I say. Instead, she seems a little dazed, focused and yet not focused on me. Like her body is here, but her mind has floated away; back to when she was standing next to me in the afterlife. My heart lifts with hope. Please, please, let her remember something…and soon. It will be so much easier that way.

When she doesn't say anything, I force myself back on track. "My Angel talked to me, but it wasn't in words. It was this kind of knowing that passed between us, not spoken aloud like in the physical world. More a transmission mind-to-mind. And everything she said made perfect sense to me. There was no confusion. Just a feeling of pure clarity and well-being. I remember just laughing and laughing because everything I'd worried about in my whole life suddenly all seemed so pointless and hysterical."

She laughs, as if she's feeling it too. I relax a little more since it seems like at least a few drops of resonance have begun to drip through her stony walls. "A lot happened when I was there. So much really that it's hard to make sense of when you try to fit it inside four minutes. But time isn't the same there. Space isn't either. But I can go into all of that later. Because right now we *are* limited by time and I don't have enough of it in this one free period to explain everything. So, I'll just get to the part about the letter. The part about you."

She sighs heavily, sits back in the beach chair, clutching its arms with both hands as if she's preparing to be blasted off into outer space. Which is not a bad analogy, since what I'm about to describe is a whole other dimension than what's here on Earth. Whether or not she believes me…well, that's another story.

"My Angel Guide led me to what felt like some kind of precipice. In front of me was a vast endless dark ocean of space and behind me was more solid ground, the path I'd walked down to get there.

I somehow understood the two planes represented my past and my future. Then we stepped out further into the darkness and it was like I was standing inside the world's hugest diamond. All around me were millions and millions of facets. All these geometrical shapes with white glowing rays shooting out, coming together in points, then shooting off into more shapes, more fractals of possibilites."

"She explained each ray was a possible decision I could make. Each one led to another and another and another, forming these millions of pathways of choices that would make up my future life." I huff a laugh, remembering the enormity of it all. "My God, there were so many of them it would make your head spin, but at the time, it didn't feel overwhelming. It just felt like freedom and spaciousness and endless, wonderful possibility. At the intersection of some fractals, I could make out these fragments of scenes, like a really quick movie being played over and over. My Guide told me they were important moments that would affect the entire trajectory of my life."

Annie just barely nods, the rest of her body frozen in rapt attention.

"After I looked around for a while, she gave me a choice. She said I could stay there with her or go back to my life here on Earth."

I'm not sure Annie is even breathing now, but I can't worry about that because the more I stay in the feeling of being with my Angels the easier it is for me to speak. Of course it's easier, I remind myself. They're still here with me now.

"Right away, I said I wanted to stay with them." Out of the corner of my eye I see Annie stiffen, as if I've somehow betrayed her for admitting such a thing out loud. I whirl to her. "But you have to remember how sick my body was. How much pain I'd been in just moments before. The thought of leaving that place of such bliss, such pleasure…well that seemed impossible to me. I couldn't go back to my old body."

I wait for her to give any indication that she understands, but she just sits there, unmoving.

"Then my Angel said they would take care of my sickness for me.

That I was only choosing between whether I wanted to play some more here in the physical realm or come home."

"Play?!" Annie huffs. "They call life *playing*? What is this? Some kind of game to them?" Again, I smile. I suspected she was going to have a hard time with that concept.

"No, not at all. They cherish every little part of us. They're so grateful for all we do here. But yes, this is also still fun for them. That's why they were so excited when I got there. They were telling me how much they were enjoying experiencing life through me, in my personality as Theo."

She scrunches up her face, clearly not buying it.

"We can argue about that later," I tell her. "Again, let me get to the letter before I wear the treads off these sneakers."

"Can you sit down for a second?" she asks. "I'm getting dizzy watching you pace back and forth."

I consider saying No. My overwrought energy feels too huge to confine to just one place. But then I see her scoot her chair just a smidge closer to the one opposite her, and I understand what she's really asking. If I sit down, my legs are so long they will have to press up against hers. She's asking me to touch her.

Knowing that, I practically leap into the chair. And when our knees press together, the energy coursing through me smooths and begins to loop rhythmically. She lets out a long shuddering breath and I know she feels the same sense of relief as I do. I know that, even if there's no way to rationally explain it, the two of us have just become one and the same.

∞

"So where was I?" I stammer, realizing I've been sitting here in silence, basking in the pleasure of Annie's touch for way too long.

"Um, you were choosing between life and death." She gives me a wry smile.

"Ah, yes. How could I forget?" I have to tear my attention away from the heated point where our skin touches so I can think clearly again. "So even though they said they'd fix my body, I was still considering staying. But then I turned my head and caught sight of this path my Angel called—" *No, I can't say that.* I hesitate, trying to pick my words carefully. "Of uh…this path that seemed to shine brighter than all the others. A path that felt so beautiful, so special, it nearly broke my heart open, it was full of so much love. Which is saying a lot since my blurry light body was already pretty much in ecstasy."

I stop for a moment and think back on the wonder of seeing that path for the first time. Remember how my Angel Guide had been so excited about me finding it, she'd actually jumped up and down like a little girl, making her jewelry tinkle like wind chimes from her ears and wrists. (Although I'm still baffled by why an angel would need to wear that much jewelry. But I guess even perfect entities are allowed to have their own sense of style too.)

Annie looks anxious, so I go on. "It's hard to describe, but this path." *The one intertwined with yours.* Goodness, if I described it that way she'd be running for the hills in two seconds flat. I need to tone it down a bit. Again, I recalibrate. "This one path was calling to me with a much stronger force than all the others. I mean, don't get me wrong, all the paths were wonderful but this one…this one was like super intense."

"I told my Angel Guides I wanted to go back for that life. The extra special lit up one. So they showed me a snippet…like a little movie of a moment in time that would help me find the first step on that path."

"A movie?" she repeats skeptically.

"Yeah. I know it sounds weird. But it was a flash of a possible future. Just a few seconds of a moment that would change the course of my life." Inwardly, I cringe. I wish I hadn't made it sound like such a big deal. With the way she sees herself, Annie will never want to be part of something that seems too important. She still insists, all because of that one night, she's someone who can't be trusted.

"So, as you've already figured out," I rush on, "I came back and they kept up their end of the bargain. They healed my body. Within days of my incident, my organs regained their function and my bone marrow went back to normal and the leukemia cells in my blood diminished. And within a month, I was completely cancer free. The doctors still can't explain what happened. They consider my recovery some kind of fluke. But, of course I know the truth. My mom does too. But when I tried to tell my oncology doctor what I'd experienced, I could tell he didn't believe me. He said that what I saw was all just a reaction from chemicals that were released when my heart stopped. That it was a delusion. A trick my brain played on me. That my NDE hadn't really happened. But believe me, what happened there was more real than anything I've ever experienced here in my physical body."

In the distance, I hear the metal clunk of canoes hitting the dock, the swell of voices at the waterfront as the kids come in from the lake, a signal that our free period is ending soon. Annie glances over her shoulder, noticing it too. She presses her knee harder into mine as if she wants to keep our circuit intact a little longer.

"So, I was back, and I was healed, and it was a miracle, and Hallelujah," I quickly recap, waving my hands in the air for emphasis. "It should've been a time of bliss and rejoicing. But instead, I became obsessed with trying to figure out how I'd ever find that one path full of love I'd seen on the other side. I got all practical and logical and went back to focusing on how the odds were against me and how unlikely it was that I would ever get each decision supposedly 'right'," I air quote myself. "So as soon as I was strong enough, I asked my mom to bring me paper and pen and in the hospital bed I scribbled down everything I could remember from that one snippet in time I'd been shown that would start me on that path. It wasn't a lot to go on." I take a deep breath, knowing there's no going back after I say what I have to next. "Just the image of a beautiful, blonde-haired girl tying some kind of green string on my wrist...touching me and making goosebumps run down my arms."

She swallows hard, the implications of what I've just said slowly sinking in. Terrified by all I've just revealed, my next words wobble out of my mouth. "Having the paper…capturing all those details helped me calm down. Made me feel like I had something that would help me remember. So if the moment ever did come, I'd know without a shred of doubt that I'd finally found the girl I'd seen on the other side."

My heart pounds furiously as I wait for her to say something. It's a lot to process, I know. But it's hard to sit still. I want to *do* something…*say* something. Explain more, convince her more. But something deeper within me tells me to stay quiet. To let her have space to take in all I've told her in. No matter how much I want to, I can't control whether sharing my experience will draw her closer or push her further away. I can only trust that whatever happens next will be alright in the end.

She furrows her brows, looking down at where our legs are pressed together, where the electricity still whirls and sparks between us. This is the point in all my fantasies when the girl from my memory leaps up, embraces me in a hug, and tells me she's been waiting all her life to find me, too. Then she tells me she remembers everything and can't wait for the two of us to start our adventure together…to find our happily ever after together…for however long that might be.

But the frown plastered firmly on Annie's face tells me that's not how this is going to go.

I take a deep breath. It's okay. She just needs more time. My God, even though I sensed what was coming, I still felt like I was about to pass out the first time I saw her: The long-awaited girl from my memory…standing right *there* in the middle of Camp Boundless' dining hall. Just after she'd tied that bracelet on me, I'd slipped off and found the paper in my duffel and read an exact description of what had just happened, predicted by a past version of myself. Talk about time and space collapsing into itself. That paper was like a portal between two worlds.

She abruptly sits back, breaking our connection, staring broodily out over the lake. The emotions warring across her face makes my stomach churn. I already sense what's coming next.

"So, *I'm* a part of your path then?" She narrows her eyes at me, looking wary about playing such a role in my life. "There's something about me that's important to you finding this super special life of yours?"

I knew she wasn't going to like that part.

"Yes, but don't get freaked out, okay?" I know it wasn't a coincidence how she just pulled away from me. "We don't have to turn it into some big deal. Or try to figure out why our meeting means something. We can relax and just go with it and see where it leads us next."

"Relax and just go with it?!" she shouts. "Have you even met me, Theo? I'm not the kind of person who *relaxes* and *just goes with* anything!"

"Yeah, but you could start now. If you wanted to," I offer hopefully.

She huffs and sputters, clearly frustrated with me.

"There's a first time for everything, right?" I interject just as she's about to shout at me again.

"Not for me Theo! I'm not like you! I need a plan. Some solid reasoning. Some assurance about what's going to happen next."

"Why? Why do you need to know how everything's going to turn out ahead of time?"

"Because…because…" She throws her hands up, exasperated. "Because you clearly know why! When I'm left to my own devices, things don't go so well!"

"That's not true. Don't be so…"

"…hard on myself? That's easy for you to say, Theo. You've only known me a few weeks. You don't know how messed up I really am."

I open my mouth to argue, but she raises a hand to stop me.

She stares up into the canopy of trees above us, fighting to form words for what seems like an eternity.

Luckily, whatever she sees up there must calm her because when she speaks again, her voice is more even. "This is all a little crazy. I thought I was going to come here, and you were going to tell me some story of having a dream about me years ago, and that alone was going to be weird enough. But all this." She shakes her head, still looking so discombobulated. "You dying and coming back to life and talking to angels and seeing me when you were there. I mean, you have to admit, that's a lot to absorb."

"I know! And I completely understand. It's definitely going to take some time for you to process. I'm not asking you to say anything or make any big decisions. I just felt like I should tell you." It's killing me not to ask what I truly want to: Do you believe me?

She cocks her head, staring at me with a funny expression on her face. Almost like she heard my silent plea.

And then I see it. The recognition of something. It's only there for a split second, but it's there…I swear it's there. She just remembered something. Something that happened when we were together before. The question is, will she admit it to me?

Seeming dazed, she takes my hand in hers, holding it almost reverently. "Yes, I believe you, Theo." Then she shakes her head as if she's surprised by what just came out of her own mouth.

A rush of relief passes through me so forcefully I sway in my chair. I hadn't realized how badly I needed to hear those words until they were out of her mouth.

She goes on. "I mean, I don't *want* to believe you because it's not at all like me to give in to that airy fairy shit about God and Angels watching over you. But for some stupid reason, once again you've made me do something I said I'd never do." She laughs weakly, as if this entire conversation has exhausted her. "So there. You got it. I'm pissed as hell about it, but goddamn it, I believe you."

I squeeze her hand hard. "Thank you. You don't understand how much that means to me."

She shrugs, waves me off brusquely. "Actually, this might explain a lot about why you're the way you are." She scoots to the edge of the chair and stares deep into my eyes. "Maybe you're an angel too."

I laugh, stopping myself just before I blurt out, *Not quite yet.*

Again, her brows furrow, almost like she heard my thought again. Could that be possible?

I'm considering asking her if she just read my mind when she abruptly leaps to her feet.

"You know what? I better get back now or else I'm going to be late for Arts & Crafts." She claps her hands together hard, the sharp sound signaling the end to our conversation. She stiffly folds up her lawn chair and props it up against a tree. And just like that, it's as if a steel wall has been dropped between us. I sit there stunned, watching her, wondering if I've imagined all I just felt pass between us. The warmth. The connection. The fleeting sense that she somehow remembered our brief time together and the pact we'd made to find each other again.

For some reason, the mystery postcards I'd received in the mail just before I left for camp pop into my head. The little watercolor landscapes that look so familiar and feel like they mean something important. Although I have no idea why. I'd wanted to ask Annie about them, but now with the way she's acting, the timing doesn't seem right.

She bustles around the platform, kicking off sticks that fell in last night's storm, making a point of not meeting my eyes. Again, I tell myself she just needs some time to process everything. That she'll come back around, eventually. I need to give her some space. I'm glad I'd left out the part when the Angel told me our path could affect many lives. That would've really sent Annie over the edge.

We're just about to leave when a fully formed sentence whispers melodically in my head.

Tell her more.

I freeze in place, barely breathing. I know exactly what my Angel is asking me to do. She asking me to tell Annie about the one minor detail I'd omitted from my story. A detail that Annie is not going to like one bit. Geez, and I thought telling her this much was hard.

Are you sure? I ask inside my head. *Don't you think telling her that part will be too much?*

But the tinkling voice comes back even louder this time.

She has to know so she can make her decision.

As if in slow motion, I watch Annie turn back to me, face scrunched up like she's wondering why I'm not following her. It has to happen now. I can't think. I have to listen and trust and do as I feel. I have to just say it.

"There's one more thing I need to tell you."

CHAPTER TWENTY

ANNIE

I'M JUST ABOUT to step down off the platform when I swear I hear the faintest voice say, *Tell her more.*

I stop in my tracks, spanning the dappled forest to see where it came from. Tell her more? Tell *who* more of *what*?

I turn back to Theo and he's standing frozen in the middle of the deck, mouth moving just slightly like he's having some kind of internal argument with himself. When I give him a funny look, he startles back to life. Then he says, "There's one more thing I need to tell you."

I slump exaggeratedly. "What the hell else could you possibly tell me? That after you woke up, aliens abducted you, converted into a robot, then dropped back into your hospital bed with instructions to go forth and shower the planet in love?"

He laughs, then says flatly. "Yes, that's exactly what happened. I can't believe you guessed every single detail correctly." He slips into a mechanical voice, jerking his arms like they're hinged by bolts. "I… am…now…a…love…robot. Come…closer…so…I…can…shoot… you…with…my…laser…of…love."

I honk a loud laugh. "Have I mentioned that I love it when you're sarcastic? You really don't do it enough, but I think if you practiced, you could get really good at it."

He shakes his head, looking both exasperated and relieved. I think he's glad I'm laughing and not running full speed down the trail to get away from him. Believe me, I'm just as surprised as he is that I'm still here. There are so many warning bells going off in my head, telling me to get as far away from this boy as possible, that I'm surprised he can't hear them himself. But ever since he said that one sentence, I'm having trouble listening to reason anymore.

Do you believe me?

The second the words came out of his mouth, it was like a key clicking open a rusty lock inside my head. Suddenly I was back there, on the night when Caroline had called for me to come to the hospital to say goodbye to Mom. I'd tried to get to her. Truly I had. But just as I was about to leave, I stopped to check my reflection in the bathroom mirror and that's when the magnitude of what was about to happen hit me. One second I was okay and the next my heart was beating too fast and I was crying and sobbing so hard that I couldn't draw a full breath. I honestly felt like I was suffocating. And no matter what I did, I couldn't get my heart and my lungs and my weak legs back under control. Eventually, it got so bad that I must have either fallen asleep or passed out from lack of oxygen…I have no idea. But that's when the dream came. And I felt it…the overwhelming magnitude of love. The warm presence beside me. That's when I heard the instruction that for years I've been trying to understand:

When he comes…believe him.

I'd always thought my addled mind had made the whole thing up. But now, after the way I'd felt when Theo asked me that question, "Do you believe me?" I'd somehow known, without a doubt, that this was the moment I'd been waiting for.

Theo nudges my shoulder, startling me back to life. "Do you want to hear what else I have to say or not?"

"Oh, yeah, yeah, Lay it on me," I say absently. "After everything you just told me, nothing can surprise me anymore."

He tips his head back and forth like he's weighing the odds of whether or not that's actually true. My stomach drops sensing something foreboding coming my way.

He clears his throat. "So, remember when I said my Angel Guide gave me a choice? I could stay there or come back?" I nod and he continues. "Well, there was one little caveat to coming back I didn't mention before."

He hesitates like he's still not sure he wants to go on. "Which was?" I twirl my hand in front of me, prompting him on.

He lets out a heavy sigh then blurts, "She said if I came back I would die young."

It feels like someone just punched me straight in the gut. Hard.

"WHAT?!" I shout when I finally catch my breath.

Theo laughs. He actually fucking laughs. What the hell is wrong with him? "Yeah. That was the condition. I'm going to die young." He shrugs as lackadaisically as if he's just told me the price for coming back was stubbing his toe on his bedside table once a year.

"What does that even mean?!" I rage, hoping that any minute he's going to tell me this is another of his lame jokes. "Young? How young?"

"I won't live past twenty-one."

It's like the floor just dropped out from under me and I'm freefalling through the air. No. No. *No.* This can't be happening. There must be some kind of mistake. Theo can't die young. He's standing here right in front of me with so much vibrance, such life pouring out of him. Someone as healthy as him? No. It's not possible for him to be gone.

But then I remember how unfair God or the Universe or Satan or whatever you want to call the powers that be that make stupid decisions like this are. And suddenly snatching a young, beautiful soul like Theo back into their grips seems exactly like something they'd do.

I don't even realize I'm swaying on my feet until Theo comes closer and grips my elbow to steady me. "Are you okay?"

"Am I okay? Am I okay?" I blink at him, dumbfounded. "No, I'm not okay! You just told me you're going to die in what…like two years? That's kind of bad news, Theo. I mean, even *you* understand how much that sucks, right?"

Again, he hesitates, like he has to think it over. Why would he have to think it over?! Dying is bad. Everyone knows that!

"I mean…yeah, I can see why, from your perspective, it doesn't seem ideal…"

"I can't believe you can find a way to make even this into a positive!"

"I mean, it's all positive, Annie. Life is always…"

"Ugh! Just stop talking for a second!" I wail, pulling my arm out of his grip. "I need a second to think!"

I walk to the railing and look out over the lake, which I suddenly hate for having the nerve to look so glimmeringly beautiful at a moment as horrible as this. Behind my back I can feel Theo bubbling with everything he wants to say, but I have to give him credit, he somehow manages to keep his big trap shut.

Now I wish I hadn't said I believed him earlier. Then I could just brush off this latest revelation as the crazy rantings of a madman. But his story had felt so real, so right to me. And those words…that guidance that came from somewhere that felt so much bigger than me. *Believe him*, she'd said. Now that I've followed that instruction, it's hard to go back.

I curse at the water, the trees, the rocks….the entire world for a while. Goddammit. I can't believe the one time I let my guard down, the one time I let myself have feelings for someone, I find out they're going to die on me, too. Isn't that just rich? I gotta give it to you, Universe. You've got one sick sense of humor. I should've known this was a trap. I should've known better than to let myself actually care about someone again.

I spend way too long feeling sorry for myself before I remember there's one person on this platform who has it worse off than me.

Turning to Theo, I ask, "Do you know *how* you're going to die?" I hold my breath, part of me not wanting to know the answer.

"No. I've just kind of always assumed the cancer would come

back." He shrugs again. He actually fucking shrugs again. "I don't know exactly. They didn't give me any other details than that."

"AND YOU DIDN'T ASK?!"

He looks up in the air as if the thought had never occurred to him. "It didn't seem important at the time."

I stomp back and forth across the deck, throwing my hands in the air, mouth flapping as I try to form a coherent sentence. Leave it to a man to not to ask for directions!

He rushes over matching his steps to mine, bending in front of me, trying to force me to look into his eyes. "Don't freak out, okay? It's not like I'm going to drop dead any minute."

"No, but you're already nineteen. You only have two years left!"

He winces as if he knows I'm not going to like what he has to say next. "Actually, I only have a little over one year left. I turn twenty in a couple of months."

He leaps out of the way when I take a swing at him. Which is also the most selfish reaction in the world. What the hell is wrong with me? He's dying, for Christ's sake. It's not like it's his fault. But wait a minute. It kind of is his fault, isn't it? After all, he chose this life for himself, right?

Before I can interrogate him further, he barrels on. "But don't worry Annie! I still have a lot of life to live. I can feel that. When I was there, looking out over all those fractals of choices, there were still plenty more ahead of me. But then they all stopped at the same spot. When I asked why, my Angel Guide explained that was the end of my life. I mean my life in this body because of course, we're all eternal. We go on forever and ever. Because there is really no death, per se, there's only…" He trails off when he notices my face getting redder and redder.

I grab my head in frustration. "Ugh! Theo! I can't handle all this right now."

"I'm sorry. I know it's a lot. Forget about that eternal stuff. We can circle back to that later if you want."

I grab his arms, press them into his sides. "I swear to God if you shrug one more time when you're talking about dying, I'm going to kill you myself!"

He makes a goofy sorry-about-that face, and despite the horrible circumstances, I can't help but smile. God, how I love him. My blood runs cold, hearing my own words. Oh, this is bad. This is so, so, bad.

"How can you be so blasé about this!?" I yell.

"What do you expect me to do?"

"I don't know. Fight it somehow! Can't you take extra vitamins? Get x-rays every month to catch the cancer before it comes back? Ask your doctors to give you some kind of preventative treatment to keep it away? There's got to be something!"

"And spend the time I have left fighting against something that's not even here yet?" He shakes his head hard. "No. That's not how I want to live my life."

I hate to admit it, but he's right. When my mom first got her diagnosis, we were all thrown headfirst into the machinery of the medical system. We tried all kinds of different treatments, spent so much time in doctor's offices and hospitals, always getting our hopes up, just to get them dashed back down again. But after a while, Mom said she felt like she was only living half a life. That her sickness had consumed her.. not just physically, but mentally, too. She decided she didn't want her entire identity to be about fighting the disease. So, she went back to being her normal upbeat self. She went back to her painting, along with getting her treatments, and it was only then that she found some relief.

"Do you really believe it's true?" I ask once I calm down. "Do you really think you're going to die young?"

"Yes. That was what I saw when I was on the other side."

"So, knowing that, why the hell would you ever agree to come back?"

He starts to shrug, but quickly stops himself when I give him the evil eye. "You have to remember, it's pretty awesome there, and I was kind of planning on staying anyway. So coming back into physical form for a while seemed like fun. I figured, what's the risk? I could come, have this intensely beautiful experience here, then go back to pure bliss and ecstasy there. It seemed like a Win-Win situation to me."

I roll my eyes. "Well, when you put it that way, sign me up too!"

"It doesn't work that way," he says dryly. "You have to make your own deals with your own Angel Guides, Annie."

I lunge like I'm about to throttle him, but he dashes away, laughing way too hard for a person in his situation.

"I don't know how you can be this happy knowing you're going to die."

He huffs a little laugh. "Uh, I hate to break this to you. But one day, *you're* going to die too."

I sputter at him, so frustrated I can't form a comeback. "It's true though!" he cries. "You just forget that fact most of the time. I'm lucky because I'm fully aware that my time here is limited. And because of that, I get to enjoy my life way more than most people do."

Hearing his explanation, images begin flashing through my mind:

Theo stopping to watch a spider spin its web.

Theo crouched in front of a wheelchair, waiting patiently as Jenny struggles to speak.

Theo stopping mid-sentence to listen to two mourning doves calling back and forth to each other.

Theo with his eyes closed, licking marshmallows off his fingertips crooning "Is there anything in the world better than a perfectly toasted marshmallow, Annie? I think not."

Now I understand why he takes such time to soak up the nuances of the world around him—the tiny, little details of life that so many other people miss. He notices everything because he's aware each one could be his last.

And what do I do? I make fun of him for it. Tell him to stop acting like a three-year-old boy and hurry up already. Hasn't he seen the sunset a million times before? Why does he have to go on and on about how beautiful it is every damn night? It annoys me, the way he over-appreciates things. But now I understand why he's the way he is. He's aware he doesn't have much time, so he wants to savor every second he has left.

A wave of shame washes over me for my reaction. "I'm sorry. I shouldn't have yelled like that. It's just…I don't like surprises. They make my heart race all crazy and it reminds me of…." *The breakdown I had the night my mom died.* "It reminds me of things I don't want to think about. That means when something really shocks me, I tend to lash out before I think."

He wags a finger at me. "Yeah. I know that about you."

It's true. He does know that about me. But how? How do we both know each other so well in such a short time? It feels like I've known Theo for lifetimes…for eternities. But how is that possible when I just met him a month ago?

"What I should ask is, how are you Theo? Like truthfully. How are you doing with all this?"

He looks off wistfully. "I'd be lying if I said I wasn't going to miss this life. There's so much here to love. And that's gotten even more true since I met you."

My cheeks heat at his sincerity as he goes on. "But this is what we agreed on and…"

"We?" I interrupt.

"What?"

"You just said *We*. Who do you mean by we?"

His face turns red as he stammers to correct himself. "Oh, I meant this is what *I* agreed on. Sorry, I misspoke there."

He watches me closely, as if he's waiting for me to say something, although I'm not sure what.

"So, you consider yourself lucky?" I say, trying to break the awkward moment.

"Yeah, I do. I get extra time to soak all this good stuff in." He waves a hand at the vista before us. "My mom and I call it my Bonus Life."

At the mention of his mom, I shudder. My God, it must be so

sad for her to know her child will never get the chance to grow old. "It must be awful for your mom knowing you're going to die young."

"Yeah, I'm sure she wishes it could be different. But then again, she did watch me die. So she's happy she even got me back at all." He smiles, eyes going distant as if he's thinking of her. "She's grateful for all the life I'm getting to live now. All the time we have to be together that we wouldn't have had if I'd never come back. And she feels the same way I do. That every moment I've been given is an added blessing."

"Wow. She seems like a really amazing person." I marvel at how anyone could be at peace with such a horrible situation.

I stand there, taking Theo in. The sun at his back illuminates his long wavy hair, lighting up the edges of his slender body with an almost otherworldly glow. I'd made that crack about him being an Angel as a joke, but now, thinking of how he sees life so differently than the rest of us, I wonder if I'm not so far off base.

Part of me wants to rage against what he's just told me. But then I wouldn't be able to believe that my mom is now living in complete joy and happiness. And now that I've tasted that kind of relief, I'm not ready to give that up yet. So as much as it sucks, I guess if I'm going to believe one part of his story, I'm going to have to believe it all.

Theo is going to die. And soon. And that really sucks. Even if he doesn't agree with my assessment of the situation.

It suddenly hits me. How close I came to making a really huge mistake. Thank the Lord I didn't tell Theo I had feelings for him that day in the boat. Or give in to my urges and kiss him at the party. Or tell him about this maddening attraction I have to him that seems to be getting stronger every day.

Thank God I'm still safe. I can still get out of this unscathed. All I have to do is slowly distance myself from him. I won't hang out with him as much. And I'll make up excuses as to why I can't come here to The Lookout with him anymore. Then, over the next months, we'll naturally grow apart. Which means once camp is over we'll go our separate ways and I'll never have to see him again. He'll die and I'll never even know about it. It sounds cruel, but it's the only way I can survive this. Because there's no way I can endure what I did with my mom all over again.

"Listen, let's not worry about how long I have left." Theo catches my hand and pulls me closer. It's hard to meet his eyes knowing all the shameful plans I've just made to abandon him. "What's more important is that you still believe everything I told you, right?"

"Yeah, of course," I mumble, mind still reeling from all that's happened this past hour.

"And have I talked you into waiting to see why my Angels have brought us together? You know? So that maybe we can find that extra special path together?"

Shit.

"Oh yeah…that," I say, heart sinking. "This lit-up path of yours that's obviously going to be very, very, short?"

"Yeah, that's true," he admits. "But on the bright side, it means you won't be stuck with me for long."

I glare at him. "You and all your bright sides."

I'm not sure what my face is doing, but it makes him laugh really hard. Which makes me shove him again. Then the two of us agree we had better get going so we're not late picking up our campers. We'll have time to talk about this more later.

Although what Theo doesn't know is, if I stick to my new plan, that might not be true.

CHAPTER TWENTY-ONE

"I'LL GO GET it. I don't mind," I tell Susan, when she realizes she's forgotten a camper's insulin in the dining hall refrigerator. It's late and the girls are already in bed, which is where I should be after a long, hot day like today. But the idea of being alone in the woods for the fifteen minutes it takes to walk to main camp is too enticing to pass up. With the way this past week has gone, I desperately need some time to myself to sort out this tangled up head of mine.

Today was the summer solstice, so even though it's late, pastel light still seeps through the leaves into the dusk mist, making the path before me glow pink and fuzzy like something out of a fairy tale.

We'd celebrated the solstice with a party on the dining hall lawn. The kids made flower crowns and sun catchers; feasted on fresh fruit and homemade bread; sang songs around a roaring bonfire. Some of the campers had convinced Theo to dress up like a woodland fairy and dance with them as part of the evening entertainment. Always the good sport, he'd worn a pink tutu over his shorts, and let them braid his hair with pastel ribbons and replace his normal red headband for a crown of daisies. He looked ridiculous, but of course he hadn't minded. He threw himself into their choreographed dance, twirling around their motorized wheelchairs. Bowing and kissing the back of their hands and leaping in the air like a backyard Baryshnikov.

At first, we'd all laughed at the groups' antics. But then the music became more poignant, and Theo stepped aside to let the girls take center stage, where they somehow mastered a magical, swirling ballet from only their spastic fingers on electronic controls. And when the troupe ended their performance with a dramatic bow—and Theo throwing rose petals at their feet before collapsing like a dead swan in the dirt before them—there wasn't a dry eye in the house. (Or the *woods* as it were.)

If it had been last week I would've probably helped Theo with his costume. Maybe even been the one to braid his hair. But since I've been avoiding him for the past week, the entire performance was as much a surprise to me as it was the rest of camp. And I hated it. Not the dance…that was beautiful. What I hated was being left out of Theo's life. I hated not knowing what he was thinking, what he was doing. Even though I'm the one who has pushed him away.

The day after he'd unloaded all his otherworldly agendas on me, he'd asked me to go to The Lookout with him like always. But I'd already switched my time off with Greta, so I'd have an excuse as to why I couldn't go. In the days since, I've pretended to be busy whenever he's tried to talk to me and declined his offers for rows to the cove, and swings in our hammocks, and Cokes at the Indian caves. When I turned him down this afternoon I expected him to confront me, to tell me to stop acting like a child and quit avoiding him. But being his typical gracious self, he'd only nodded and said "I understand Annie" before leaving me alone exactly like I'd asked.

Sometimes I hate how he listens to me.

When I get to the dining hall, the lights in the kitchen are on. It's probably Maeve, the camp baker who sometimes works the evening shift after the cooks have gone home. I smile, looking forward to getting to spend a few moments basking in her good cheer. She's from Ireland, so she tells the best stories in her thick Irish brogue. Stories her Nan used to tell her about the old Irish folklore. Come to think of it, we should've had Maeve come tell stories around the campfire earlier. She surely would've had some wonderful tales of fairies and leprechauns and sprites.

I purposely slam the front door as I come in so I don't scare her. I doubt she's used to having company at this time of night.

When I push through the swinging door to the kitchen she looks up from where she's kneading an enormous pile of dough. "Howya! What's the story with you tonight, missy?" Her black hair is swept up in a bun and flour streaks her cheeks. She likes to call that look her baker's blush. "Cheaper than makeup and more alluring, don't ya' think?" she'd told me the last time I'd caught her working away in a cloud of dust.

I point to the little fridge in the corner reserved for medications. "I just have to grab some insulin we forgot." Weaving around the stainless-steel tables, I sniff the sticky air, coming up with a nose full of sweetness and cinnamon. "Ahhh…I have a feeling I might be getting my favorite cookie tomorrow!"

"If your favorite is oatmeal, then you're in luck. Although I can't make it the way my Nan did…full of nuts and raisins and the lot. Too many allergies with you delicate Americans. I still say you still aren't raising your kids to eat enough dirt. My Nan always said a little earth in the diet gives a child a strong constitution."

I laugh as I grab the vial out of the door, checking the fine print to make sure I've got the right one. So far I haven't killed any campers, and I'm hoping to continue that streak.

"Oh, believe me, I agree with you!" I say. "My parents raised me in the woods. I barely knew how to use utensils until I went to kindergarten. I just shoved it all in my mouth with my dirty little hands." I mime my caveman eating. "Now I'm as healthy as a horse."

She chuckles at me, turning back to attack the blob on her countertop once again. Maeve may be a bit pudgy around the middle, but the woman's got biceps of steel from all the kneading she does.

I hear the giggles of a toddler just outside the back door. "Is Ewan here with you tonight?" I walk over to look out the window into the dimly lit side yard. Ewan is Maeve's four-year-old son. I don't know all the details, but apparently Maeve is raising him alone. She came over on a short-term visa, hoping to earn money and then going to culinary school in the states.

"Yeah, he comes with me now. I lost my babysitter at home, but luckily I found someone here to help out."

A muffled voice calls out from around the corner, startling me with its familiarity.

"Wait a minute…is that…"

The next second, Theo jogs into sight, scooping Ewan up around the waist and twirling him around, sending him peeling with laughter.

"Yeah, Theo was here the night I found out my babysitter quit," Maeve calls over her shoulder. "I was moaning and complaining like some idiot about how I didn't know what I was going to do. So he said he'd take care of Ewan on the nights I had to do my baking here." Maeve only comes in to make cookies and bread for the campers every other night. During the day, she works as a nanny so she's able to take Ewan with her to her job.

She stops and wipes her hands on her apron, walking over to peer at the two of them playing together on the swing set outside. "He was a lifesaver, that one," she says, smiling fondly at Theo. "Ewan loves him. And the lad doesn't even let me pay him. Can you believe that?"

"Yes, I can believe that," I mumble into the window.

A warmth grows in my chest, watching the easy back and forth between Theo and Ewan. How does he do it? After a full day's work. After giving everything to his campers all day long, how is he able to give even more?

Ewan shouts, "I want a Mammy cookie!" and runs to the door. Before we can barely back away, he and Theo burst through the door like two rambunctious puppies.

When Theo sees me, he does a double take. "Oh, hey. It's you." He seems flustered by the sight of me.

"Yes. It is, in fact, me," I reply lamely. I hate how everything feels so awkward between us now. It was the quality about us that was always so special: How easy things felt when we're together. We were smooth and rounded. Like a river rock whose rough edges have been whittled away by years of running water. Now I've gone and ruined everything by avoiding him like some coward.

Theo stays focused on Ewan. He gets him a cookie and a little plastic cup of milk and shoos him into the main room.

"Here Buddy, let's eat this out here and let your mommy…I mean your *mammy*…do her work." Then he's gone without a backwards glance. Which I suppose I deserve after freezing him out all week. But still, it hurts.

I stand there feeling tender and stung by how he'd just ignored me. Thinking about how much I miss him. Of how much I wish we could go back to the way things were before.

To my horror, tears begin welling in my eyes. When I blink to clear them, I see Maeve standing right in front of me, cocking one eyebrow like she knows exactly what's going on. Oh God, has Theo talked to her about me?

"Don't ya' think you should go out there?" She tips her head to the other room.

"I uh…I'm not sure…I should…"

"Let me rephrase that." She brusquely cuts me off, grabbing my shoulders and roughly aiming me at the door. "Go out there. *Now.*" She gives me a hard shove. Yeah, this lady is way stronger than she looks.

The loud flap of the swinging door, and my graceless stumble through it, makes Theo look up. He sits on the bench of the only table left in the room—all the others have been cleared away for the janitors to mop—throwing a big blue ball across the empty space for Ewan to chase. He gives me a quick smile, then goes back to his game of catch.

I pause for a moment to watch him. He's wearing shorts, and a tank top which is stuck to his chest with sweat, his hair extra curly from the humidity. Though he's laughing and cheering Ewan on in a sing-song voice, I can tell from the slowness of his blinks he's tired.

And all I want to do is go to him and hug him and tell him to lay his head on my shoulder so he can rest.

But I only have the guts to do the first part.

"Hey," I say, sitting down next to him.

"Hey," he says back, not looking at me.

"I just wanted to say I'm sorry for being such a jerk this week."

He opens his mouth to speak, but I cut him off. "And I know you're going to say I'm not a being a jerk, but I know I am. And I know you're going to say it's alright. But it's not. And I know you're going to say I'm being too hard on myself. But I deserve to be this hard on myself. And I know you're going to say…"

He raises a palm, and I finally stop rambling. "Should I just leave?" he asks. "Because it seems like you're having this conversation all by yourself, and you don't need me at all."

I hold my breath, not sure if he's mad or not. I can't tell because Theo's never been mad at me before, so I don't have any reference to go by. But luckily he gives me a little wink and I slump in relief.

He lurches off the bench to catch a wayward throw from Ewan. As he tosses it back, I can't help but notice the curve of his biceps, the patch of smooth skin that flashes when his shirt rides up in the back. *I want to touch that.* The thought is so primal it shocks me. When he sits down next to me again, I pray he doesn't notice my red cheeks, now blazing as hot as today's noonday sun.

"I was just trying to say, before you so rudely interrupted me." I nudge my shoulder into his. "That I'm sorry."

"Annie, seriously. I meant it when I said I understand. I've had years to come to terms with all this craziness. I don't expect you to just accept it all in one week."

"You don't?"

"No. I mean, I miss you. And I wish we could at least hang out while you're thinking this over."

"But that's just it. I don't know what I'm supposed to be thinking over. What exactly do you want me to do?"

He shrugs. "I don't know."

When I groan loudly, he goes on. "I know those are the three words in the English language you hate the most."

I smile because he's right. If there's one thing I hate, it's uncertainty.

"It's crazy, how open and unknown it all seems," he says. "But I've found that if you pay attention, there are whispers that guide you. Clues scattered everywhere if you just stop and take the time to notice."

I can't help but scoff. He makes it all seem so easy. As if life is all one big game, like one of the elaborate treasure hunts my mom used to play with me. Not the hardscrabble existence I've been eking out ever since she died.

He must pick up on my resistance because he quickly changes tactics. "Besides, all I really want is to be near you. And I think that's what you want too." He cocks an eyebrow at me. "Even though you're doing a pretty good job of pretending otherwise."

I'm not surprised that, just like always, he's seen right through me. "You're right," I admit. "This past week has been agony."

He immediately brightens, and I immediately feel the need to squelch his hope. "But don't get a big head about it. I just want you around because you push my campers up from the lake for me. It has nothing to do with your charm, good looks, and how much joy I get out of making fun of you."

He laughs hard, tipping his head up at the ceiling so the sound echoes through the cavernous space. Hearing Theo, Ewan bursts out laughing too, even though he has no idea why it's funny. He flops his little body over the plastic ball and rolls around while he giggles along. The two of them are so sweet that even a hardened curmudgeon like me can't help but join in.

After we catch our breath, Theo says, "Don't worry about the details, Annie. I think if we keep spending time together, whatever is supposed to come next will somehow reveal itself to us."

I consider that for a moment. "So let me get this right. You want me to just be all chill and spontaneous…to blindly go with the flow, with no plan at all? Even though I have no idea where it will lead in the end?"

"Yeah. That's it!"

"Okay. I'll think about it."

We both burst out laughing at my predictable response. Oh, how I wish I didn't always have to always be so wary and scared. Oh, how I wish I could be as trusting as Theo.

The ball gets stuck behind the trash can, and Ewan wails. Theo slowly gets to his feet. "I'll be right there, Buddy! Start counting… see how long it takes me." He lowers his voice. "That usually buys me some time."

I smile, but the words hit too close to home. *Buying him some time.* But nothing can truly do that, can it? All of Theo's time is slipping away and there's nothing he can do to change that. And there's nothing I can do either. It's all completely out of my control.

Maeve comes out under the guise of checking on Ewan, but I see her watching me say goodbye to Theo. I give her a little nod of thanks when Theo isn't looking, and it's odd because even though she's probably only a few years older than me, that warm sense of mothering that pours off of her soothes an ache I've been nursing for such a long time.

I feel better as I leave Theo to his babysitting and head to the door. I'm glad I stopped being so childish and told him how much I've missed him. (Even if I'd couched it in a sarcastic joke.) Still, I've wasted so much time this week. Ducking behind bushes, avoiding him, and making excuses, when we could've been having fun together. Now tomorrow is Friday, and the session is over and we won't see each other for another two days. Even though he's still in the room with me, I already miss him.

The logical part of me says to keep walking, reminding me that distance from Theo equals safety. But for once I don't listen. Yes, entanglement with Theo is dangerous. He's going to die…which is literally my worst nightmare. And yet, maybe I need to give in and admit the truth: Even with all I know of his future, I don't want less of Theo. I only want more.

You have a choice, you know.

The voice in my head sends a pleasant trill along my skin. I'm hearing that voice—the one filled with such love and benevolence—more often now. The voice that reminds me so much of…No. It can't be. That would be impossible.

I suddenly think of Theo telling me the world is a friendly place… that it's okay to trust it. Then an idea pops into my head with such force it stops me in my tracks.

"Hey Theo," I call out before I ruin everything by thinking too hard about what might happen next. He wants me to be spontaneous? Well then, I'll give him spontaneous.

"Yeah?" he calls back, propping the ball under his arm.

"This weekend."

"Yeah. What about it?"

"Do you want to come home with me?"

CHAPTER TWENTY-TWO

"CAN YOU LIKE…MAKE it a little less poofy somehow?" I plead, gesturing to Theo's wild mane. He's had his window down the entire way to Caroline's house and now his hair has swollen to such great heights it's practically taking up the entire passenger seat.

"How's this?" He pats his head, trying to tamp it down; to no avail. Oh God. I can already hear Caroline's sardonic whine. "Oh Annie, why didn't you tell me you were bringing Bon Jovi to dinner? I would've made lasagna."

I slap his hands away. "Here, let me try." I hope to hell Caroline's not looking out the window, witnessing the drama unfolding in her driveway. I finger comb his hair back into perfect waves, marveling at its silky softness, its sweet flowery smell. (Covertly though, so Theo doesn't catch on to how much I truly like it.)

He closes his eyes as I fuss over him, chin tipped up, a hint of a smile playing on his face, and dammit, he looks so cute it pisses me off. I feel like he intentionally ditched his glasses for contacts and wore his tight faded jeans and the light green polo shirt that shows off his beautiful arms on purpose, just to entice me. I'm especially mad because it's working. It takes everything I have not to lean forward and plant a kiss on his perfect lips that are waiting…*right there* for me to devour them.

Have you forgotten about Greta? the nasty voice in my head lectures, dumping a bucket of cold water right on my throbbing crotch.

Oh yeah. Greta. I'd seen the worried look on her face as she watched Theo get into my car earlier. Now, I wish I hadn't bragged to her about all the guys I'd unceremoniously dumped in my lifetime. Even if she wasn't in love with Theo, I'm not the type of girl anyone wants hanging out with their best friend. I'd felt horrible as Theo and I had driven off together. Still, I'm not doing anything wrong. After all, Theo and I are only friends. And I'm determined to keep it that way. Even if my body seems to have other plans.

Realizing I'm way too close to him, I sit back in my seat and slap my hands together. "Okay, I'll grab the wine since you're an underage little boy." He rolls his eyes since I'd already made the same jab twice in the liquor store parking lot. "And you grab the groceries. Then we'll reconvene by the front bumper and lead the charge as a unified brigade."

I'd briefed Theo on the way to Caroline's about how he was about to enter a household with a toddler, a nine-month-old baby, a sister who's even more sarcastic than I am, and a husband so starved for adult companionship he's likely to be kidnapped and forced to talk for hours on end about why scotch is a whiskey but not all whiskey can be called scotch. (Or is it the other way around? I'd blacked out when Jonathan had tried to explain it to me before.) All of which means he probably won't be getting as much rest and relaxation as he normally does on his weekends off.

"Don't worry about me," he'd assured me. "I just want to be with you. Plus, you know me. I get along with everyone. I'm sure I'll love your family."

He hadn't quite understood that I wasn't so much worried about what he thought of my family as about what they thought about him.

When I'd called Caroline to ask if I could bring a friend home this weekend, she'd happily agreed. Of course, when she'd found out it was a boy coming with me, she'd had to needle me. "Yeah right. You two are just friends."

She has good reason to be suspicious, since every guy I've brought home as a "friend" before has slept in my bed. But I'd assured her that this time, things were different.

"He's younger than me," I'd said by way of explanation. Caroline knows about my proclivity for older men, so I was sure that would make her back down. Then I'd added for good measure, "And he's nice too."

"Nice?! *Nice?!*" she'd raged after she'd stopped choking on her coffee. I've always been clear that niceness is a huge turnoff for me. Usually the bigger the asshole, the stronger the attraction for me. Caroline and her half-finished psychology degree insists it has something to do with being rejected by my dad as a little girl. A thought I've wished I could scrub out of my mind ever since she said it.

After learning of Theo's niceness, Caroline had laughed uproariously. "So should I tell this poor guy he's a goner when he first walks in the door, or wait until after dessert?"

I'd spent the next five minutes bribing her with free babysitting to keep her from embarrassing me. She'd agreed to behave, but I'm still wondering if I've made a huge mistake inviting Theo into my life outside of camp.

We lug our stuff straight into the living room. The noise of our arrival makes Caroline call out from the kitchen. "So how much stinky laundry did you bring me this week?"

She appears in the doorway with baby Emma perched on her hip. Even without makeup, wearing a shirt stained with God knows what, she's beautiful. Her dark hair, falling out of a messy ponytail, comes from my dad. But in every other way, she's all my mom. High cheekbones, blue eyes, skin that tans instead of burning like mine.

"Double the amount," I say, as both Theo and I hold up our bulging laundry bags.

I watch her take Theo in. I can tell she's purposely not letting her eyes linger on him too long, so she doesn't give me the satisfaction of showing any surprise. But I know her well enough to see my very uncharacteristic choice of a guy has surprised her.

"Just…uh…throw those in the basement before I have to fumigate the whole house."

I heave my bag down the stairs, then grab Theo's and chuck it down the same way. It thuds all the way down, landing with a loud crash at the bottom, which I'll have to investigate later.

Theo's eyes go wide at the commotion. I guess his family doesn't throw things down the stairs like ours does? Duly noted.

After I formally introduce Caroline to Theo, he asks, "And who's this?" reaching a finger out to the baby.

"Oh, this is Emma," Caroline says, shifting her daughter on her hip so Theo can see her better. "She's very shy, so don't be offended if she…" She trails off as Emma reaches both arms toward Theo, grinning big.

My sister and I exchange a stunned glance. When strangers come over Emma usually buries her face in her mom's neck, refusing to even make eye contact until she gets to know them better. Even when I come home on weekends it takes a while before she warms up to me. But now, it looks like she's about to launch herself into Theo's waiting arms.

"That's weird," I say. "Emma usually doesn't like new people."

Theo shrugs nonchalantly. "Babies love me."

I stage whisper to Caroline. "Yeah, pretty much *everyone* loves Theo. It's really annoying."

Theo ignores me, choosing instead to be his easy-going self and compliment Caroline on her lovely home and the way she's decorated it so stylishly. I feel an odd sense of pride that he's noticed her gift. Caroline got all Mom's artistic skills and has put them to use decorating her house in a beautiful palette of soft colors and fluffy furniture and interesting knickknacks from her travels to Europe after college. (All now stored above toddler height.)

"I love your pottery," he points to the bookcase in the corner. "Are those pieces Raku fired?"

Caroline practically levitates off the floor at his interest. She immediately drags him over for a closer look, chattering excitedly about how she made the all the pieces herself.

I let out an internal groan. Dammit. I can't believe I'd forgotten to tell Theo the cardinal rule of visiting Caroline: Never ask about her pottery! Once she gets going, describing the throwing, the glazing, the firing, every little nuance of each vessel, he'll be trapped for hours. Although maybe he deserves it. *Is that Raku fired?* Where the hell did he come up with that?

Luckily, five long minutes into Caroline's presentation, little Jack bursts into the room. "Mommy, Mommy! Outside. Outside now. You said you'd push me in my swing."

Caroline looks crushed to be interrupted. It's rare she gets to discuss her pottery, since both Jonathan and I have learned to stay far, far away from the topic.

"We have a guest here, Jack," she says. "This is Annie's friend, Theo."

Theo crouches down to look Jack in the eye as he says hello.

Jack scans him with a look of wonder. "You have a lot of hair!"

We all laugh. "Yeah I do," Theo says, grinning widely. "I have to. It helps keep me warm in the winter." He pulls a hunk down over his shoulders, pretending it's a blanket, and Jack giggles. Then Theo invites him to touch it if he wants.

After patting Theo's head like a dog, Jack informs him, "My daddy's hair is prickly, but yours is soft."

Theo glances up at Carolyn and she explains. "Jonathan likes to keep his hair very short. I mean, not that he wouldn't want it to be longer. It's just..." She lowers her voice, pointing to the crown of her head. "It's a little sparse in one spot. Makes him a bit self-conscious."

Theo nods. "Oh, believe me, I know how he feels."

Caroline shoots me a confused look, but I wave it off. I've already decided it's not my place to tell them about Theo's past. If he wants to share about his cancer, that's his story to tell.

"You know who else has hair like this," Theo says to Jack, waiting wide-eyed for the answer. "A lion!"

He roars loudly and chases Jack around the living room on all fours, tossing his hair like the king of beasts. Jack laughs hysterically while baby Emma kicks her little legs frantically like she wants to get in on the fray.

Once Theo finally stops and stands to catch his breath, Jack tugs his arm.

"Theo, Theo, go outside with me!"

"Oh no honey, Theo needs to rest," Caroline explains, awkwardly trying to wrench Jack's vice-like grip off Theo's hand.

"I'd love to take him outside," Theo offers brightly. Caroline insists (a bit weakly, I note) that he doesn't have to, but Theo's already leading Jack to the sliding glass doors that open to the backyard.

"No, seriously, I want to." He bends down to Jack, pointing outside. "I see a slide. A swing. Oh my gosh, is that a sandbox? How could anyone stay inside with so many fun things to play with out there?!"

"I know! So many fun things! How could I stay inside?" Jack parrots back like the rest of us are fools.

Caroline tries to argue more, but I tell her it's pointless. "Theo has a lot of energy. Like a very strange, superhuman amount of energy. Just let him go."

Theo shoots me a wry smile, then says to Caroline. "And Annie likes to talk about me as if I'm not in the room."

I roll my eyes and push him toward the door. But before he slips outside, he turns to Caroline. "Can I take Emma too?"

"What?! No. I couldn't make you take them both!" Again, Caroline's outrage sounds awfully stilted.

"It's no big deal," Theo says. "My brother has three kids, so I'm used to it. Plus, I know how hard it is for you staying home with them. You probably never get a moment to yourself."

Caroline keeps up the weak 'I could never!' act, so Theo pushes more. "C'mon. Let me take them. You deserve a break." He reaches out and Caroline nearly tosses Emma into his waiting arms. Then she catches herself and pretends it's simply killing her to let her go. I have to bite my tongue to keep from laughing.

Once Theo has the baby, Caroline and I both hold our breaths, waiting for Emma to start screaming. But after Theo expertly whisks her outside with her brother, all she does is giggle and kick in Theo's arms.

Caroline stares out the window, looking stunned. I join her and we both watch the scene unfolding in the backyard with matching awe.

"Did he just say he wanted to take my kids because I needed a break?" she murmurs.

"Yeah. That's what he said."

"Is this some kind of act? Like, is he trying to impress me or something? Because let me be the first to say…it's working."

I huff a laugh. "Oh, believe me. It's no act. It's just the way he is."

She gives me a look of disbelief.

"I know," I say. "Weird, huh?"

"Weird for you, that is. I mean, he's definitely not your typical Flavor-of-the-Month man, that's for damn sure."

"I told you. We're just friends."

She cocks an eyebrow at me.

"What? It's true!" I protest, unconvincingly. I sound like I'm twelve again, insisting it wasn't me who cut off all her Barbie's hair.

Theo is dancing around, arms and legs flapping like they're made of rubber as he sings a silly song. Apparently he's switched from imitating a lion to an octopus now. Emma squeals delightedly on his hip, yanking a handful of his hair in her tiny fist.

"I know what he reminds me of!" Caroline cries, pointing at Theo through the glass.

"What?"

"A really handsome Muppet!"

I burst out laughing. "Oh my God! You're right. That's the perfect description of him!"

After our laughter dies down, Caroline studies Theo for a while, not saying much, just staring. I've got a bubbly feeling in my throat because I can tell she likes him and that makes me really proud. Which is stupid because Theo's loveliness has nothing to do with me. I don't want to come right out and ask her what she thinks of him. That would feel too much like I'm asking for her approval, and I don't want to her to know I care. Still, after she doesn't offer any more, I nudge her with my elbow.

"So? What are you thinking?"

"Oh," she startles a little, as if she hadn't realized she'd zoned out. "I was just thinking that he has a very nice body."

"Caroline!!"

"And like a super tight ass." She makes a lewd gesture, like she's cupping each of Theo's ass cheeks in her hands. I shove her sideways, laughing uproariously. She joins in, cackling just as loudly.

"I can't believe you!" I yell, "Lusting over a nineteen-year-old boy! I'm going to tell Jonathan!"

"My God, I'm not an old lady Annie. I'm only twenty-six! Besides, Jonathan won't mind." She waves a hand through the air. "He just wants me hot and bothered. He doesn't care how I get that way."

I pretend to be even more outraged, and she continues. "Hey, can't I have a little fun? I'm stuck in this house all alone, being drooled on and nursed from all day long. What's wrong with letting me enjoy a little entertainment when it shows up at my door?" She gestures to where Theo is now pushing Jack in a swing, singing another ridiculous song that he's most likely made up on the spot. And yes, looking quite sexy as his tan arms flex with each shove.

My stomach flips, watching him. Out of nowhere, the scene in front of me—Theo laughing and playing with the kids—sparks a quick flash of déjà vu so strong it throws me off balance. I see the image so clearly. It's of him. And me. And not Caroline's kids. But our own.

I brace a hand on the couch, trying to regain my equilibrium. What the hell was that? The image disappears as quickly as it came, yet the sensation it leaves behind is so thrilling I catch myself grinning wildly out the window at Theo. He sees me and waves all crazy (exactly like a really handsome Muppet) and I wave back the same way. And it's like my chest is filled with a bunch of little bubbles all swelling and popping, and popping and swelling over and over again, which feels so damn good.

Caroline glances over at me. "You look so happy."

The word catches me by surprise, sending me careening back to reality. "Oh, we had Mexican food on the way down. Must just be indigestion," I deadpan, patting my belly.

She shakes her head at me. A few second later she says quietly, "You're allowed to be happy you know."

I roll my eyes the way I always do when my big sister annoys me.

Still, she stares. Whatever she sees on my face makes her say, "You should go outside and be with him."

You should be with him. A sweet whisper in my ear agrees.

My heart whirls at the thought of being close to Theo again. Then I remember all the reasons that's a terrible idea.

"No, I can't." I don't realize I've said the words out loud until Caroline shoots me a puzzled look.

"Why not?"

I quickly try to cover my slip. "Oh, I just mean…uh, I can't go out there because there's too much laundry to do."

Flustered, I tear myself away from the idyllic scene out the window and force myself down the stairs and into the basement, where the darkness feels more like home.

CHAPTER TWENTY-THREE

WHEN JONATHAN COMES home from work, he shouts a quick hello into the kitchen where Caroline and I are prepping dinner. Then he runs upstairs to change out of his suit into his "play clothes" as he calls them, reappearing a few minutes later in khaki shorts and a REO Speedwagon concert shirt. He gives his wife a kiss on the head and me a rib-cracking bear hug, which I wholeheartedly return.

It's strange how much easier it is for me to show affection to my brother-in-law than to my own sister. He's a mushy guy and over the years, he's worn me down with his unwavering good cheer. So much so that I actually look forward to his hugs now.

When my mom was dying and afterward, when Caroline and I weren't getting along so well, Jonathan was the steady voice of reason that held us together. The person who reminded my sister and me how much we needed each other; how important it was to our mom that we stayed close. And eventually that we were both incorrigibly hard-headed, and he'd '*had it up to here*' with refereeing our Most-Stubborn-Sister contests. I'd never thanked him for being there for me during those hard times. And for still being here in the better ones now. But I'm hoping the way I squeeze him back extra tight is enough to convey the words I can't say out loud.

"So, this is the new guy, huh?" Jonathan peers out the kitchen window into the backyard where Theo and Jack are racing each other back and forth from the swings to the garden shed, Emma having been put to bed a while ago, after falling asleep in Theo's arms. Lucky girl.

Unlike when he raced Greta, Theo is letting Jack win. At least most of the time. It seems my super chill friend has a bit of a competitive streak he lets slips out every once in a while.

Jonathan turns to where I'm slicing tomatoes, his eyes wide at what he's just seen. "Wow, he's—"

"Not her type? I said the same thing!" Caroline interjects.

"I told you we're just friends!"

My sister turns from where she's forming hamburger patties and shoots me a look like she knows I'm bullshitting myself. Then she tells Jonathan in a haughty tone. "Theo likes my pottery. And he knows how hard I work every day. And he thinks I need some time to myself every once in a while."

Jonathan huffs and rolls his eyes behind Caroline's back. I giggle at his mugging as Caroline glares. She always accuses Jonathan and me of ganging up on her. "And he has a super hot body," she snaps at her husband in retaliation. "And Annie has agreed to let me borrow him later if I want."

"I did not!"

"Oh, just play along," she hisses. "Jon will up his game if he thinks he has some competition."

"Alright fine!" Jonathan says. "So what kind of duel should I challenge this…this…" he glances at Theo loping across the yard, sun-streaked hair blowing back in the wind. "This rock star that Annie has obviously kidnapped off his world tour?" He grabs Caroline's hand, still globbed with hamburger meat and tries to kiss the back of it. "I need to make sure I keep my fair maiden's hand."

Caroline pulls away in horror. "Stop! Don't get that in your mouth. I saw on Oprah last week that a woman died after accidentally ingesting raw hamburger when she was making meatballs! You're going to kill yourself with your stupid jokes."

After she orders him to the sink to scrub his contaminated fingers,

Jonathan calls over his shoulder to me. "So, what do you think, Annie? Do I challenge this boy toy of yours to a wrestling match or a chess tournament first?"

"Well, since I have a feeling he could beat you at both, I'd try to come up with something else."

"Fine." Jonathan dries his hands, then snatches the plate of burgers off the counter. "A grilling competition it is! No one can beat me at flipping meat over an open flame. I'd like to see him try."

Caroline rushes after him, gloppy hands sticking out to her sides and gives him a kiss on the cheek. "Go get 'em honey! Show him who's king of our backyard!"

Jonathan charges out the door with dramatic flourish, leaving Caroline and I giggling together like when we were in middle school whispering in our twin beds over who's cuter, Sean Cassidy or Leif Garret. I can't believe I was worried about bringing Theo here. It seems trite to say, but he makes everything better. I don't think I've had this much fun with my sister in a long time. And the weekend's only just begun.

∞

When Caroline and I finish our meal prep, we pour ourselves glasses of wine and lean on opposite counters, idly catching up on our week. My sister begs me for stories about camp. "Please bring me news of the outside world! My life is so boring now!"

I oblige, curating my memories to make them more entertaining. Wiping butts and inserting catheters isn't so exciting. But Honey Bear slipping on the trail down to the lake, then purposely log-rolling the rest of the way, arms stuck out in a Superman pose just to make the kids laugh. Now *that's* a funny story.

A little while later, Jonathan breezes through the kitchen doorway and points out the window where Theo is waiting for him by the grill.

"I love this guy!" he announces loudly.

Caroline throws her hands in the air, sloshing some wine on the floor in the process. "Dammit, honey! You've done it now."

Jonathan winces as if he's just realized his mistake. "I mean…uh… this guy is a real tool, Annie. A good-for-nothing son of a bitch. Don't you ever…and I mean *ever*…bring him back to our house again!" He shoots a wary glance at his wife. "How'd I do?"

"You're about as convincing as Jack promising he's going to make it to the potty instead of peeing his pants," Caroline says dryly.

I shake my head at them. "Nice try. But I know what you're doing. The old reverse psychology trick." I turn away, reaching for the paper plates in the cabinet behind me. "And I know, I know. Theo's wonderful, but don't get too attached to him."

"Why?" they both ask in unison.

"Because. Once camp is over you guys are never going to see him again."

As I pull napkins from the plastic wrapper, I hear the faint sounds of whispers and wild gesturing behind my back. "I know you're talking about me," I grumble. "Can you please just wait until I leave the room to bitch about me?"

"Fine," Caroline huffs. "But I know you're just doing this to punish me. I finally find someone who appreciates my pottery, and you want to take him away from me? I don't know how you sleep at night, you monster!"

"Yeah, you can be stupid and dump him," Jonathan says, coming to his wife's defense. "But you know what? We might just get his number and invite him back when you're not around."

"You probably should," I say, as we all file out the sliding glass door to the backyard. "He's obviously a much better babysitter than I am." I wait for them to correct me, but unfortunately, they both stay silent.

We gather around the grill, *oohing* and *ahhing* over Jonathan's amazing prowess poking things with his spatula and opening and closing the grill lid. (Which apparently is some kind of skill?)

Later, we eat our burgers and chips on a picnic table under the shade of an old oak tree; Jack occupied enough with his sandbox to allow us a few minutes of grown-up conversation.

When Caroline asks Theo why he decided to be a nurse, he tells them about his cancer. How the support of his nurses got him through the really tough times. And how he hopes to one day be that kind of support for kids like him, too.

It makes me think about the afternoon at The Lookout when I'd questioned him about why he'd even pursue a degree that he'll likely never get to use.

"I still like learning," he'd explained. "And I get to be in the hospitals, helping where I can." He'd told me that, during the school year, he volunteers as an aide on the cancer floor where he once was a patient.

"Besides, I don't want to let what I know about the future influence my choices," he'd said when we were alone. "I want to live a normal life. Exactly how a person who expects a long life does. I don't want to waste my time here constantly thinking about when it's all going to end."

I'd pretended that his reasoning made perfect sense, but I still don't understand how he can be so accepting of the shitty hand he's been dealt. If I were him, I'd be bitter as hell. Heck, I'm bitter as hell now and I don't have things half as bad as he does. Which just goes to show how selfish and ungrateful I am.

After Theo finishes telling Caroline and Jonathan he's now in remission, I push my salad around on my plate, waiting for their reactions. I hope they don't pity Theo the way I know he hates.

Luckily, it's admiration, not pity I see in their eyes.

"Wow," Jonathan says after taking a moment to absorb Theo's story. "That must have been quite an experience to go through so young."

Both he and my sister's eyes stray to Jack, playing with such exuberance across the yard. I realize from the haunted look on their faces where their minds have wandered.

"Yeah. It was something that's for sure," Theo says in his infuriatingly casual way. "It certainly made me appreciate how precious life really is."

He makes a point of not looking at me and I take a long drink of my wine, try to clear the lump rising in my throat at the thought of the ever-shrinking time he has left. Oh, if Caroline and Jonathan knew the real reason I'd warned them not to get too attached to Theo.

"I'm sorry about your mom," Theo says to Caroline.

"Oh, yeah. Well, thanks," she says brusquely. "It was awful losing her so young. But what're you gonna do, right? Cancer sucks." She throws back a huge glug of wine so she doesn't have to say anymore. It seems my sister and I have similar approaches to dealing with our emotions.

Theo watches her, green eyes sharp like he's all too aware of her turmoil. "I know it's hard. But I also know that your mom is still…"

He glances at me, hesitating. I know he wants to say his normal shit about our mom still being with us, but knowing how much I hate hearing that, he adjusts himself. "That your mom is still a big influence in both of your lives."

He squeezes my knee and I give him a warning look that says, *I'll tolerate that much, but don't push it, Buster.* A phrase he's heard me repeat many times now.

Last week he'd prodded me to reveal why the thought of my mom still being aware of me was so upsetting; pestering me long enough that I'd finally blurted out, "It pisses me off when you say that because I loved my mom. And I thought she loved me. So when I can't feel her or hear her like you say I should, it makes me feel like something's gone wrong. Like she's forgotten me. Or that she didn't really love me as much as I thought she did after all."

My outburst had stunned him into silence for a second. Then he'd said in a tender voice, "Oh Annie, of course she loves you."

"Then why won't she talk to me?" I was glad we were both lying flat in our hammocks at the time so he couldn't see my quivering lip.

"Believe me, she's trying. You're just having a little trouble hearing her right now, that's all. But don't worry. You'll get better at it. You just need a little more time."

When I'd scoffed loudly, he'd gone on. "Do you usually feel sad when you think about your mom?"

"Of course I do! She's dead, Theo!" My shout had echoed across the lake. Lowering my voice, I'd added, "And not only is she dead, but she also suffered a long, horrible illness before she died, so it's kind of hard not to feel sad when I think about her."

"Well, there it is. That's why you can't hear her. Your mom doesn't feel sadness or regret or pain or any of those negative emotions anymore, so when you do, you aren't able to hear her."

I stiffened against the netting supporting me. In other words, Theo was saying it was all my fault. It was me who was fucking everything up again. Yeah, that sounded about right.

Not picking up on my distress, he'd kept on explaining. "Remember when I described how wonderful and loving and peaceful I felt on the other side? That's how your mom is feeling right now, too. All the time. So, if you want to hear her, you have to feel that way too. You have to tune to where she is *now*. Not where she used to be."

At that point my molars were nearly cracking I was gritting my teeth so hard. Why did he make everything sound so easy? *Just think differently, Annie. Go against all logic. Life is friendly. You can trust it.* Damn him and his sunny outlook on life…and now his sunny outlook on death, too.

At the table, Theo opens his mouth to say more, but luckily Jack climbs up next to him and starts eating a stick of butter like corn cob. And when Caroline tries to get it away from him, he throws a tantrum so loud it makes even Theo wince. Caroline and Jonathan apologetically rush him inside for bath and bedtime while Theo and I clean up.

After the dishes are done, Theo slips upstairs to call his mom while I amble around the house, picking up toys and idly thinking about how nice it is to have Theo here with me. Even though I know I can never invite him back again. It would be too much of a good thing, letting myself get even closer to him. Letting myself actually believe all the nice things he keeps saying about me. I'm not sure I deserve to let myself off the hook like that yet.

Eventually, I head upstairs and find Theo in the hallway looking at the pictures on the wall with an odd look on his face.

I have no idea why he's so puzzled. "What is it?" I ask, coming up behind him.

He startles as if he hadn't heard me approach. "Oh, it's just…uh…this is your mom, right?" He points to a candid photo I'd taken of my mom in her studio. It's one of my favorites because I'd been able to not just capture her image, but the essence of her as well. In the picture she's smiling really big with her arms flung out wide, so excited by what she'd just painted that she's practically glowing. That's just how she was. Always so in love with life.

"Yeah, that's my mom," I say proudly. His brows are still furrowed, so I go on. "I know why you're confused. The blonde hair throws you off, doesn't it? Caroline actually looks more like her than I do, even though I got her hair color. But their faces are more alike, don't you think?"

He studies my face, then my mom's. "Yeah, I guess. But I see the resemblance in you, too." A faint warmth blooms in my chest at being compared to her. My mom was beautiful. The kind of woman that made people do a double take when she walked by. Although I always thought it was way more than just her physical features that drew people in.

"Is that a coat she's wearing?" Theo asks.

"No, silly." I give him a little shove. "That's an artist's smock."

"Oh. It's very….uh…very colorful."

I laugh at his accurate description. "Well, it started off light blue. See?" I point to the edge of her sleeve. "But every time she accidentally got a blob of paint on it she would take her little paintbrushes and transform it into a flower. She said she found a lesson in those small transformations. She believed there were no mistakes in life. Just opportunities to learn and make things more beautiful the next time. And as time passed, the little messes grew into this whole smock of brightly colored flowers. It was kind of her philosophy on life. You can turn anything bad into something good with a little time, a new perspective, and a fresh coat of paint."

Theo nods still gazing intently at the picture. I'm not sure what he's trying to figure out, which is making me kind of nervous. "Yeah, she had a kind of garish sense of style." I laugh, wondering if that's what's intrigued him so. "She loved bright clothes and dangly jewelry. The more outrageous, the better. Those earrings she's wearing in the picture were her favorites. See? They're hummingbirds."

He leans in, recognition growing across his face. Recognition and some other emotion I can't quite name.

"Oh yeah. I see it now. Hummingbirds. Yeah…they were hummingbirds. Of course." He huffs a faint laugh.

"She was a very talented painter," he says, repeating the same comment he'd made earlier as I'd drug him around the house, pointing out all her paintings on the walls. The muted landscapes so detailed you could almost hear the lap of the water on the shore, the call of the whippoorwills lilting through the air as you gazed at them. For an instant during the tour, I'd considered retrieving the little postcard sketches she'd left me in her will. For some reason it had seemed important for Theo to see them. As if he of all people could somehow help me solve the mystery of why she'd given them to me. Which makes no sense at all, since Theo never even met my mom.

He's still blinking at the picture and acting kind of weird. I can't figure out why he keeps staring at her like that, face all scrunched up and mouth flapping, like he wants to say something but keeps stopping himself.

I give his hand a tug. "We're supposed to play cards now. You coming?"

He straightens as if he's just remembered himself. "Uh…yeah. You go ahead. I'll be there in a minute."

I head down to meet Jonathan and Caroline, thinking of how nice it was to talk about my mom to Theo like that. It felt so natural. Not as painful as it always has been in the past. Theo makes everything easier. In fact, I think I've talked more about my mom in the past few weeks with him than I have in the past three years since she died. Chalk that up as just another of the many ways being around him has changed me.

I'm still musing about how good Theo makes me feel when I get to the bottom of the staircase. I stop and glance back up. He's still standing in the exact same spot, transfixed by the picture on the wall.

CHAPTER TWENTY-FOUR

THEO

"I THOUGHT YOU said you were good at cards," Annie grumbles, leading me up the stairs to her room.

"Usually I am. I guess I was just off my game tonight." I don't tell her the truth: that I couldn't think straight because I was too distracted by what I'd seen in the hallway earlier. That for the last two hours my mind has been ping-ponging between "How can it be?" and "Of course, that makes perfect sense," with such ferocity that I didn't have any bandwidth left to remember the nuances of Euchre strategy.

"It's just I hate when my sister beats me at Euchre," she says. "She's such a gloater! And the way she snaps down the edge of her card each time she takes a trick?" She shudders like the memory physically pains her. "Ugh. It's so fucking annoying!"

She pauses at the top of the stairs, turning to where I've stopped on the step below to scrutinize my face.

"I'll be better next time," I assure her, flushing from the heat of her stare. Even to my burning ears, my excuse isn't all that convincing. But again, my mind's a bit preoccupied by how the hell I'm going to tell her what I've just figured out. I've surprised her with a lot of things so far—my cancer, my Near-Death Experience—but those things are nothing compared to the bombshell I'm about to drop.

She takes off down the hall toward her bedroom. Or what she always calls "the room where I stay when I'm here." She doesn't say, "where I stay when I'm *home*." It's always "where I stay when I'm *here*." As if Caroline's house is just another way station along all the other temporary stops in her life.

As for me, I'll be staying on the pullout couch in the basement tonight. An arrangement which seemed to surprise her sister. I have a feeling that all the guys Annie has brought home in the past have slept in the same bed as her. But not me. She's still adamant that the two of us are just friends. Even though I'm not sure if either of us truly believes that anymore.

When I pass by the watercolor paintings on the wall and the photograph of her mom in her studio, I idly touch the envelope I'd slipped in my back pocket before coming up here. After we'd lost the last hand of cards and said our goodnights, I'd pulled Annie aside and told her I really needed to talk to her. *Now.* She was the one who suggested her bedroom. And as she glances over her shoulder, biting her lip like she's nervous, I wonder if she's regretting choosing such an intimate place for us to be alone.

"Here we go." She ushers me inside and closes the door behind us.

She'd showed me the room on our tour of the house earlier. I'd been surprised at how pristine and uncluttered the space was. The shelves were all empty and dresser tops bare; the pale earth tone bedding way too mature for the tastes of a teenage girl.

Now I ask the question I'd held back before. "So, did they turn this into a guest room after you moved out?"

"No. This is the way it was when I lived here."

"But where's all your stuff? Didn't you have concert posters and pictures and books everywhere? I certainly did! In fact, my bedroom at home is still a mess. My mom claims she likes it that way. It makes her feel like I'm still there whenever she walks by and sees it."

When Annie turns away, I discreetly slip the envelope from my pocket and set it on the empty dresser top. I'll need that later. If she's still speaking to me by then.

"Oh, in my old house I had all those things." She smiles wistfully, gazing around at the artfully adorned walls. "But when we had to sell it, I didn't keep much. I didn't want Caroline to have to deal with storing my junk. And I didn't put up anything personal here because…" She looks down at the ground, choosing her words carefully. "Well, it's not really my room, is it? I didn't want to mess it up and be even more of a burden to her and Jonathan. They were already doing so much just by taking me in."

I nod like it makes perfect sense, but inside my heart breaks a little. How can Annie think of herself as a burden? As someone who doesn't even deserve the right to claim her own space in the world? Especially when, to me, she's the exact opposite. Someone I'd gladly let take over my entire universe.

This room is like a visual representation of how she thinks of herself. Everything so neatly contained. So regimented, so as not to create any waves. From the way she'd described herself as a child, she wasn't always this uptight. In fact, she said her mom always used to call her a wild child, always so loud and expressive. Unapologetically venting her anxiety by yelling and tantruming her way through life, never holding anything back. But now it's like she's purposely bottled up her true nature just to feel the pain of the constriction. Like she's trying to pay penance for some made-up sin she thinks she committed by letting her mom down in her time of need. Oh, if Annie's mom were here now, she'd tell her how wrong she's gotten it all. I know that for a fact.

"So lay it on me," Annie says, flopping down on the edge of the bed. "What's so important that you couldn't concentrate long enough for us to beat the pants off my pompous sister and her poor doting husband?"

She leans back on her arms, looking up at me with wide eyes. She's wearing a flowered sundress with spaghetti straps, and all I can do is stare at the flawless point of her shoulder and think of how badly I'd like to lean down and kiss it. Then I'd gently brush back her long blonde hair and kiss up her slender neck, to the soft spot behind her ear, then down along the curve of her jaw until I got to...

"Theo?"

I startle back to life to find her looking at me with a funny expression. If I wasn't already frazzled enough by what I'm about to tell her, seeing her on the bed below me in that tiny dress that would only take two, maybe three moves to slip off...well that's just making things even harder.

She sits up, puts her hands primly in her lap with just the hint of a satisfied smile playing on her mouth, almost like she's read every thought I'd just had. And liked them all.

"Sorry, sorry." I shake my head, trying to clear my thoughts. "Give me a second. It's just. What I'm about to say...it's a lot to take in."

"I think I can handle whatever it is you have to give me."

We both flush and look away, the unintended innuendo registering at the same time.

I distract myself by pulling the desk chair from the corner closer, try to rid myself of these lurid thoughts that have no business creeping up at a time like this.

I need to remind myself that Annie has always listened to me in the past. Which has been such a blessing (and surprise) so far. But this time...well I might be pushing the boundaries of her beliefs to their very limits. I only hope that what I was told on the other side will still hold true. That I won't be doing this all alone.

I settle on the chair in front of her and force myself to start. "So do you remember how I told you in my Near-Death Experience there was this one main Angel Guide that came to me?"

She furrows her brow, thinking. "Yeah. The woman with the bright coat and all the jewelry."

"Yeah, well..." There's no easy way to say it, so I might as well just get it out. "That Angel Guide was your mom."

She gapes at me, mouth hanging open, body so still I'm not sure she's even breathing. She stays frozen that way for so long I eventually reach out and ever-so-lightly place my hands on her bare shoulders.

"Breathe, Annie. Just breathe."

"What did you just say?!" she finally shouts. And even though I expected her to be surprised, the sheer volume of her voice still jars me.

"Your mom is my Angel Guide." When I repeat the words, her eyes go wider than I thought humanly possible. "I didn't know it was her until I saw that picture on the wall outside." I rush on, pointing to the hallway. "But the moment I saw it, I knew your mom was the same woman I'd seen in the afterlife."

She shakes her head, blinking at me in disbelief. "But how is that possible?"

"I don't know. But I'm telling you, it was her." Once I saw her mom in the picture, all the details that had once been so blurry in my memory instantly filled in. It was like her face triggered a flood of memories I previously hadn't been allowed to recall.

Annie's mouth flaps open and closed, as if she can't quite form words. "But…but…how…why? This makes no sense. Why her? You didn't even know her." She cocks her head at me. "I mean, you didn't know her, right?"

"No. I never met her. And I have no idea what the connection is between us. When I was there, she said something about us not meeting in the physical world this time around, but there's still a connection between us, Annie. All of us. I felt that when I was there."

She swallows hard, fighting to digest the magnitude of what I've just told her. I want to hug her for how hard she's clearly fighting to stay open-minded and not automatically discount my claims as the rantings of a madman. But from the look on her face, I'm not sure the scales have tipped all the way in my favor yet.

"I was just as confused as you are when I first realized it," I say, trying to make her understand. "But in the picture it was her. Remember how I thought it was some kind of colorful coat my Angel was wearing? It was actually the artist's smock with the painted flowers like you told me about. And the jewelry, it was all the same. The hummingbird earrings. The bracelets. All the details filled in. Her hair… her face…her smile. I'll never forget it. Even the way you described her…so happy and carefree. It was her Annie. I know it was. Your mom is my Angel Guide."

She stares around the room, looking at everything but me. This time I'm the one holding my breath, silently praying that something will click with her. That the memory of the two of us standing side by side, choosing to take on this challenge together will come back to her. My Angel said the memories would return at just the right time. And dammit, I'd say now is about the rightest time there could possibly be.

Suddenly she sits up tall as if she's just thought of something. "Theo, what day did you have your Near-Death Experience?"

The question sets a warning bell off in my head. I know where she's going with this. Annie is asking for some concrete proof. If my NDE happened after her mom died, then she might accept it as possible. If not, well…I don't want to think about where we'll go from there.

I hesitate to answer, because what Annie doesn't understand is time doesn't work the same way in the afterlife as it does here. Which means my answer could either give her the evidence she needs, or ruin everything between us. All I can do now is pray someone out there has my back.

"February 4, 1986," I whisper.

She sucks in a sharp breath.

Her reaction sends my heart soaring. But she says nothing. She just sits there, clutching the edge of the bed like there's a good chance she might fall off any minute.

"Annie," I prod, desperate to know where we stand. "What day did your mom die?"

"February 4, 1986."

We both nod at each other dumbly, words woefully inadequate

at a time like this. I can almost hear the sound of two puzzle pieces clicking into place in the air between us.

"This is crazy," she breathes.

"Yeah, I know," I admit, even though I shouldn't be surprised since I was the one who remembered more than her. Still, the odds that we've even gotten to this moment are so staggering I'd say my awe is well deserved.

"It's hard to believe," I say. "But somehow, on that day, all of us were able to come together and decide on this path."

"Wait a minute. What do you mean, *all of us?*"

"You don't remember?" I ask gently. I know my Angel…uh, Annie's mom… said I had to take it slow with her, but there comes a time where everything needs to be out in the open once and for all.

"Me?" Annie asks. "Why would I remember anything about *your* NDE?"

I reach out and hold both her hands in mine, as if that might be enough to brace her for what's coming next. "Because you were there too."

She recoils, jerking out of my grip. "I was not!"

"Yes, you were. Standing next to me. The three of us. We were all there together."

She struggles to stand, but I'm leaning too close. She gives my shoulder a hard shove. "Can you give me some space please?!"

When I oblige, she leaps to her feet and begins pacing around the foot of the bed, squeezing her bottom lip between her fingers as she thinks.

"No. No. This can't be," she mumbles, staring down at the carpet. "I didn't die. How could I have been there too?"

I sit quietly, begging inside my head, *Where the hell are you? You think you could give me a little back up here?*

Just be patient. The tinkling voice says. *She's coming around. The part she needs to remember is there. We'll just have to see if she's open enough to let it in.*

On her next pass by, Annie stops abruptly, a dawning slowly spreading over her face.

And Bingo! There it is, my Angel says. Although I guess I shouldn't think of her as just my Angel anymore since she's obviously Annie's Angel too.

Annie swallows hard, working to compose her features back to their normal reserve. For a moment, I'm sure she's going to deny whatever it was she just remembered.

But then she comes back and sits down on the edge of the bed, taking my hand in hers this time. The strong, soothing pulse of our combined energy swells, making me feel like, no matter what happens next, everything is going to be okay. For both of us.

"What did you just remember?" I ask tentatively, still not sure how much information she was allowed to keep.

A smidge now. A smidge later. And if you two get further…well then…

I want to ask my Angel what that means, but before I can get the question out, Annie starts talking.

"Um, I'm not sure exactly. But the night my mom died I had a really vivid dream." She gazes over my shoulder, eyes going vacant, as if she's drifting back in time. "Or at least I thought it was a dream. But now, I don't know. Maybe it was more than that?"

I nod, not wanting to break her revery by speaking out loud.

She goes on. "I told you how I started crying really hard, and it was difficult for me to breathe, and I'd collapsed on the bathroom floor. That's when the dream came. I was standing in the middle of a bright orb of light and my mom was standing in front of me, smiling with such radiance I could barely see her face. I felt this overwhelming sense of peace and happiness pouring out of her and, and…" Her eyes well up as she struggles to go on. "I couldn't help it. In the dream, I started crying again. But this time the tears weren't from sadness, but from joy."

She searches my face for some sort of confirmation. I whisper softly. "Yes, that's exactly what it feels like there." My eyes well too, remembering that state of pure bliss.

Relieved, she goes on. "My mom hugged me to her and she felt so…so real. And the best part was she was healthy again. Just like her old self before the cancer. In fact, she looked like she did whenever she came out of her studio after finishing one of her paintings, wearing her flowered smock and clogs, all that crazy jewelry she loved so much." Ragged laughter seeps out around her tears.

"Then she said something to me. She said *Don't worry about me, Buttercup*." She stops to explain. "That's the nickname she called me when I was a little girl. Which I hated. I always got so mad when she used it when I was a teenager. But believe me, I was so happy to hear her say it again that night."

"I can imagine."

Her face goes slack as she resumes her story. "She said…. *Don't worry about me*." Her voice hitches. "*I'm free now*."

Annie cries harder, and I pivot out of my seat to sit beside her on the bed. "See?" I throw an arm around her shoulder and hug her tight. "She *did* talk to you. You told me you could never hear her, but you did that night."

Her head bobs against my chest. "I didn't believe it, though. When I woke up I told myself it was only a dream that it was just something I made up to ease my guilt." She pulls back so she can look me in the eye. "But now you're telling me it was real? That it was really her?"

"Yes, it was really her, Annie. And she *is* free now. She really doesn't want you to worry about her. Or feel guilty about anything."

Hearing those words, her body goes slack underneath my arms as if the years of tension are physically draining out of her. She suddenly feels so much lighter, fragile almost. Like I'm cradling a hollowed-out eggshell. I ever so slightly loosen my grip.

We stay that way for a while until she sits up and heaves a heavy breath, eyes red-rimmed but so much brighter than before.

"What else do you remember?" I ask, not voicing the question I'm dying to know. *Do you remember me?*

"I remember standing there for a while talking to her and," she furrows her brow. "Then I noticed another presence there, standing next to me. Except when I turned to look, the light was too bright in my eyes and I couldn't make out who it was."

I raise my hand, smiling big. "That was me!"

She scrunches up her face. "I still don't know how that's possible, Theo. I was alive. And you two…well, you weren't."

"I don't know how it happened either. But it's okay. Maybe all the vast mysteries of life aren't meant to be understood by our tiny human brains."

She doesn't seem very pleased by that explanation. But she continues, speaking slower now, as if the memories are getting hazier. "Anyway, I know we all had a lot of fun together…and there was a lot of laughing and joking around?" She says the last part like she can't quite believe it.

"Yeah. That's how it is there. Very light and carefree. You're doing good. Anything else?"

"Eventually, you two started fading away."

"Actually, you were the one who faded away first. But never mind that. It's all just semantics."

"I didn't want you to go because it felt so good being there next to you," she mumbles, as if she's working it all out as she goes along. "It's hard to explain. But I still feel it now when I'm near you. It's like this really pleasant feeling of warm accompaniment. This feeling of someone who knows every deep-down part of you and yet still loves you anyway."

She pulls away from me, cheeks flushing as if she wishes she hadn't let that part slip out. I hadn't missed how she'd used the present tense when speaking of me. Like it wasn't just the Dream Theo she wanted to be near, but the me that's sitting next to her right now.

"So anyway," she rushes on. "There was more, but I can't remember much else. But I do remember the one thing my mom said to me right before I woke up." She pauses, smile growing as more puzzle pieces click into place. "She said, *When he comes....believe him.*"

Goosebumps run down my arms. Suddenly, everything makes sense. Why the normally so skeptical Annie has believed every part of my outlandish, illogical, un-verifiable story. I'm so damn proud of her I could burst. Because not only did she hear her mom's guidance, she'd done something much harder: She'd listened to it.

She blinks at me like she's seeing me for the first time. "You really are the Him she was talking about?" Her voice is filled with wonder.

"I'm the Him," I repeat, my heart nearly bursting by what I see in the depths of her eyes.

She shakes her head, still fighting to make sense of it all. "I tried to tell myself it was ridiculous to believe something I heard in a dream. But sometimes, whenever I was lonely at night, I'd let myself dream about you. I'd wonder what you'd look like. Who you'd be." She gives me a playful nudge on the shoulder. "And when the hell you'd ever get your act together and come find me!"

We laugh together and a weight lifts off my chest. She believes me. She doesn't remember everything. But even with as little as she has to go on, she believes me.

"You're finally here." She leans closer, tipping her face up to me. "I've waited for you for so long."

Her eyes drop to my mouth, a clear asking in her eyes. And without thinking I answer… bowing my head and ever so slightly brushing my lips to hers. When our skin meets, an even greater surge of energy pulses through my body, unlike anything I've ever known. Her lips are soft and luscious, a thousand times more delicious than I've fantasized about. (Which is saying a lot since I've fantasized about this moment for a long time now.)

Our kissing starts off slowly as we get to know each other with soft grazing brushes. But soon Annie grabs the back of my head and pulls me down with a fierceness that surprises me; her mouth opening wider to my probing tongue as if she desperately needs more of me inside of her. There's nothing fragile about her now. She's no longer an eggshell but a runaway fire. Her desire strong and unwavering; leaving no doubt about her feelings for me in its wake. I greedily match her determination, my body humming and hardening from the force of our combined heat. And all I can think as we finally give in to each other is, *This is right. This is right. This is so, so right.*

But just as I'm about to be carried away by the sheer ecstasy of the moment, she pulls away.

"We shouldn't be doing this," she pants, pulling up the strap of her dress which had fallen in our flurry.

It takes me a second to remember how to form a sentence. "Why not?"

"Because of…" It seems like she's warring with herself. I see desire and longing and, for some reason, guilt, all jockeying for position on her face. "Just because. It's not right."

I'm unhinged. Barely able to focus on anything outside the narrow scope of her mouth, her lips, her tongue. I move closer until my own lips are only a whisper's breath from hers once again. "But it was so good. And everything good is right." I vaguely remember someone telling me that once.

"Ugh, I know," she groans. Then, as if she can't help herself, she voraciously claims my mouth again. "It's so, so good," she murmurs in between kisses. Then she roughly forces herself away once more, her expression so pained it's like she's being torn apart from the inside out. Her blue eyes frantically search my face. Whatever she sees there makes her grab a fistful of my shirt and jerk me back to kiss me again. And again. And again.

With another loud groan, she pushes me away and lurches to her feet. "We have to stop! This is bad! We need to figure out what the hell is going on here, not doing *this*!"

She paces like a caged animal around the room. I wonder if her body's throbbing like a live wire, like mine is now. I'm not sure why she thinks giving in to our feelings for each other is such a bad thing, but she's clearly upset.

"You're right," I tell her, more to soothe her than because I actually agree. I hate being the cause of her angst. "Let's calm down and think about what all this could mean."

She's still tense, clutching her arms around herself as she stalks by, as if she has to physically hold herself back from touching me again. I smile to myself, secretly delighting that she wants me as much as I want her. A possibility that even in all my optimism, I haven't let myself consider until now.

"How about we take a second to review what we know?" I suggest.

"Yeah, that's a good idea," she says, looking relieved by my distraction. "In fact, I know exactly what we should do." She wags a finger at me, all business now. "Let's make a list!"

∞

After Annie retrieves a notebook and pen from the desk drawer, she comes back to sit on the bed beside me. "I always think better when I can look at the facts in black and white," she says curtly.

She balances the notebook on her lap and writes: "Things We Know For Sure" at the top, then underlines it with two sharp strokes of her pen.

She looks up at me, blinking her long lashes expectantly. I guess I'm supposed to start.

"Okay uh…number one." I fight to shuffle my thoughts back in order. "I chose to come back because I saw a really bright loving path that supposedly will affect many people's lives."

"Right," she scribbles that on the pad.

When she's done, she stares up at the ceiling, tapping the pen on her bottom lip as she thinks. She abruptly starts writing again. "And number two: That path starts when you meet me."

"Yes. That's definitely something we know." Eager to keep the flow going, I quickly tack on. "And that path ends sometime before I turn twenty-two."

She winces, and I internally kick myself for reminding her of that incriminating fact. I hurry on, trying to distract her. "And, although we don't really know what's on this extra special path, we do know that the two of us agreed to do it together."

She stops writing. "Wait a minute, wait a minute. You've alluded to that before. But I don't remember ever agreeing to anything."

"Oh, shit. You don't?"

She shakes her head, so I try to jar her memory. "Yeah. You were definitely in on it. In fact, your exact words were 'Sure. Why not? Sounds like fun!' And then we tried to shake on it, but it didn't work because our bodies weren't really physical at that point just all misty and so our hands just passed through each other's and…" Her eyes are as round as saucers, so I stop myself. Yeah, it must be awfully strange to have someone tell you about something you said, but for the life (or death) of you, you can't recall.

Her face has gone pale and she looks like she might be sick.

"What's wrong?" I ask. "This is good. We're both on the same page now. And we have all this information." I gesture to the notebook.

"You think this is a lot of information?!" Her eyes are still huge as she scans down at what she's written. "So far, we have a glowing path, a vague mission, and a ghostly handshake. Oh yeah. That makes everything crystal clear! We definitely have a rock-solid plan now, Theo!"

I chuckle at her outrage, which she doesn't take kindly to. It must be killing her to feel so out of control. And I'm starting to wonder if that just might be the point of this whole adventure.

"But we have your mom helping us too," I say. "Put that down. That's got to mean something, right?"

She poises her pen on the paper, but hesitates, an emotion I can't quite name clouding her face.

"What? What's wrong?"

"It's just…the whole thing with my mom…"

I stay quiet, give her time to sort out her words.

"Before, when you said I was involved with you finding this path of yours, it felt like I could just do my part and be done with it. That my only role was meeting you, starting you off on your trajectory, and that was it. I wouldn't have to actually go on the path with you because it was only about *you* finding your way."

I knew this was coming. Annie has been careful to keep a wall between us. Maintaining her boundaries not just by keeping us as friends, but also by making it clear that at the end of camp we'll go our separate ways and never see each other again. I can hardly blame her. Caring for a person who is scheduled to die soon is not for the fainthearted. And after what she's been through with her mom, it almost feels cruel to ask her to open herself up to such pain again. For the first time ever, I wonder whether I'd made the right choice in coming back. Because just by being in Annie's life, I'm now destined to hurt her.

Annie goes on. "But now with my mom involved. With all this you've told me about us all meeting up in some kind of dream-heaven-limbo space and making some kind of big agreement, it feels like whatever happens next is as much about my life as it is yours. And I know it's probably stupid to say, but that freaks me out. It feels like too much pressure. Like I'm being forced into this…this…whatever it is. And I can't say no without messing everything up for everyone. Why did they choose me for this? Mom should know I can't be trusted to do anything right!"

I reach for her. "Annie, I told you she doesn't blame you for what happened that night. That means nothing to her now. You have to let that go."

She turns away, refusing to meet my eyes.

"But it wasn't just that one night," she says quietly. "I haven't told you everything, Theo. I haven't told you how mean I was to her sometimes. How I used to snap at her whenever she tried to talk to me. Or make some kind of stupid sarcastic comment instead of having a genuine conversation with her while I still could. I actually avoided her. Can you believe that?" Tears spring to her eyes again. "Once Aunt Lydia came to help take care of her, I spent as much time at school and at parties drinking myself into oblivion because I couldn't stand to watch her wasting away. Honestly, I was furious with her for getting sick! Like it was her fault or something. But still, that's how I felt sometimes. I was so fucking angry that she was leaving me. Good God...who thinks such horrible thoughts as that? I have to be the worst person in the world!"

Her agony is so palpable I feel its ache in my own chest. "Annie, a lot of people have those same feelings when someone they love gets sick. We all want to think we'd act all noble and caring when push comes to shove, but the reality is we're only human. And being human means we have a whole, huge range of different emotions. And we're allowed to feel them all."

She still doesn't look convinced, so try again. "I know that for a fact because when I was sick I treated my mom like shit, too."

"You? Perfect Saint Theo?" she snaps in disbelief.

"Believe me, I was no saint then. I was at my worst...so mad at the world for what had happened to me I took it out on mom. The person closest to me. Who was giving up her whole life to take care of me." My stomach turns, thinking of how badly I treated her. "But she doesn't hold a grudge. Just like your mom doesn't. Maybe neither of us can comprehend that kind of love because we don't have kids yet. But somehow moms just understand."

Her shoulders drop just a fraction of an inch, making me think she's heard at least part of what I've said. "And as for your other worry," I go on. "You have every right to say no to all this. You're free to walk away right now and not speak to me for the rest of the summer if you want. You can forget you ever met me and I would understand."

"You know that's not what I want." It comes out as more irritated than loving. As if she's pissed at herself for liking me so much. She must hear the harshness in her own voice because it lightens as she tries to explain. "It's just you want more from me than I can give, Theo. And I can't. I just can't. I can't go through that again."

"I don't expect you to! Seriously, no commitment." I hold up my palms in surrender. "Let's just stay open and see what happens next, okay? I promise in two months you can walk away. No strings attached."

"Are you sure?" she asks. I hate how relieved she looks. It makes it even more clear that if anyone's a burden in this lifetime, it's me.

"I'm sure," I say. "If I get a few months with you as friends, I'll consider myself a lucky man."

She looks at me as if I'm speaking a foreign language. As if I'm nuts to see a silver-lining in what seems to be an awfully dark cloud.

But now that she's no longer obligated to watch me die, she seems to relax. Giving her a playful elbow in the ribs, I prompt, "Besides, aren't you curious about what's next? We've got eight more weeks together. Who knows what adventures we could have in that time?"

"Yeah. I guess so," she begrudgingly admits. "But where do we even go from here?" She scans down her written list again. "If this is all we have to go on, it seems like we're already at a dead end and we haven't even started yet."

"Actually, I don't think we are." I lift a finger in the air. "In fact, I think I may have already gotten our first clue."

Annie gives me a puzzled look as I make my way to the dresser. Hmmm. What's the best way to drop this next bombshell? Thank God, it's the last one.

I keep my back to her as I nervously finger the edge of the white envelope. "I got this in the mail right before I came to camp. I had no idea what it meant at the time, but now that I've been here and seen your mom's paintings, I'm pretty sure these have something to do with her and what we're supposed to do next."

I slip the two watercolor postcards into my hand, then whirl around, holding them out so Annie can see.

"What do you know about these?"

CHAPTER TWENTY-FIVE

ANNIE

I STARE DOWN at what Theo is holding in his hand, barely able to register what I'm seeing.

The next instant, I'm seething. "Why do you have those?!"

The nerve of him. I can't believe he had the balls to rummage around in my bag and take my two most prized possessions without even asking me first.

I open my mouth to blast him for being so presumptuous, so… so *intrusive*, but the words die on my lips. Because when I look closer, what I realize makes my blood run cold.

Those aren't my postcards in Theo's hand.

They look almost exactly like my postcards. They're the same size as my postcards…the same watercolor palette…were obviously done by the same artist, who just so happens to be my mom. But the two sketches Theo holds depict different scenes than the ones she left me. My studies are of a shaded inlet and a huge birch tree at the intersection of two trails. His studies show some kind of cave entrance and a wide expanse of a lake with a beach barely visible off in the distance.

My mouth hangs open as I stare at him in disbelief. Suddenly it feels like the room around us has dropped away, and I'm floating in a tunnel of white light with only Theo and me suspended at its center.

Then I blink again and with a loud *whoosh* in my ears I'm back in the bedroom with him. *What the hell was that?*

His lips are moving and I can tell he's trying to explain more, but nothing makes sense anymore. It's just sounds and gestures and impossibilities playing out like some kind of theater production I'm looking down upon from my seat in the rafters.

I shake my head hard, trying to force myself back into my body. Whipping my legs underneath me, I crawl backwards on the bed. Trying to get as far away from him and those…those…pieces of my mom that I've never seen before that he has absolutely no business possessing, in his hands.

"Where did you get those?!" I shout, finger shaking mid-air as I point.

From the way he sighs, I have a feeling he's already explained himself while I was trying not to pass out. "I told you. I got them in the mail right before I was getting ready to leave for camp."

He seems to be forcibly pressing his lips closed, like he wants to say more, but knows I need some time to let that information sink in.

"My mom painted those," I say dumbly.

"Yeah, I know. I figured that out when I saw all the paintings here." His words are gentle and even. But he looks scared. Like he's genuinely afraid of what I might do next.

I look down at myself and realize I'm perched on all fours, shaking like a cornered animal on the far edge of the bed. Lowering myself down on my haunches, I take a deep breath, working to get myself back under control.

Theo sets the postcards on the dresser behind him (as if not seeing them is going to help anything) then holds a palm out to calm me. "It's going to be okay. I'm sure we can figure this out."

He sounds like he's trying to talk someone off a ledge. Which is pretty much how I feel right now. With what I've gone through in the last ten minutes, I'm definitely fighting a severe case of vertigo.

First, there was the shock of finding out my mom is Theo's Angel

Guide. Then the thrill of knowing he's the mysterious figure I've dreamed about all these years. Then there was the kiss…oh my God… the kiss. It was so perfect, so right. I nearly fainted from the sheer passion of it. Then came the guilt about Greta and how wrong it was to kiss Theo like that. And now, I've circled all the way back around to shock again after seeing something that shouldn't be possible staring me right in the face. No wonder I feel like I've just been thrown inside a dryer set to high heat tumble.

"How? How could you have those?" I stammer.

"Honestly, I don't know."

"My mom died three years ago, Theo. And even though I know you claim she's still 'always with me'," I air-quote furiously. "I know for a fact she can't send *mail* from where she is now!"

He huffs a laugh. "I know she can't send mail from heaven. I won't argue about that. But there's something more." He winces, like he's afraid of my reaction. "Either she, or someone who sent those postcards, also wrote me a note."

My stomach rolls as he retrieves his evidence. No. There's no way that Theo—a guy I met by sheer coincidence a month ago just because I took a job at some random camp—might have an actual note from my mom. That is completely and utterly impossible.

I gingerly crawl across the bed toward him, gasping when he finally unfolds the notebook paper. "Oh my God! That's my mom's handwriting."

"I figured," he says, annoyingly cool, like always. As if getting mail from the afterlife is some kind of daily occurrence for him.

Hands quivering, I take the note from him. As I read her words, a clanging rings through me like my entire body has become one gigantic bell.

This is only one half of the puzzle. It reads. *You'll have to work together if you want to understand the rest.*

"So? Do you have any idea what she means by one half of the puzzle?" Theo asks, pale eyes boring deep into mine.

"Do I have any idea?!" The shrillness of my own voice hurts my ears. I don't know why I'm yelling at him. It's not like he planned this himself. I mean, he didn't, did he? No. He couldn't have. Could he?

"Actually, I do have an idea," I say, softening my tone. "Wait until you see this."

I awkwardly scoot-hop off the bed to where my duffel rests on the floor. As I dig out the manilla envelope I keep with me at all times, I think of how, when Theo was looking at the paintings in the hallway earlier, I'd gotten the urge to show him these. Had that been some kind of cosmic nudge from my mom?

I take my postcards out of the envelope and hold them out to him. "These are the other half!"

Theo's eyes go wide as he rushes over to get a closer look. "Wait a minute. These scenes are different than the ones I have."

"Yeah, these are what my mom called studies. Little sketches she used to do to plan out her compositions before she tackled the full-sized paintings."

"You mean she did bigger paintings of these pictures?"

"Yeah, that's what Caroline told me when I asked her about mine. She helped Mom organize all her work in the last few months of her life, so she knows more about them than I do. I guess these were a series of landscapes she did when she was just starting out."

"Where are they now? Maybe if we looked at the finished paintings, we could figure out what to she wanted us to know."

I make a face. "Yeah, I had that idea, too. But we don't have them anymore. She sold them all when I was little. I don't remember ever seeing them in real life."

He visibly deflates, looking as frustrated as I'd been when I'd questioned Caroline about the paintings three years ago.

"Theo, this still doesn't explain how in the hell you got these in the mail a few weeks ago." I gesture to the top of the dresser. "Wait a minute. Can I see that envelope? Maybe the return address will give us something to go on."

"That's not the envelope they came in. I transferred the cards to a smaller one so they'd fit in my bag."

"Do you remember anything about the original one?"

"It was in a big manilla envelope like the one you have there. I still have it at home. I looked at it, but I didn't have time to do any research before I had to leave for camp."

I let out a loud sigh. Now what the hell are we supposed to do?

"Although there was something weird about it," he adds.

I try my best to remain patient as he furrows his brows, thinking. But after only a few seconds, I snap, "Which was?"

He startles out of his stupor. "Oh. The return address was from Montana."

CHAPTER TWENTY-SIX

CAROLINE HAS POSITIONED herself in the corner of her dining room as far away from Theo and me as possible.

"I feel like I'm in an episode of *The Twilight Zone*," she says, staring at us like she's just seen a ghost.

On the table between us sits the four postcards and two hand-written notes. Which (judging from the terrified look on her face) Caroline must believe have just been delivered from the underworld by Hades himself.

"This…this whole thing." She swirls a finger at our collection of evidence. "I just don't understand how it's possible."

"None of us do," I tell her brusquely. "But believe me, we're about to find out."

The second Theo had uttered the word Montana back in my bedroom, I'd known exactly who was involved. Aunt Lydia.

I'd thundered down the hallway and pounded on Caroline and Jonathan's bedroom door, not caring if they were awake, asleep, or having the most earth-shattering sex of their lives. I just knew I needed help and I didn't want to do this alone.

"I'm sure there's a perfectly good explanation," Jonathan says languidly, while I try to ignore the fact he's wearing only boxer shorts below his ratty Metallica t-shirt. Sitting next to me, Theo nods in agreement. For the first time I notice how similar he and Jonathan are. Both so easy-going and unflappable, which I guess is the kind of guy it takes to put up with the high-strung antics of Caroline and me.

Jonathan is wrestling the cords of the phone and some contraption he'd brought home from work weeks ago; tugging and untangling until it reaches the middle of the dining room table. He claims he can hook the phone up to this black box and it will become a speaker so we can all hear Aunt Lydia talk, just like when Charlie talks to his Angels on TV. I'll believe it when I see it. Or hear it, as the case may be.

"Are you going to sit down?" I ask Caroline, who's still huddled in the corner, looking like she might bolt out the sliding glass door any second. I guess I was a little abrupt when I'd tried to catch her up to speed earlier. Once we'd shown her the postcards, we'd had to tell her about Theo's Near-Death experience.

And about how Mom is his Angel Guide.

And about how I passed out the night Mom died and somehow spoke to both her and Theo in some kind of cosmic meeting room.

And about how I apparently agreed to join Theo on a mission which has to be completed before he dies in a little over a year.

So, yeah. I guess Caroline has good reason to look a bit shell-shocked right now.

"Sorry for piling that on you all at once," I say, patting the chair next to me. "We can explain more later if you want."

"Now do you see why I took my time telling you everything?" Theo mumbles in my ear.

I roll my eyes at him as Caroline finally relents and settles next to me; her gaze still glued to the miniature watercolors before us.

"I know I'm acting a bit unhinged," I tell her. "But we have to hurry. Montana's two hours behind us, but it's already pretty late. And there's no way I'm going to bed until I figure out what the hell is going on."

"Well, now that you've dragged me into this, neither am I," Caroline says. She takes a deep breath, a steely resolve replacing her former shakiness. "Hand me the phone, honey," she says tersely to Jonathan.

"We're going to get to the bottom of this. Right now." Hearing her take-charge voice—the one that usually grates on my last nerve whenever it's aimed at me—makes me thankful I got her out of bed.

As Caroline dials the number, I think back to the last time I talked to Aunt Lydia. I'd gotten the notion to call her a few weeks before camp started. I've always been close with my aunt. We share a love of horses and the outdoors. Lydia spends a lot of time trail riding in the Montana wilderness with her friends when she's not working as a nurse, so we always bond over the antics of her three horses and all the various wildlife she sees on her trips. Still, it hadn't been typical of me to call her out of the blue like that. Normally when we talk, she's the one who reaches out first. With all I know now, I wonder if the idea to make that phone call hadn't come from me alone.

Caroline sits on one side of me, Theo on the other, Jonathan standing so he can fiddle with nobs on the speakerphone. The first ring from Aunt Lydia's line blasts through the black box at near deafening levels. Jonathan and Theo cheer as Caroline hisses "Turn it the fuck down before you wake the kids!"

As we wait for her to pick up, I mutter to my sister. "I swear to God, this better not be one of Aunt Lydia's practical jokes."

Lydia was the kind of relative who used to wrap boxes of coal for us at Christmas, giggling uproariously as we cried in disappointment. Then, once she'd gotten a good laugh, she'd suddenly whip out some amazing gift, like a Star Wars light saber I'd been asking for. Or a ping-pong table she'd set up in the basement overnight. We never knew what the hell to expect from her. Which is why I'm a little leery about what this conversation is about to reveal.

"Well, don't be too surprised," Caroline warns. "You know what a warped sense of humor she has."

There's a click on the line and the four of us suck in a collective breath when we hear Lydia's almost combative hello.

Caroline starts with traditional pleasantries. "Hi Aunt Lydia! It's Caroline. Sorry to bother you so late. How are you…"

"Did you send a letter to a boy in Indiana a few weeks ago?!" I shout over the top of my sister.

Lydia bursts out laughing. Theo and Jonathan immediately chuckle along, while Caroline and I hit them with our most vicious death stares. Our aunt laughs harder and harder. I think I might even hear the sound of a hand slapping jeans, which only serves to irritate me more.

"Answer the question!" I wail. This lack of information is killing me. I feel like a fish dangling on the end of a line, not knowing whether it's going to be thrown back or eaten for dinner. I need to know what's going on *now*.

She finally catches her breath. "So, it looks like you two finally found each other, huh? Oh, your mother is going to be so happy!"

I start to correct her the way I always do when she speaks of Mom in the present tense, but then I remember how lately inside my head I've been referring to my mom in the same way. Lord, am I becoming a believer like her and Theo now?

"Yeah, we found each other!" Theo shouts beside me.

Jonathan puts a hand on his shoulder. "Uh, you don't have to talk so loud, dude. She can hear you if you use your regular voice."

"Oh, uh…sorry," Theo says sheepishly. He leans closer to the black box, speaking softer, but a lot slower this time. "This is Theo…Aunt Lydia…I'm…the one…you sent…the letter to…"

"Again, you can just speak normally," Jonathan whispers patiently. "It's like a regular phone. Just not pressed up against your face."

Theo shrugs and smiles goofily at me. I can't help but smile back. He's just so damn cute.

"Nice to meet you, Theo!" Aunt Lydia shouts way too loudly back. Jonathan shakes his head, looking too exhausted to correct her. "But I'm going to tell you right now," she continues to bellow, "there's no way in hell I'm going to even attempt to say that last name of yours, son. My God, when I saw Grace writing it down, I thought she was just scribbling down random letters of the alphabet in a delirious haze.

Why in the hell would anyone need to have a name with that many consonants lined up in a row, anyhow?!"

Theo laughs. "I'm Polish. We like to use as much of the alphabet as we can. Makes us feel like we're getting our money's worth!" She cackles loudly as he explains more. "And if you ever want to give it a whirl, it's pronounced Teodorczyk… teo…dork…sick."

"Oh well, that's not so hard. Teo—"

"Wait a minute," I cut her off, picking up on something way more important than nonsensical last names. "Did you say Mom was the one who addressed Theo's envelope?" My mind feels like it's gone haywire, all its circuits overloaded with too much incongruous information all at once. Theo said he and Mom had never met in real life. So how could she have known his name and address before she died?

I start to ask more, but Caroline puts a hand on my arm, stopping me. "Let's not jump in with a bunch of questions all at once," she says firmly. "First we need to summarize what we know, then we'll hear Aunt Lydia's side of the story. Then after that we'll open up the floor to questions, alright?"

I'm so taken aback by Caroline's lawyer-like demeanor I can't even pop off a sarcastic comeback before she charges on.

"So Lydia, as you can imagine, we are all quite confused by this turn of events."

Turn of events? I mouth dramatically at Jonathan, who looks away, fighting back a smile.

"Here's what we've got for facts," Caroline says. "Right now, we're sitting here at my table looking at the two little watercolor paintings that Mom left Annie in her will and a note that says," Caroline picks up the paper and reads aloud. "*When the time comes, you'll understand. And remember, stay open to life, Buttercup. Let it show you where it wants you to go.*"

She sets my paper down and scoots Theo's paper closer. "And we also have two different watercolor studies and another note, clearly written by Mom, that says: *This is only one half of the puzzle. You'll have to work together if you want to understand the rest.*"

"Uh huh," Lydia says, not sounding one bit surprised.

Sticking with her just-the-facts tone, Caroline goes on. "And those two postcards were delivered to Theo only five weeks ago, with a postmark from Montana. Therefore, we can conclude that you clearly have some involvement in this. So can you please explain yourself?" She slaps a hand down on the table like a gavel. "Aunt Lydia, you now have the floor."

Again, I make a face at Jonathan and he stage-whispers, "Your sister likes to watch a lot of courtroom dramas on TV."

Lydia chuckles a little more, taking her blessed time before speaking. I don't think she's being annoying on purpose. I think she's genuinely as flabbergasted by these turn of events as we are. But that still doesn't keep me from wanting to reach through the phone and squeeze the answers right out of her throat.

"Alright, alright. I'll tell you everything I know. Settle in pardners. This is going to be a wild ride."

Theo glances at me, eyes as bright as a four-year-old about to be read a bedtime story. Even though I know it might be a bad idea, I reach over and lace my fingers in his, pull his hand over so it rests on top of my thigh. The weight of it feels like an anchor holding me in place. The warmth of his skin a reminder that I'm not in this alone. Which is what I need right now.

I wish I could be as excited as he is. He looks so innocent and hopeful, as if he can't even imagine anything going wrong with this situation. Isn't he worried about how big this all feels? Doesn't he think about what might happen if we make a mistake? Why does he act like this is all so much fun? My God, doesn't the rest of his short life and the many lives it might affect depend on what we do next? Why doesn't this seem as heavy to him as it does to me?

"So, in those last days when your mom was still at home," Lydia begins. "Before she had to be hospitalized, she started having these really vivid dreams. She said she was talking to our mom and grandma and her other Angels and they were comforting her. Telling her they were waiting and that they would take care of her, so she didn't have to be afraid. A bunch of good stuff like that. Remember? I told you girls about that."

"Uh huh." Caroline and I exchange a guilty look. Aunt Lydia had told us about Mom's visions, but we'd never actually believed that she was 'going back and forth between the realms' as Aunt Lydia had put it. In fact, we'd laughed about it, privately making fun of Lydia for her strange beliefs. Now I'm ashamed of myself for being so cynical.

"She used to come out of those dreams so energized, so excited about whatever it was she'd just heard. It was such a relief for me to see her that way. To know she was being soothed like that because, well, you know. Those last weeks were awfully hard."

A lump rises in my throat and I have to concentrate on the whorls in the wood table to keep from bursting into tears. The reality of those last days and how my mom had suffered—slowly withering away in what seemed like the cruelest of ways—were memories I fought to keep in check every single day of my life. Now, as Theo's thumb brushes gently across the back of my hand, the tears threaten to spill over. But luckily Aunt Lydia pushes on before they escape.

"She'd wake up and tell me she knew how life worked now. And that she wasn't afraid anymore. One afternoon she asked me to bring her paper and pen and some envelopes. She started scribbling down all kinds of stuff. Folding up pieces of paper and making piles and putting numbers on them. I tried to see what she was doing, but she shoo-ed me away. Said if I saw them it would ruin all the fun." Lydia laughs. "That's exactly how she put it. It would ruin all the fun. And I teased her and said, My God, Grace. What the hell kind of fun are you planning there on your deathbed?" Lydia stops to explain. "We always joked with each other that way. If something got too serious we just laughed about it. She thought me ribbing her was hilarious.

Anyway, when I asked what she was doing, she said, I'm making one last Treasure Hunt for Annie."

With that, I let out a strangled gasp, and the tears begin falling freely down my cheeks. I shake my head in disbelief, overwhelmed by the thought of my mom making such an effort in her last days of life, just for me. Caroline roughly grabs me, hugging me hard as she sniffles too. "It would be just like mom to think of us when she was supposed to be thinking of herself," she chokes out.

I huff a laugh, letting go of Theo's hand as Caroline wrenches me tighter to her side. "Yeah, you'd think she'd have a few more important things on her mind at that moment than entertaining me," I say, voice cracking.

Lydia pipes up. "Oh, I think it was good for her to have something hopeful to focus on. Whatever she was doing, it tickled her pink. She kept laughing and saying how wonderful this was going to be. And how she knew you were going to love it."

I smile through my tears, imagining my mom thinking about me and feeling happy and hopeful. All this time, I've believed her last days were filled with disappointment in me. Even though she never once said anything to that effect. In fact, she'd tried to convince me of just the opposite. But I was too mired in my guilt and sadness to listen to her. God, why hadn't I been able to hear her when she'd held me in her arms those last days of her life and told me how proud she was of me?

Something dawns on me then. "This Treasure Hunt she planned." I glance guiltily at Caroline. "Is it just for me?"

My sister must understand why I'm asking, because she quickly cuts in. "Don't worry Annie. It's ok it's only for you. Mom and I were good. We spent a lot of time together those last months and worked a lot of things out. I'm not jealous."

"You sure? I feel kinda of bad—"

"Seriously, don't."

I must not look convinced because she gives me another rough squeeze. "Hey, listen. I'm sick of you feeling bad for everything, you dork. Besides, I think maybe Mom planned this because she felt guilty for leaving when you were so young. I think she probably wanted to do something special, so you'd have something to remember her by."

I swallow hard, wondering how Mom could ever think I could forget her. But then again, how would she know where my head was at those last months? The only conversations I could manage without breaking down were about stupid stuff that happened at school or funny shows I'd seen on TV. I refused to talk to her about anything serious, like what would happen to me after she was gone. I can't believe she felt like she had to go to such lengths—resorting to a concocting some elaborate posthumous game—just to reach me.

"So anyway," Lydia starts again. "She directed me to the place in her studio where I could find those watercolor studies you have there. By that time, she was already in the hospital going in and out of consciousness a lot. But the day before she died she became very lucid. She came out of one of her dreams and rattled off exactly what I was supposed to do step by step. And that's when she asked for the manilla envelope and wrote your crazy ass name Theo and your address too."

"The Angels even gave her my address, huh?" He laughs, not at all surprised that he's apparently listed in some kind of heavenly phone book.

"Yeah, can you believe that?!" Lydia says. "Although I did have to look up your zip code. I guess omniscience only goes so far, huh?"

"Yeah, the Angels like you to do a little legwork," Theo says. "Makes you feel like you've got some skin in the game."

Caroline and Jonathan stare at Theo, dumbfounded. They only got the Cliff Note's version of his time in the afterlife, so they don't know about his close relationship with the dead. We'll obviously have to fill them in more when this phone call is over.

I press for more information. "So, Mom gave you Theo's sketches the day before she died. What else did she say?"

"She told me to hold on to the envelope. She said I was probably going to have to wait a while. Or I might never get to send it at all.

How did she put it, exactly? She said, 'it will be up to the choices they make'. Which didn't make much sense to me at the time. But I promised her I'd do everything exactly as she asked because it seemed so important to her. She said if Annie ever called and told me she was going to a camp for disabled kids, I was to mail the envelope right away. And that's exactly what I did six weeks ago."

At the table the four of us look at each other, half-dazed. Even Theo, who rarely gets flustered, seems at a loss for words. It's hard to fathom that whatever is happening here was set into motion three years ago, when my mom was still alive. And since then, has been gently nudged along from wherever she is now. How did her convoluted plan ever get this far? The odds of us getting to this dining room table, with the two halves of our clues joined like this, seem like such a longshot it's hard to believe my mom ever thought it might actually work.

"So, you waited over three years to mail that envelope?" Jonathan asks.

"Yeah! I was losing hope. I figured you two had missed whatever path it was you were supposed to follow."

"But we didn't miss it. We listened…and now we're here." Theo's eyes meet mine and I'm pretty sure we're remembering the same thing. How we'd both felt strangely compelled to accept Mile's job offer, even though it didn't make sense to either of us at the time.

"I think your sister may have given us a little help, Lydia," Theo says.

"Yeah. That sounds like her. She's always been bossy like that."

"So what are we supposed to do now?" I ask. "What were these steps she gave you?"

"Okay. Here's how this Treasure Hunt goes." Lydia clears her throat ceremoniously. "Those four little watercolor sketches match four of her full-sized paintings. What you have to do is visit each of those paintings in person and find out their titles. Then you call me with the name of the painting and I send you a clue. Once you've collected all four clues…and not before…she was adamant about that…*then* you follow the clues to find the treasure. Easy Peasy."

Easy Peasy? All those steps seemed awfully elaborate to me.

"But wait a minute," I interject. "Mom didn't name her paintings. She only gave them numbers."

"Yeah, I know," Aunt Lydia says. "I said the same thing when she told me the rules. But I guess she actually *did* name her paintings. She just never shared them with anyone else. She said she liked to keep those to herself as a way of holding on to a piece of them that no one else could have."

"Wow? Really?" Caroline says. I'm surprised she didn't know that since she was so involved in cataloging Mom's works.

"Yeah, I guess she penciled the names somewhere on the back of each painting really lightly. I don't think most people even notice it. Your mission is to find those names, then call and tell me. If they match the titles she gave me, I'll send you a clue."

A few beats pass as we digest the information. "So do you know where these paintings are?" Jonathan asks Caroline, his face scrunched up like he's already trying to figure out the most efficient way to tackle the problem. "They're obviously a series. Maybe someone bought them all?"

Caroline scoffs. "Like Mom would make it that easy? Do you even understand what a Treasure Hunt is, Jonathan? It involves multiple steps. One leading to the other, to the other. That's what makes it a hunt."

They bicker with each other while all the various details I've just heard swim in my head. "How are we ever going to find them?" I murmur to myself. This part of the assignment worries me. My mom may have been a meticulous artist, but the business side of her artwork was always a mess. She was notorious for having receipts and cash and invoices scattered around in the most unlikely places: Paper-clipped in the pages of her sketchbooks, stuffed in drawers, hidden in the back of the freezer. I doubt she even knew where her paintings ended up.

"Don't worry," Caroline says as if I just spoke all my concerns out loud. "I'll show you how we're going to find them." She leaps from her chair and dashes off down the hall while the rest of us look at each other, perplexed.

Ever thoughtful, Theo tries to keep Aunt Lydia apprised of what's going on, shouting into the box, "Lydia, Caroline just left the room to get something! We're not sure what it is, but I'll let you know as soon as she gets back!"

Jonathan shakes his head, muttering something to himself which sounds a lot like "I give up."

Caroline comes back and plops a blue binder on the desk. "Luckily, Mom listened to me when I told her we had to sort out her shit before she died."

As she flips through the pages, Theo leans into the speakerphone. "Aunt Lydia, Caroline just came back into the room with a blue binder that's about eight inches by ten inches, with a…"

I clamp a hand over his mouth. "Just stop. Please. How about we leave some things to her imagination?"

Lydia snorts on the other end of the line. "Oh, you two are going to have a lot of fun together, aren't you? Your mom knew what she was doing alright."

When I drop my hand, Theo wags his eyebrows and I pretend to be annoyed. Mostly so I don't have to think about how thrilled I am at the thought of being cosmically paired with this lovely boy sitting next to me.

As friends, of course. I'm sure my mom only ever wanted us to be friends. Because she must have known his situation, right? That he was going to die young. Or maybe she didn't know that little fact until after she set up the game? Because Theo didn't decide to come back for a limited time only until the night she actually died, right? Although he says time doesn't work the same way in the afterlife, so maybe she knew how it was all going to play out before it actually played out?

God, this is all so confusing. My brain hurts trying to sort it all out. I want to ask Theo to help me understand, but I know what he'll say because he's said it to me before: "Why do you have to know everything ahead of time, Annie? How about you just trust the Universe? Maybe we're not here to understand our lives. Maybe we're just here to live them." Ugh. And maybe being paired up with him isn't going to be quite as much of a cake walk as I first thought, either.

I tune back into Caroline, who is explaining the book. "Mom's more recent paintings were documented in greater detail because by that time she was doing shows and had hired a business manager to catalog her work. It was her earlier work that was such a mess. That's what I helped her sort out. And that's what this book is for."

We lean closer as she flips through the pages of a photo album. In each plastic sleeve is an ordinary snapshot of one of my mom's paintings. "Her way of keeping track of her work a long time ago was to take a picture of it after she completed it and then," Caroline slips one picture out of the sleeve and flips it over. "She'd write on the back who she sold it to."

The photo in Caroline's hand isn't a rendition from one of our postcards. It's an early acrylic abstract she'd done in art school. But on the back, written in pencil, is a name and an address.

"Not quite the method I'd use," Jonathan mumbles. "But I guess it worked for her."

Caroline gives her husband a withering look. "She told me that back then she didn't think anyone would ever be interested in her work. That's why it didn't feel important to keep any records."

The thought takes me aback. It makes me sad to think there was a time when Mom didn't see the value of her artwork. How could she have not known her own talent? Especially when it's so obvious, not only to me but to all the collectors in the art world now clamoring for her work. But I guess it just goes to show how warped our perspectives can be when it comes to seeing the truth about ourselves.

Caroline explains more. "What I did was take all those old pictures of hers and sort them out and put them in this album. So, all we have to do now is find these four." Caroline points to the watercolor studies on the table. "And hope to hell she actually wrote the names and addresses on the back."

We all hold our breaths as Caroline slowly flips the plastic pages. Suddenly something catches my eye.

"Stop. Right there," I point to a painting that depicts a lake with just the hint of a beach in the distance. "That looks like it matches one of Theo's cards." I snatch the study from the table and hold it next to the picture in the album. What's in my hand is only a sketch and Mom obviously added a lot of detail to the finished product. But it clearly shares the basic composition of the painting in the photograph.

"That's it!" Theo says. "And look. That one on the next page matches this one." He pulls another card and lines it up. Caroline flips the page to find two more. The four of us are grabbing and matching and cheering and wowing, while Aunt Lydia calls out. "Hey! What's going on? Don't forget about me, guys!"

Theo fills in Lydia. "We found the paintings. Now we just have to look at the backs to see who owns them."

"Here, pull them all out of their sleeves so we can look at them all together," Jonathan instructs Caroline excitedly. She's just reaching for the first one when Aunt Lydia shouts, "Wait!"

Caroline snatches her hand back like she's just been bitten by a snake. "What the hell?" she says, clutching her chest.

"Oh, sorry about that. I just remembered. Grace said you have to do them one at a time."

I sigh loudly. "Well, that seems like an important detail you might have mentioned earlier."

"Hey, don't blame me for forgetting!" Aunt Lydia shoots back, not missing a beat. "I've had to remember this for a long time. If you two had found that damn camp earlier this all would've been a helluva lot easier for all of us!"

We all laugh and I turn my attention back to the speakerphone to ask, "So, is there any order to them?"

"Hell if I know," Lydia replies. "At this point I'd say just pick one. You've made it this far on your instincts. You might as well stick with that."

I cock an eyebrow at Theo and he nods in agreement.

I line up the four postcards on the table in front of us, then tell Theo, "Okay, on the count of three, we'll each point to the one we think we should start with."

But just as I'm about to make my pick, Theo gently touches my arm. "You're agreeing to do this then?" he asks with a serious expression.

His question stops me in my tracks. I haven't even had time to consider that I could say No to all of this. I mean, of course I'm going to follow my mom's last wishes. How could I not? But I understand what Theo is getting at. He's thinking of the concerns I'd voiced earlier about feeling like I didn't have any free will in all this. He wants me to realize that *I'm* the one making the choice to go through with this hunt. That no one is forcing me into anything. Especially not him.

"Yes, I want to do this," I say, hoping I sound more confident than I feel.

He breaks into his beautiful smile. My stomach drops out from under me at the sight of it. Oh, what am I getting myself into, committing myself to him like this for the rest of the summer?

"Let's shake on it then." He extends his hand with a playful grin. He obviously wants to remind me of when we tried to shake on our agreement during his NDE. Which apparently didn't go so well back then since both of us were mostly made of mist. At least that's what he told me.

"Fine," I say, slapping my palm in his defiantly.

When our very solid hands touch, something jolts through my body, white light bursting at the edges of my vision, blinding me for a moment. Suddenly a chant trills in my head. Two voices joined as one:

Across time and distance,
lifetimes and eternities,
always together. Forevermore.

I drop his hand like it's on fire, blinking up at him in shock. Those weren't just any voices I just heard. They were his and mine; joined as one.

Theo opens his mouth to speak, but I jump in so he can't address what just passed between us. "Can we just pick now?" I ask, waving at the postcards lined up before us.

He blows out a huge breath, obviously as jarred by what just happened as I am.

"Alright," he agrees. "Let's pick on the count of three. And remember, don't think. Just follow your heart."

"Fine, whatever," I snap, still feeling annoyingly off kilter. "One, two, three."

Our fingers shoot out, and not surprisingly, they both point to the same sketch: the scene of the lake with a beach in the distance. Caroline and Jonathan gasp, impressed by our apparent telepathy. Jonathan fills Aunt Lydia in on what happened and she whoops, telling us we obviously already have a very conducive partnership.

"Just like I said," she calls out cheerfully. "Follow your gut and everything will work out just like your mom planned."

Theo grins big and I do too, but when Jonathan and Caroline turn away to say goodbye to Lydia, he searches my face, a question creasing his brow. Even though he doesn't speak the words out loud, I can somehow sense we're feeling the same thing. A subtle nagging in the back of our minds telling us that, despite all this new information, we still don't know everything yet. That we're missing some vital piece of information that has nothing to do with sketches, or paintings, or addresses. We both somehow already know that to find the final X my Angel Mom has planted for us, we'll have to stretch ourselves further than we ever have before. And that, although it may seem clear cut on the surface, there's more to this Treasure Hunt than meets the eye.

CHAPTER TWENTY-SEVEN

AFTER HANGING UP with Aunt Lydia we all agree to go to bed and talk more in the morning. But with all that's happened tonight there's no way I can sleep. So I lie in bed and try counting backwards…and listening to the hum of the air-conditioner…and reciting prayers I doubt more than believe. But none of my usual methods for quieting my mind work. My thoughts are running too wild. Ricocheting from the sheer wonder of what my mom did for me. To all the details of her instructions for the Treasure Hunt. To that bizarre chant I heard in my head when I shook hands with Theo. To the delicious memory of kissing him in my bedroom.

Yeah. That's the memory that really won't let me sleep.

And I need to do something about it. Right now.

I rip off my covers and quietly pad downstairs.

Taking a single step down the basement stairs, I call out softly, "Theo? Are you still awake?"

"Yeah, I'm up." The response comes so quickly I have a feeling he's been lying awake staring at the ceiling, just like me.

When I get to the bottom of the stairs, Theo is pulling himself up to sitting, fussing with his pillows to prop himself up. A single lamp illuminates his bare chest, nestling shadows along the lines of his toned stomach. He smiles big, drinking in the sight of me. My lower belly aches pleasantly in response. He urges me to come closer, absentmindedly running a hand through his hair, sweeping the long waves off to the side, oblivious to how sexy the gesture makes him look. He's like some ancient Greek God, reclined on a rumpled altar before me. And the primal part of me wants nothing more than to sink to my knees and worship him until he trembles with pleasure.

Yeah. Coming down here might have been a huge mistake.

I stand frozen in the middle of open space. "Sorry. I didn't mean to bother you."

"You're not bothering me. Here." He pats the bed beside him. "Sit down."

I swallow hard and take a few steps closer but stop myself at the foot of the pull out couch. "I, uh…don't think that would be a good idea."

"Why not? I don't bite."

"No, but after what happened earlier, when we were alone. It's probably better if I stay far away from your bed."

He cocks his head to the side, looking puzzled. "You didn't like what happened earlier?"

"No. I liked it! That's the problem!"

He scrunches up his face like he can't make sense of me. Which makes two of us.

"So you enjoyed kissing me," he says plainly. "And I enjoyed kissing you. Very, *very* much, by the way. And you consider that a problem? Help me understand your reasoning, Annie."

Oh, if he only knew all the reasons I had for not letting this go any further. I flash to Greta's face that day on the beach when it was clear how hurt she would be if her Mystery Man didn't like her back. I don't want to be the cause of that. And besides, even if Theo is infatuated with me now, I'm only going to break his heart when I leave him at the end of the summer. He's better off with someone stronger like Greta, who will stick by him through thick and thin. Unlike me who, if history serves right, will only run away.

I clear my throat, forcing out the words only my logical self believes. "It's just not right… us getting involved in that way."

He sits up. "But it *is* right! And you know that!" It's the most forceful he's ever been with me. And I have to say…I like it.

"Theo, I've always been very clear with you," I stammer. "I only want to be friends. The only reason I came down here was to make sure you knew that."

He narrows his eyes at me. "Are you worried about what's going to happen when I turn twenty-one? Because I'm serious about what I said before. I promise after the summer you can leave me, no strings attached."

"But that doesn't make any sense. Why would you agree to that?"

"Because if there's one thing I've learned from my experience, it's that I want to enjoy the present moment as much as possible. I won't sacrifice what little time I have left worrying about the future. Especially when there really isn't any future, Annie. Not for me. And not for you, either. There's only ever right now."

I shake my head, not wanting his words to make as much sense as they do.

He leans toward me, voice rising. "And I know we could have so much fun, so much *love* together if all we cared about was enjoying this very moment. All I'm asking is for you to be honest with yourself about what you really want. I'm not asking for any commitment. I just want to spend as many of my *right nows* with you as I can."

"I want that too!" I blurt out without thinking. My entire body screams to go to him. To climb into his bed and forget about Greta. (She can have him in September, for Christ's sake!) Forget about the fact that he's going to die soon. To only think about how good it would feel to give in to the magnetic pull between us that's getting harder and harder to resist. But if I love him this much now, how much more will I love him when we get even closer? How much more pain will I feel when he's gone?

A cold resolve seeps through me, realizing what I just admitted to myself. Again.

It's the truth I can't deny any longer. I love Theo.

No. This can't happen. I have to keep all these futile, pointless, heart-threatening feelings of mine under control.

"I told you. I only want to be friends," I lie.

He stares up at the ceiling, clearly frustrated. I use the respite to gather myself, force the rational part of my brain to get a firmer grip on the steering wheel. There will be no more blurting out of the truth anymore. From here on out, I will follow clear reason only.

"Of course I want to hang out with you," I say gently, hating the pain I see in his pale eyes. "Obviously, now that we have this little assignment to complete we're going to be spending a lot more time together. But this whole thing is complicated enough. Let's not muddy it up even more with some messy summer fling."

He levels me under an unflinching stare, not blinking for so long I start to squirm.

"And that's honestly all you want?" He clearly knows I'm not being truthful with him.

Again, I have to force my mouth to say the traitorous words. "Yes, that's all I want."

His shoulders sag as he lets out a heavy breath. But as always, he bounces back quickly. "Well, you can't blame me for trying." His grin is more forced than normal. I return his sad smile, my stomach burning at my betrayal. I've hurt him. Which oddly enough feels exactly like hurting myself.

I wander closer to where he's propped up in bed, clutching my hands together to keep from reaching out and touching the faint shadow along his jaw. It would be so easy to just give in. Theo's so sweet he wouldn't even make fun of me for going back on my word so quickly. But instead, I squeeze my hands tighter, force myself to remember the other reason I had trouble sleeping. Maybe he can help me sort things out.

"Aren't you worried about what we've gotten ourselves into?" I ask.

He shrugs. "What's there to be worried about? It's all just for fun."

His casualness irks me. "Why is it so easy for you to expect the best all the time?"

He blinks at me, face so open and sincere. "What would be the alternative?"

His response only irritates me more. He's doing it again. Saying one simple line that reaches in and pulls the purest, most distilled truth from the depths of my soul, making me wonder why the hell I hadn't thought of it myself.

I don't want to fix you because I don't think you're broken.
The Universe is good Annie. You can trust it.
What would be the alternative?

It pisses me off because deep down, I know he's right. What would be the alternative to expecting the best all the time? Expecting the worst. Which I know from firsthand experience sucks.

"But what if we can't find the paintings?" I ask.

His smile is much more earnest now. "What if the Universe is friendly, Annie?"

I roll my eyes. "But what if no one will talk to us?"

"What if the Universe is friendly, Annie?" he repeats.

"Ugh," I groan, anger rising. "But what if we can't figure out where this supposed treasure is?"

"What if the Universe is friendly, Annie?"

I glare at him, lying there, grinning so confidently in his bed. "But what if…you know what…never mind! If you say that one more time, I'm going to slap you!" I lean closer. "Bet you won't think the Universe is so friendly after that, huh?!"

He bursts out laughing, clearly proud of himself for antagonizing me. He's so adorable, with his scrunched-up eyes and flexed stomach, that I break down and laugh at myself too. Theo always teases me about how much energy I spend coming up with my worst-case scenarios. It's the same thing my mom always scolded me for, too. And I have to admit, after what I've been through tonight, their approach—focusing on what good might come of things instead—seems like a heck of a lot more fun than my boring old doom and gloom.

But I have to be careful about how much fun I have with Theo. Because after what kissing him has done to me, I'm not sure I can physically remain rational if I let myself touch him like that again.

"I'm going back to bed now," I announce, backing away from where I've gotten way too close to him.

"Alright. But seriously, Annie, trust me. It's going to be alright."

"You promise?"

"I promise."

I give him a begrudging nod, then turn and walk away. I'm almost at the foot of the stairs when he calls out.

"You heard it too, didn't you?"

I freeze in place, terrified by what he's about to say next.

"Across time and distance, lifetimes and eternities," he chants in an all too familiar cadence. "Always together. Forevermore."

My heart beats so wildly it feels like it might explode out of my chest.

When I don't turn around, he adds softly, "I saw your face earlier, when we shook hands. You heard it too, didn't you?"

No. I can't tell him the truth. That will only make things so much harder.

Keeping my back to him, I shake my head and tell him my third lie of the night.

"No, Theo. I didn't hear anything."

CHAPTER TWENTY-EIGHT

Somewhere *else…*

HERE IN THE afterlife, Theo has just noticed something important about the lines of his possible life trajectories, glowing like diamond facets all around us: They all seem to end at one spot.

When he asks me why, I tell him the truth. "Because the life you just agreed to return to will most likely be cut short."

He laughs. Which is a typical response for visitors here. Lightheartedness is innate in this space. Knowing you'll always be reunited in an endless ocean of love tends to take away all a person's fears. Especially of death. Which doesn't truly exist, except in limited human minds. I wish more people knew that. Maybe I'll take that up with the big boss some time. Ask them: Why doesn't everyone get to remember how perfect it is here? How their true nature is not limited, but vast and eternal? Boy, wouldn't that make things easier on everyone in the human experience? But then again, we all like a little drama sometimes, right? It's the not knowing that makes life so exciting.

Theo is unperturbed by this new development. "So, I get to come back here sooner?" he says, with a carefree shrug. "Seems like a pretty sweet option to me!"

"Yeah, you get to come here," Annie grumbles. "But I get left behind." It sounds like a complaint, but her jab is bubbly, holding no venom. That effervescence is what makes jokes so much funnier here.

Theo chimes back. "That's true. But in a blink of an eye we'll be back together again, so there's nothing to worry about."

"I guess," she concedes, pointing to their Intertwined Path, glowing with such overwhelming love. "It will definitely be worth it if we get to enjoy that path in the physical world. At least for a little while."

She walks out into the darkness, investigating their conjoined path more closely. I have to hold back a gleeful giggle as her eyes land on what's been there all along, but Theo hasn't yet noticed. It seems, even here, women are more attuned to details than our male counterparts are.

"Hey, what's that?" she asks. "Why does that one line jut out from our Intertwined Path and continue past where all the other ones stop?"

Theo takes his place beside her, eyes going wide when he sees where she's pointing. The spot where a single line shoots out, then becomes an entirely separate galaxy unto itself; countless sparkling fractals of life stretching further than any eye could ever see.

"Does that mean?" he asks, hopefully.

"Yes, you two have a chance to jump timelines," I tell them. "You've been given one chance to change your fates." I pause to let that sink in.

Annie recovers her voice first. "Are you saying there's a path where Theo lives a long life and doesn't die young?"

"Yes. But you only have one opportunity to make the jump. You must somehow find a way to reach that *specific moment in time*. And if you do, both of your futures will change."

I gesture to the junction in question. Inside the fractal, a scene plays out over and over: Theo and Annie holding hands, smiling with so much love at each other. A cloudless blue sky stretches behind them and colorful garlands of flowers adorn the background. He's wearing a white shirt and a dark tie. She's wearing a wedding dress.

"You're saying that…" Annie starts.

"If we get married, I live?" Theo finishes incredulously.

I smile. I knew that would be the next question. "Well, it's not just about getting married. In many of these shorter timelines, you also get married." I gesture to the myriad of other possible paths that all end at the same spot. "And in others, you both go your separate ways and never see each other again."

They both wince when I say that part. Their synchronicity is so cute. These two are definitely meant to be together for all time.

"It's not simply the action of the wedding alone," I explain. "It's the people you are, what you've learned, and who you've become when you join together *at that specific point in time* that will allow you to change your fates. And the fates of many others, too."

They blink at each other, looking stunned. And a bit overwhelmed, too. I probably shouldn't have emphasized that 'fate of many others' part again. I don't want to scare them and make their adventure seem too serious. I meant it when I said this is all for fun. Theirs and ours alike. When I quickly remind them of that, their smiles break out again. There. That's more like it.

"This is so exciting!" he says to her. "I think we can do it!"

She nods determinedly. "Yeah. It will be challenging, but challenges are kind of our specialty aren't they?"

It's true, the two of them have always triumphed, even in lifetimes of struggles and tribulations. Which has only forged their bond even stronger. Looking off at the trajectory that awaits them this time around…*if* they find it…well, let's just say the joy and love that lies there promises that this lifetime will be about reaping the harvest they've sown in their pasts.

An idea comes to me then. "Want to make it even more exciting?" I ask. I might as well give them the option. They're the ones always blabbering on about how they hate to be bored.

They don't even need to answer out loud. Their twinkling eyes tell me they can't wait to hear what I have to offer.

"We can make it so that *neither* of you remembers this part of our conversation."

Annie grins big. "So, neither of us will know that Theo will live if we get married at that certain place and time?"

"Right. You'll have to go into it blind. Agree to get married while still believing Theo is going to die young."

"Oh! That's a good twist!" she says. "I can already tell that's going to be a tough one for me!"

I love hearing her speak from the heart of her true nature. Not the one that's been muffled by the fears she's been spoon fed all her life.

"I'm in!" Theo chimes up eagerly.

"Me too!" she says. "So, what do we have to do?"

It's such a human question it makes me chuckle. So much emphasis on *doing* down there. Still, I answer, since it's all part of the game.

"To get to that point where you jump timelines, you'll have to agree to love each other despite believing your physical partnering won't last. You'll each have to learn to trust not only yourselves, but each other, and the Universe too. To truly believe that you're strong enough to survive whatever circumstances arise in your life. To trust that you'll be taken care of no matter what. And when you get to that point, that's when you'll find true freedom. That's when you'll truly begin to live. Because trusting without proof, is love in its purest form."

"Wow," they both marvel in unison.

"That sounds beautiful," Theo says, waving a hand to the beyond. "Thank you for showing us all of this."

Annie nods, adding wryly, "Although I guess it was kind of pointless since we're going to forget it all anyway, right?"

"For a while, yes. But if you get to that one moment in time, it will all come back to you. But don't worry. I won't leave you all alone." I wrap them both in my arms and give them a big, blurry hug. The conjoined energy of the three of us sends the light surging to near blinding whiteness around us.

Letting go, I gently usher them back toward the whirling tunnel of light. "You have to leave now. But I'll still be with you. And I've got a little something planned for the two of you that I think you're going to like. Consider it a little game to help you along."

They begin fading, but I can feel their joyous anticipation permeating the air as they dissolve.

"I can't guarantee my little hunt will get you to that exact point in time," I call softly after them. "But it will definitely be fun. And I have a feeling that…if you allow yourselves to listen and trust…together, you just might find your way."

∞

To Be Continued…

Dear Reader,

I hope you enjoyed the first book in my *Treasured Love* series. Yes, I left you with a bit of a cliffhanger there. If you want to find out what happens on Annie and Theo's otherworldly Treasure Hunt—and whether or not they will find that fateful moment in time their Angel showed them—run (or click) to get the final book:

US, Fatefully

Available wherever books are sold!

And since I'm already asking for favors, if you can leave a review for this book on Goodreads or Amazon, it would help me immensely. If you're unsure of how to do that, I'll leave a few prompts below to get you started, but feel free to say whatever is in your heart. I truly appreciate your help!

Love
Kiersten

If you're thinking, "I have no idea what to include in a book review," maybe answering one or more of these questions will spark some ideas:

1) Were there any specific plot points, characters, or themes of this book you liked?

2) How did you feel as you were reading it?

3) After you finished reading, what were some takeaways you got from the story?

4) Who else might enjoy a story like this?

ACKNOWLEDGEMENTS

This story came to me with such friendliness at a time when I needed it the most. I was just finishing up my debut romance series and—as many of you who have been involved in a big project probably know—there is a sadness that comes with finishing something you've poured your heart into for so long.

Luckily, even before the last word of *The Playlist Diaries* was written, this new story jumped in to distract me from that melancholy. It seems Red and Will had decided it was time to pass the baton off to Annie and Theo. And with that, I was off and running, following these characters on their otherworldly adventures, so grateful to keep my writing momentum flowing. (And also, to have an excuse to lock myself in my office again and be alone for hours on end!)

So, my first thank you is to this story itself. Bless you for showing up and trusting me to bring you to life on the page. I hope I did you proud.

But there are also a lot of *real* people I'd like to thank too!

To my writing friends, Michele and Denise. I love that I can share my creative ups and downs with you and you understand what I'm going through! I'm in awe of your talent and so grateful to you both for beta reading this book and giving me such thoughtful feedback. Here's to many more years of sharing our love of this crazy pursuit called writing together.

To the Canton Library Writing Group (a.k.a Salon) who kept me accountable and inspired me through your own creative works. And also cramped my brain with questions like, "What truly is beauty?" (I'm looking at you Mike!)

To my sister Kendall whose daily chats inspire me and make me laugh and remind me that it's okay to go down rabbit holes and love what you love for no other reason than that you love it! Your unwavering support keeps me going when my confidence wanes. Thanks for always being there for me…only a Marco Polo away!

To my kids, Lauren, Andy, Ben, and Sam and their partners Scott and Alli, thank you for being genuinely interested in my creative pursuits and cheering me on along every step of my journey. You all inspire me every day with the kindness and grace you share with the world. Our deep talks around the kitchen table are so much fun! (It almost makes those crazy toddler years worth it…)

To my grandchildren Finn, Abel, Julien, and Otto, thank you for reminding me of how life is supposed to be lived…free, loud, messy, (and a lot of times naked?) I'm lucky to have you all as my role models! (Although I'll keep my clothes on, thank you very much…)

To all those who have read my books and reached out to say an encouraging word or show up at a Zoom call or book signing, you will never know how much that meant to me. Writing a book can sometimes feel so vulnerable, and presumptuous and yes, even cringey! But you all took care of me when I needed you the most. Theo would be so proud of your simple acts of kindness!

And last but not least to my husband Andrew, the best cheerleader and editor a girl could have! Being able to talk about this story with you in all its various stages has been almost as fun as writing it. (Which is saying a lot because I really love writing!) We are a living testament to what a summer camp romance can turn into. There is so much of our story woven in these pages and I have no doubt we will always be together…forevermore.

Kiersten Schiffer grew up on a farm in Indiana and now lives in Connecticut with her husband. She is addicted to stories in every form (especially books and TV shows) and enjoys writing essays about creativity and spirituality and how the two intersect. When she's not immersed in her latest writing project you can find her reading her favorite Romantasy series, bingeing the latest hot TV series, taking walks down the dirt road she lives on, playing with her grandkids, or enjoying her favorite pastime: napping!

She loves making new friends so make sure to reach out and say hello on her socials:

@kierstenschiffer

@kierstenschiffer.com

@authorkierstenschiffer

@kierstenschifferauthor

www.ingramcontent.com/pod-product-compliance
Lightning Source LLC
Chambersburg PA
CBHW032251310726

48973CB00008B/2371